Arucard

BARBARA DEVLIN

Copyright © 2015 Barbara Devlin

Published by Barbara Devlin

The Brethren of the Coast Badge is a registered trademark ® of Barbara Devlin.

Cover art by Lewellen Designs

Library of Congress Control Number: TX 8-051-659

ISBN: 0-9962509-6-4
ISBN-13: 978-0-9962509-6-2

TITLES BY BARBARA DEVLIN

BRETHREN OF THE COAST
Enter the Brethren
My Lady, the Spy
The Most Unlikely Lady
One-Knight Stand
Captain of Her Heart
The Lucky One
Love with an Improper Stranger

Loving Lieutenant Douglas: A Brethren of the Coast
Novella

BRETHREN ORIGINS
Arucard
Demetrius

KATHRYN LE VEQUE'S KINDLE WORLD OF DE WOLFE PACK
Lone Wolfe

DEDICATION

To the late Tonya M. Rupell of Stone Soup Designs. I met Tonya through the indie author community, and the minute I saw her fabulous work, I knew I had to commission custom swag from her. Tonya was a loving and generous person who took pride in her artistry, and she collaborated with me on some wonderful pieces, which I gave as prizes to my readers. My dear friend passed away during the composition of this novel, and she was taken far too soon. Godspeed, Tonya. We will meet again.

CONTENTS

Prologue   1

Chapter One   7

Chapter Two   23

Chapter Three   41

Chapter Four   58

Chapter Five   74

Chapter Six   91

Chapter Seven   108

Chapter Eight   125

Chapter Nine   137

Chapter Ten   146

Chapter Eleven   160

Chapter Twelve   171

Chapter Thirteen   180

Chapter Fourteen   189

Chapter Fifteen   196

Chapter Sixteen   202

Chapter Seventeen   207

Chapter Eighteen   220

Epilogue   229

PROLOGUE

La Rochelle, France
Friday the Thirteenth, October
The Year of Our Lord, 1307

Hunkered behind a stack of barrels, Templar Knight Arucard de Villiers hugged his sword and prepared to lunge, as King Philip's guards searched the undercroft. When the pile of casks shifted, he crouched lower and uttered a silent entreaty, as he gazed at his tormentors through a crevice in the mountain of containers. At the age of seven and twenty, he had fought hard for his patron Pope Clement V, and never in his life had he cowered from peril. But desperate circumstances necessitated drastic measures, if he hoped to survive the Crown's connivance against the warriors of the Crusades.

WANTED: DEAD OR ALIVE

In the dim light of the braziers, he peered at the warrant, which commanded Arucard, along with his brother knights, to surrender for interrogation, regarding unfounded accusations of heresy, sorcery, and unspeakable acts of sexual perversion, the whole of which were false. But he knew too well the true motives upon which the malicious conspiracy had been launched, and it had naught to do with the heinous claims. Rather, King Philip needed money, and he craved ownership of the vast Templar treasure.

"It is as I told thee, good sir." Arucard's marshalsea on land and second in command on sea, Pellier bowed. "My lord departed on Thursday last, and he never returned."

"*Merde.*" The soldier gritted his teeth. "Then I suggest thou vacate the premises, at once, as His Majesty hereby confiscates these properties, forthwith."

"Of course." Again, Pellier made his obedience. "If we might have enough time to gather our personal effects, given a handful of servants remain in residence, we shall leave the keep to thy good service."

"Thou mayest have until the morrow." The guard dipped his chin, gave the vaulted cellar a final cursory glance, and then directed his men. "Let us ride for Moncel Abbey."

From the safe haven of his hiding place, Arucard smiled, because Morgan, the lord of Moncel, along with Geoffrey and Aristide, had retreated to his ship at dawn and already should have cast off for the prearranged meeting point, northwest of the *Golfe de Gascogne.* Soon, Arucard would withdraw to join his hunted brothers, as they sailed the Channel and sought asylum in England, whither Edward II had outlawed torture.

The estimable empire may reject the once esteemed Order of great men, but it could offer sanctuary. And if his brothers could find a new supporter, their legacy, along with their necks, would persist. It was with that thought in mind that he sheltered, despite a deep-seated desire to fight—to defend the honor of his brethren, present and past.

"My lord, they art gone." Grunting and groaning, Pellier removed three empty barrels, so Arucard could emerge from the haphazard refuge. "And we should make haste to the docks, given the royal patrol executes Philip's decree, as thou were warned. Wherefore didst thou not flee when thee first learned of the scheme?"

"Because we needed to give our brothers a chance to elude the Crown. Didst thou deposit the gold for our citizens who have chosen to stay in France?" In the kitchen, Arucard assessed the remaining stores. "If they art careful, they can subsist for years, to come, on the profits from their trade, as I will no longer be able to protect them."

"Indeed, sir." With a sigh, Pellier frowned. "My father vows to oversee the funds, in order to preserve the village, in thy absence."

"Art thou sure thou dost wish to journey with me, my friend?" How Arucard loathed separating his men from their families, which is wherefore he asked only the unmarried seamen to join him, as they risked everything to avoid persecution by association. "As thou could always grow a beard and take up farming or the smithy."

"Beg thy pardon, my lord." Pellier opened his mouth, closed it, and then grinned. "Thou dost joke, sir."

"I do." However inappropriate, given the gravity of the circumstances, he could use a little levity, at the moment. "Now let us away, as we have no time to spare."

The back hall led to the scullery, which egressed to the yard and the gardens, whither Arucard often engaged in weapons practice. In the cool evening air, as dew kissed the lawn, he strode the path and climbed the rise, which opened to the grove, whither his destrier, Pellier's rouncey, and the sumpter horse loaded with Arucard's few intimate belongings had been tied to the trees.

Gaining his mount, he steered for the muddy road, which had deteriorated after the previous day's heavy rains, to the port. On normal occasions, normal being the dearth of troops out for his head, Arucard would have carried a torch to illuminate the route, as the sun set on the horizon, but he could ill afford such luxury, so he maintained a slow but steady pace. When they reached the hilltop, he reined in to take one last look at his home, which he suspected he would never enjoy again.

"Lights in the meadow, sir." As his horse shifted, Pellier pointed to the east and cursed. *"Mon Dieu.* It is the patrol."

"By the saints. They must have doubted thy account, else fortune frowns on our endeavor." In a flash, Arucard heeled hard the flanks of his stallion. "We must hurry, if we art to escape."

To avoid wagon ruts, he kept to the grassy verge, with Pellier in his wake. His heart pounded, beating in rhythm as he pushed his destrier harder and faster. They veered left, then right, and then left again, snaking amid the sludge with the King's guard in their tracks. At last, the dense foliage yielded to sparse outbuildings, heralding they neared the quaint seaside town, whither the lanes improved, and Arucard picked up speed.

Racing through the marketplace, which was closed for the day and thus sparsely populated, he glanced over his shoulder and discovered the King's guard had gained valuable ground, and he swore under his breath. "Ride for the ship, Pellier. Do not stop until thou hast boarded the *Olifant.* And tell the men to throw off the ropes and weigh anchor, as we must sail, immediately."

"Aye, sir." At the docks, Pellier abided Arucard's orders, signaling with a mock salute.

"To arms! To arms!" In turn, Arucard pounded the boards, to sound the alarm and alert his brothers. "Onward, Demetrius. Randulf, abandon the wine, as thou must go—now. Philip's patrol nears."

At his proclamation, sailors scrambled in all directions, toppling bags of flour and rice, as they ran for their respective transports. The original plan had been to trail the merchant vessels, which ventured on the morrow tide, to avoid rousing even a mere soupçon of consternation, but they could not wait for dawn, so he altered his tack.

Charging the gangplank, he brought his stallion to a halt and slid from the saddle, as his single-masted cog slipped from its berth. When the wind caught the canvas, he took the helm and set a course for the open seas. But he could not rejoice, as Demetrius remained dangerously close to the docks, within striking distance, and young Randulf, reluctant to relinquish the cask, had just pulled his lines, when the archers took aim.

Then, to his unutterable horror, soldiers rolled in three carro-ballistas and launched a hailstorm, in rapid succession, of flaming bolts into the air. Cries of terror formed a morbid cacophony, echoing on the gentle breeze. Helpless to aid his brothers, Arucard clenched his fists and gnashed his teeth, as first Demetrius and then Randulf's ship caught fire.

"What can we do, sir?" With a grimace, Pellier rubbed his neck. "How can we save them?"

"It appears Demetrius has extinguished the small blaze that threatened the *Tigus*, but I fear thither is naught we can do to assist the *Spearintine*, as the hold is engulfed, and the gadling founders." Even as he voiced the obvious, he prayed he was wrong. With his thumb and forefinger, Arucard stared into the twilight and touched his forehead, chest, and left and then right shoulder, as the King had just claimed a victim—the first of many, no doubt. "May the Almighty Father have mercy on Randulf's soul."

In what seemed as several painful hours, but was in reality a few minutes, the knarr sank beneath the water's surface, disappearing bit by bit until not even the masthead remained visible. On the outside, he maintained his composure, as his crew relied on him for guidance, but inside he wept for his friend, a regrettable cost—a human sacrifice exacted by Philip's cursed lust for wealth and power.

As the *Olifant* rode the waves, gliding in a graceful dance as the craft passed the *golfe's* foreland, a familiar sight that had always soothed his often frazzled nerves, he fixed his attention on the bow, on the road that lay ahead, and vowed never again to surrender one of his brothers in the name of greed. And so it was with that train of thought he gave his attention to the charts.

"Sir, dost thou ever believe we will go home, again?" Leaning against the rail, Pellier stared a-stern. "Or dost thou think Edward will kill us, on sight?"

"We have no home, Pellier." Listing with the motion of the ocean, Arucard swallowed hard, as a crude reality set in with a vengeance just then. Yet all was not lost, and he coveted hope to be won in a foreign land. "But if we art to endure, mighty England is our future, and if she will have us, we shall serve her with honor until we breathe our last."

CHAPTER ONE

England
The Year of Our Lord, 1312

L ocked in the tiny stone cell in the tower keep for an untold period, which he estimated at well nigh five years as marked by the canonical hours, Arucard gazed at the azure morning sky, gave thanks for another day above ground, and wondered how his brothers fared in captivity. Were they alive and well, or had Edward executed them for the blasphemous but fallacious allegations that threatened the once great Order of Knights Templar?

The rasp of the metal lock and the screech of the hinges had him bracing for the final sentence, as he broke his fast at dawn with a customary light sop, and the bells had yet to signal sext, so he had not anticipated the noon meal. Had the Crown's men, at last, come for him? "Thither who goes?"

"It is Brewer, Sir Arucard." The steward, who had been very kind throughout Arucard's imprisonment, entered along with a small army of servants bearing a large ancere, a stack of linen cloths, and buckets of water, in the company of a familiar, much-welcomed face. "Thou art to prepare for an audience with His Majesty. I bring thee a square of barilla soap, a sharp blade for shaving, and a change of clothes, which the King requests thee wear for the singular occasion."

"Am I to be tried for Philip's spurious claims?" On edge, he charged the poor soul but drew up short, as Brewer was not to blame for Arucard's predicament. "Am I to dress for my death?"

"His Royal Highness does not see fit to apprise me of his intentions, Sir Arucard. As I am but a fleak, I do His bidding, naught more." Brewer directed the attendants and then loomed in the entry. "Thou hast an hour to tend thy needs, and then the royal escort will convey thee to St. John's Chapel. That is all I know, sir."

Once Brewer departed, Arucard and Pellier locked forearms in companionship. "My friend, it is good to see thee."

"And thou, sir." Misty-eyed, and a bit worse for wear, Pellier smiled. "The crew has been tormented by thoughts of thy demise, as we have had no word of thee."

"Thou art housed together?" Releasing his comrade, he stumbled back and gave thanks in silence. "The men prevail?"

"Aye." Drawing a shaky breath, Pellier dipped his chin. "By the benevolence of God, we art all well and accounted for, sir. Even when young Thomas caught the ague, the King sent a physician to treat the boy. And I am summoned to assist thee in grooming for an important event."

The revelations did much to soothe Arucard's nerves, as it made no sense for Edward to maintain the crew's health and Arucard's appearance, if the Crown intended to kill them, in the end. Glancing at the steaming tub, he doffed his linen underclothes and woolen stockings.

As he sank into the water, he savored the experience, as

baths were a rarity in confinement. For a Templar Knight, cleanliness was a priority, second only to his daily devotional, and the denial of what most deemed a simple pleasure had actually served only to intensify the wretched conditions of his cell. After a thorough scrubbing of his body and washing his hair, he emerged as a new man, stepped into clean braies, and sat with the patience of a saint, as Pellier shaved the long beard and cut the tangled locks.

"Thither, sir." With hands on hips, Pellier admired his work. "Thou dost look as thee did the night we departed France, if a tad older."

"So thy humor remains in fine form." With a chuckle and a much-improved spirit, Arucard donned the chausses, the linen shirt, the calf-boots, the navy wool cotehardie, over which he pulled on the matching doublet bedecked in gold braids. The fur-lined cloak of equal splendor left him perplexed, as did the ailette, fashioned of leather and bearing a unique wind-star design foreign to him, which was typically laced to the shoulder, over armor, and bore the bearer's coat of arms. "Well, what dost thou think? Am I fit to receive the King?"

"I cannot say, sir." Pellier shrugged and then flinched, as the steward returned. Retreating to the small table, whither Arucard partook his meals, the marshalsea frowned. "But I pray fortune smiles upon thee, and we meet tomorrow to celebrate glad tidings."

"If thou wilt follow me, Sir Arucard." Brewer inched aside. "His Majesty awaits thy presence."

Without a word, Arucard strolled into the dark corridor, and an escort armed with shields and pointed halberds surrounded him. Stiffening his spine, he promised to withstand, with grace and honor, whatever Edward had in store, as he would not embarrass his ancestors. The stone passage, aglow in the soft amber light from cresset lamps spaced in equal distances on the wall, led to a narrow winding staircase, which he ascended.

At the landing, the guards turned left, and a vast expanse spread before him.

Huge glazed windows filtered the sun's bright rays, and vibrant tapestries decorated the great hall. Servants and elegantly garbed nobles scurried in various directions, sparing nary a glance at him. At a double-door entrance, a sentry set wide the heavy panels, revealing a vaulted chapel—not a block for beheading.

Four massive columns connected by plain arches, and decorated with naught more than pedestrian carvings of scallop and leaf designs, flanked either side of the wide aisle, and an identical combination of similarly ornamented thick round piers, on a smaller scale, formed the apse. But it was the group of men identically uniformed and gathered before the altar that gave him pause.

"*Brothers.*" With splayed arms, he greeted his fellow Templar Knights, and they exchanged fraternal salutations and hearty backslaps. "Demetrius, Aristide, Morgan, and Geoffrey, dost my eyes deceive me? Am I dreaming?"

"Hither we art, but I am concerned for thy mental state, if thou dost resort to fantasies of me to pass the time." Ever the wit, Demetrius elbowed Arucard in the ribs. "As it stands, I summoned visions of tables overflowing with roasted pork and smoked herring. And what I would give for a tankard of beer, as we have been restricted to wine and Adam's ale, which I wilt argue is cruel and unusual punishment."

"Well I like that." Aristide shuffled his feet. "On the verge of our demise, thou dost think only of thy belly."

"And that surprises thee?" Geoffrey snickered. "I wager Demetrius expected food fit for a king, not a disgraced and exiled knight."

"But thou art no longer disgraced or exiled." At the railing of the second floor gallery, His Majesty inclined his head. "While Philip burned at the stake some fifty-four knights, in May of thirteen-ten, the Vatican Chinon Parchment, issued by Pope Clement V, absolved the

Knights Templar and Grand Master de Molay, though he remains a prisoner of France, and we anticipate will suffer the same fate."

"And what of us?" Peering at his brethren, Arucard compressed his lips, as King Edward strolled to the rear and then descended the stairs. "Art we to be treated thus?"

"Although our French adversary refuses to recognize the Papal Bull *Vox in Excelsis*, which suspended thy order, or the *Ad Providam*, which redistributed thy assets to the Hospitalliers, save the fortune thee brought to my shores and so generously donated to my treasury, we would offer a proposal to serve our combined purpose." His Majesty's voice echoed on the stone walls of the chapel, as he navigated the aisle. "As thou dost seek to live, and we require warriors of unmatched prowess upon whom we can rely, let us collaborate in noble endeavors. In recompense, we shall reward thee with thy own distinguished order, the benefits of royal favor, and our unadulterated protection."

The bargain sounded too good to be true, and Arucard raised his defenses and gazed at his brothers. "Given our devout beliefs, if I may beg thy indulgence, what would thee ask of us, Sire?"

"As we recall, Sir Arucard, thou dost shepherd thy men." The King narrowed his stare. "Thine is a courageous occupation, and we do not envy thee, but at present our needs art simple. We require an oath of loyalty, obedience in all matters of state, and unimpeachable allegiance, but we art not ignorant of thy faith, so we shall bear that in mind when issuing decrees. That is our agreement, else thou mayest retire to thy quarters and spend the remainder of thy days, however many or few that may be, in reflection and solitude."

Thither was no mistaking the veiled threat, and for a few minutes, Arucard searched his mind for a response. Were his choice limited to his future, alone, he would answer without delay, as he would rather die with his soul intact than risk eternal damnation for a prolonged existence of comfort and prestige he neither demanded nor desired. But he could not ignore his crew and the consequences his response might mete upon them, so he would gladly sacrifice himself to keep them safe from harm. With his course determined, he studied his friends for any sign of reluctance, and each conveyed their acceptance in a nod of affirmation.

"Well, then." With a fist pressed to his chest, Arucard knelt, his kindred followed suit, and so it was done. "On our honor, we art at thy command, Majesty."

"Given thy reputation, which precedes thee, absent Philip's attack on thy character, we take thy word as thy oath." In that second, the King unsheathed an impressive sword, which he tapped to each man's shoulders. "Then arise most virtuous knights of the Order of the Brethren of the Coast."

"The Brethren of the Coast?" With a grimace, Geoffrey quirked his brows. "Never have I heard of them."

"That is because we created the appointment to accommodate our new men-at-arms." Edward waved to his minion, who carried a tray draped in blue velvet, which the King drew back with a flick of his wrist. "The official seal of thy occupation, for our Nautionnier Knights. Thine ships remain whither thee docked them, and we have seen to their care, as we engender immediate departure, following a ceremony of some importance to solidify our ties."

"Gramercy." Arucard studied the heavy gold object and frowned, as it struck him as garish for a humble servant. "Thou art most kind, Sire."

"See to their comfort in chambers befitting their station," His Majesty stated to the attendant. "As we have a private matter to discuss with Sir Arucard."

Now that caught his attention, and he gulped. Was it

not enough that he would surrender his life for the Crown? When the King ushered Arucard to a side room, he halted before a small table, upon which sat a crystal decanter and goblets. After pouring two portions of wine, Edward turned. "May we offer thee a refreshment? As we believe thou wilt need it."

"Gramercy, Majesty." With quivering fingers, he grasped the stem, as his thoughts ran amok. What more could the King want? "To what shall we toast?"

"Thy wedding."

#

It was a brisk fall morning in London, and the wind whispered and thrummed in the trees, casting a shower of leaves on the path, as Isolde de Tyreswelle shivered beneath her threadbare wool cloak and filled two buckets with water from the well. Balancing the shoulder yoke, she huffed and puffed, as she carried the load into the undercroft of her family's town dwelling and struggled with the weight as she shuffled into the scullery.

"Lady Isolde, thou art not a maid." After wiping her hands on her apron, Margery, who worked as a steward, of sorts, folded her arms and frowned. "Thy mother, God rest her, would be furious with thy father, as he has not done right by thee."

"And thou wilt tell him that?" she inquired, with a grimace at the prospect.

"To see thee suffer the consequences of my forthrightness?" Margery scoffed. "Not on thy life. Yet I would not permit thee to toil as a commoner, when thou art of noble blood."

"But he ordered a bath, and I dare not tarry, else he will not hesitate to spill my noble blood." With a grunt, she hoisted the pail to a pot for boiling. "Thou dost know well his temper."

"Let Anne do it." Margery wrinkled her nose. "Oh, whither is that daggle-tailed girl? *Anne*?"

"Didst thou call me, ma'am?" With a wide-eyed

expression, the timid servant, wearing more cinder soot than clothing, curtseyed, and Isolde bit back a rebuke. "Lady Isolde, that is my responsibility."

"Sorry, Anne." Pondering her father's strange mood, Isolde yielded the chore with reluctance, as she had no reason not to return to her chamber, and she rued a chance encounter with her sire. "Then I should leave thee to it."

Mustering a smile, she nodded and walked into the kitchen, whither the cook plucked a whole chicken. Whistling a frisky little ditty, Isolde strolled through the central hall, ensured the table had been cleared and cleaned, adjusted a couple of chairs with precision, and then continued to her private apartment, which functioned as her sanctuary.

So many times, she had considered running away, but whither could she go? Despite her impressive connections, no one would have sheltered a fleeing female, given the law had defined her as the earl of Rochester's property. And her lone attempt to escape, which she had ventured a few years ago, had resulted in the abrupt dismissal of a beloved nanny and a sound beating Isolde would never forget.

Breathing a sigh of relief, as she had nary a glimpse or signal of her father, she hurried to her room. After closing the door, she turned—and shrieked.

"What is wrong with thee, chitty-face?" The lord of the manor scowled, and she raised her guard.

"Father, my apologies." With a bow of her head, she averted her stare, as he did not like her to look at him. And on the rare occasion she forgot his peculiar edict, he reminded her in his favorite manner. "I supervised the preparations for thy bath, and—"

"Not my bath, thou stupid girl." As he neared, she could not stop shaking. When he grabbed her chin and brought her gaze to his, she swallowed hard as he scrutinized her. "Wash, and make thyself respectable, as I may finally have found some use for thee. Thither art new clothes, which thou art to wear tomorrow, for a very special occasion, which His Majesty has seen fit to bestow upon thy unworthy hide. And if thou dost embarrass this house and disappoint the King, thou wilt not live past the sunset. Dost thou understand?"

"Aye, Father." Trembling uncontrollably, she digested his proclamation. In that instant, she noticed a sapphire blue gown draped over the footboard. Made of sumptuous velvet, with gold embroidery and piping on the sleeves, bodice, and skirt, pearls dotted the neckline of the elegant frock. It was the finest, loveliest garment she had been given. "How should I—"

"Thou art not to ask questions, as I owe thee no answers." The force of his blow to her cheek rendered her unsteady, and in agony she fell to the stone floor. "Do as I tell thee and naught more, else I wilt cut out thy tongue, and thy future husband wilt, no doubt, thank me."

"My future husband?" Dazed and confused, she spoke before she realized she had opened her mouth, which she clamped shut, and the bitterness of blood pooled in her throat and almost gagged her, as she crawled to the four-poster and dragged herself to sit atop the mattress.

"Indeed, thou art to marry." Perched in her reading chair, the man who gave her life, and then resented the very deed that resulted in his wife's death, stared at her with unveiled contempt, and she shuddered in fear. Didst he not know she would gladly trade places with her mother? "Edward wishes to garrison troops on the lands that border ours, and he seeks an alliance through thy union with one of his knights, to solidify the Sovereign's authority. I know naught of the man, and neither do I care, as thou shalt be his burden, and I wilt at last be rid of thee. My only concern is the power and prestige my heir shall enjoy from the connection, as William is to be made an earl, in his own right. What say thee?"

"What pleases thou pleases me, Father." Was it

possible? Could someone want her? Tracing the pattern on the damask coverlet, she dared not object, but what a revelation. Indeed, fortune smiled upon her, and it could not have happened soon enough, because Isolde believed he would eventually kill her in a drunken rage, which occurred with far greater frequency as the years passed. "And I am most happy for my brother."

"Art thou?" With a countenance of sadness, which surprised her, he toyed with his signet ring. "Often I have wondered how our lives would have been different, had thy mother survived thy birth."

"Really?" Shocked by his unusual candor, as he never spoke of her mother, and starved for a kind word from him, Isolde dropped her defenses. "So have I. What was she like?"

"Custancia was the most beautiful woman in all of Rochester." Father stared at the floor and sighed. "As thou can imagine, she was quite sought after, too. For some reason I could never fathom she chose me as her husband, and our parents negotiated our betrothal. When she bore my heir, I was never prouder of her. Indeed, she was the heart of our family, and hers was a great loss."

"Everyone says she was a very fine lady." And so many of those same persons declared Isolde the exact personification of her mother, which provided a shred of comfort in solitude. Lost in the moment, she gazed at her father and smiled. "How I wish I could have known her."

From the earliest years she could recollect as a young girl, she had conjured visions of her mother, always extending support and solace during the harsh reality of Isolde's precarious existence. With only her father and brother as kin, she had tried and failed to form spiritual bonds with those who should champion and protect her. Instead, her sibling had become her worst tormentor, second only to her sire. But perchance they had finally forged a connection, however late, and she should rejoice.

"I see her in thee." For a scarce second, he studied her

with a softness she had never glimpsed in him. Then his posture stiffened, his expression sobered, and she quivered, as she knew well what would happen next. "Thou art the reason she is gone." When he stood and unhooked his belt, Isolde's spirits plummeted. "Now take off thy tunic, kneel on the floor, and let me give thee a wedding gift, that thou might remember me after thou hast departed this house and art no longer subject to my control."

#

So much had changed in so little time, and in some ways his tiny stone cell had offered a measure of security he now lacked. In one minute, Arucard was locked in White Tower and a prisoner of the King, and thither was no uncertainty in the four stone walls that defined his world, as well as his limitations. In the next instant, he wore the insignia of a knight of the realm, he enjoyed the Crown's favor, and he was betrothed, and thither was naught certain about any of the accompanying responsibilities, as freedom could be a double-edged sword. It was the last aspect of his newfound status that gave him the most concern and left him wondering if it might have been easier to burn at the stake, because he bore a specific stigma as a cross, and he knew not how to resolve the flaw in his character prior to his wedding.

Telling himself thither was naught wrong with a thirty-two-year-old-virgin, Arucard decided he had no worries—unless, of course, he was the virgin in question. As a Templar Knight, he had no interest in or use for women. In fact, he had taken a vow of celibacy on the same day he joined the order, because only the most chaste knights could ascend to the glorious hereafter. But the Templars were no more, and his tenuous position in England necessitated a marriage to protect those for whom he was accountable and to prove his loyalty to King Edward.

And as he suspected, it had been five years since he fled the Continent with his fellow warriors of the

Crusades. Five years since the Templars had been hunted, tortured, and killed during Philip the Fair's Inquisition. Of an estimated two thousand knights, only five persisted, as far as he knew. Five Templar mariners—all remained wanted men by the king of France.

The mantle in his grasp bore the familiar red cross centered on a field of white and matched the modest, unadorned cloak that was the standard attire of his once great knighthood. How he had worn the uniform with pride, how he had cared for the pristine fabric as though it were a second skin. In a sense, it had been a part of him, a part of his identity, every bit as much as his own flesh. Yet it could define him no longer. With a flick of his wrist, he sent the garb to join the other clothing that burned brightly in the fire.

After a healthy gulp of ale, which he needed, he studied the badge of the Brethren of the Coast, the fledgling order formed by his new master, a price paid to accommodate the fighting men without a home. The seal, fashioned of gold, featured a wind-star design, a large blue diamond at the center, and the Latin phrase *Nulli Secundus*, Second to None, as was their motto.

The bejeweled piece was similar to his current uniform in its splendor. His fur-lined cloak and rich blue mantle festooned, haphazardly, with gold braids violated the tenets by which he had long existed. As a Templar, he had been taught that unnecessary excess led to immorality. While he understood that his survival in a foreign land, his allegiance to a foreign king, and his union to a creature, who for all intents and purposes was foreign to him outside the maternal realm, required equally foreign customs, he kept his hair cut short and his face clean-shaven, true to his Templar ascendants. And despite the King's generosity, Arucard much preferred the simple, understated clothes.

"I found it," Demetrius stated proudly, as he pulled up a crude wooden stool and sat before the fire, whither the men gathered to toast—or rather roast Arucard's impending nuptials. "My grandsire wrote an oath when first he entered the military, and I am certain it is contained within these pages."

"What is so important about an old oath, brother?" Geoffrey shifted his weight, as he peered at the antiquated log.

"History," Morgan responded as he neared. "We art the last of our generation and the first of our kind. Never again will the Knights Templar sail as Templars, but neither will we sail quietly into the night, shrouded in deceit and disgrace. We shall live on as the Brethren of the Coast."

"Precisely." With a snicker, Aristide clutched a pitcher and refilled the goblets. "And we must never forget from whence we came."

"Especially as we face the future." Given fate posed a far more dangerous prospect than his past, Arucard lifted his chin and sighed. "And all of its uncertainties."

"When dost thou wed?" Morgan made a pitiful attempt at concealing a smile, and Arucard had the sudden urge to punch him in the nose, as his brothers found sport in his predicament.

"Tomorrow," Arucard replied, as a chill settled in his chest, and he fought nausea. "In the morrow."

"So soon?" Geoffrey rolled his eyes and whistled in monotone. "Hast thou seen her?"

How had he known to expect that particular query? Arucard shook his head. "I have not."

"Thine is a precarious situation, brother." After flicking through the pages, Demetrius abandoned his search momentarily and raised his goblet. "Better thee than I."

With a grin, Aristide ventured to ask, "Dost thou, perchance, know her name?"

"Isolde," Arucard replied with a shuffle of his feet. "She is the daughter of a nobleman, or some such."

"Oh, no. Not a pampered princess." Unaware that he had just voiced Arucard's chief concerns, Morgan frowned. "As it is safe to assume she has not seen thee, let us hope she has a sense of humor."

"Let us hope she can cook," Geoffrey said, as he tore a piece of bread from a loaf. "As we art at thy command, and Demetrius hath quite the appetite."

"Let us hope she is fair," Arucard corrected. "Else all shall be for naught, for I will sail to the end of the Earth to escape her."

His response garnered a chorus of laughter, and, for a scarce second, Arucard's spirits lightened. Yet the fact remained he was trapped in an arranged marriage he neither wanted nor welcomed.

"How many babes dost thou intend to get on her?" Oblivious to the discord he had just wrought, Demetrius flipped through the torn pages of the mangled tome. "Five or six?"

"Babes?" And so Arucard returned to the plight foremost on his mind, as he swallowed hard. Before he could beget children, he had to learn how to copulate. While he was not ignorant of the physical requirements involved in the primitive act, he had no clue how to please a woman, and London was filled with dissatisfied ladies, as evidence by the unwanted attention he garnered during dinner at court. "I-I have given it no thought."

"Well, thou hast better think about it." With an arched brow, Demetrius cocked his head. "And what wilt thou do should the damsel fall in love with thee?"

Flames crackled, and Arucard gazed into the blaze.

Love?

A violent shudder rocked his frame, as he considered the daunting prospect. Although he was quite familiar with the brotherly love upon which his knighthood was founded, he was entirely unfamiliar with the emotion as defined by the relationship between a husband and a wife. Naught on the battlefield could have prepared him for such a predicament. He was a Templar Knight, a creature of habit, and a no-nonsense man who preferred an equally staid existence. In the end, he knew only one way to live.

Pray.

Eat.

Weapons practice.

Repeat.

Then retire.

And thither was no vacancy for a woman.

"Brothers, I fear we have secured our freedom on very hard terms." With a terrible grimace, Morgan scratched his cheek. "Very hard terms."

"I fear we shall all be expected to wed," Geoffrey added.

"Not on thy soul," Demetrius said with an air of cold determination.

"Never." Aristide pressed a clenched fist to his chest. "I should sooner end my own life than take a wife. Regardless of what the English believe, no one shall convince me, not even the King, that a matrimonial commitment is worth eternal damnation."

Perchance now was not an appropriate time to tell his brother knights that, indeed, the King had commanded just that, Arucard pondered in silence. The shock of his imminent nuptials had yet to wear thin, and the road ahead would be paved with similar hardship and resignation, he suspected. His marriage to Isolde was just the beginning.

"Found it!" Demetrius stood, clutching the tattered captain's log. "Gather round, brothers."

In desperate need of distraction, Arucard extended a hand, palm down, and his fellow Nautionnier Knights followed suit, one atop the other, forming a tight bond forged of blood, flesh, and bone. "Brothers, we have fought the good fight, but we have lost the first skirmish. Yet, despite those who would wish otherwise, we survive. Mighty England is now our home, and her King is now our commander, but our destinies belong to us, and we shall not sink into the annals of history, remembered only by our dishonor. From this day forward, let it be known that the Templars remain, though mayhap by another name. We art the Brethren of the Coast. As our Heavenly Father is my witness, in times of war and chaos, we will be revered and feared."

A roar of concurrence erupted, and from the surrounding woods the strident cry of some nocturnal beast echoed in agreement. Amid a crescent of oaks, beneath the stars, by the light of a fire, the Knights of the Brethren proclaimed their own oath. It was a promise written by men long dead but not forgotten.

Love, honor, and devotion were the beginning of our Order. Bonds of kinship and friendship, all-important. We uphold these principles embrace for embrace, desire for desire, for one, for all. For King and Country we stand, for love and comradeship we live.

CHAPTER TWO

Stifled beneath the heavy gown of blue, the traditional color of purity, with the complimenting wimple and bejeweled veil secured by an identical pair of quatrefoil pins, Isolde gasped for breath as the family carriage came to a halt before the east entrance of Westminster Abbey. Seated in the squabs across from her, and ignoring her as he had over breakfast, her father gazed out the window and frowned. When the footman opened the door, the earl descended and then turned to help her down.

A canopy of gray clouds blocked the sun's rays, so the afternoon was dreary and cold, which matched her mood. The previous day's beating, unusually brutal and lengthy, had left her back covered in raw welts and open cuts, and she fought uncharacteristic weakness, because it had been years since the discipline incapacitated her. Given the weight of the plush velvet garment, in combination with the scarf that obscured her vision, she tripped.

"Watch thy step, clumsy girl." Father squeezed hard on her arm, and she winced. "If thou dost shame me, I will—"

"Aye, Father." As she gained her footing, she clenched her teeth against the searing sting from her fresh wounds. "Thou hast made thy position quite clear, and I bear thy reminder, so thou mayest rest assured I will not fail thee." As he steered her to the cloister walk, which they strolled until they reached a double-door entry topped by a Portland stone tympanum, she inhaled and attempted to relax her shoulders.

Lingering to the left, a group of impressive knights, all mountainous men with clean-shaven faces and short hair, wearing identical attire, the shade of which matched her garb, gathered before the Chapter House. When Archbishop Winchelsea loomed as a specter of ill tidings, preparing to dispatch her to her doom, Isolde's knees buckled. Everything happened so fast, and while she tried to be brave, the pitiable truth was she shivered with terror, as she had no time to adjust to the change in her situation.

Despite societal customs, no marriage notice had been posted for the requisite forty days, and her father boasted the King—not her family, provided her dowry. So her personal items had been packed into a small trunk, which had been tied to the coach, and never again would she return to her home or her familiar and comforting friends.

As she scanned the witnesses, she wondered when her groom would arrive. Hoping for an aged, dull, and feeble noble in search of an heir, a chatelaine, and naught more, and possessed of a deep-seated abhorrence for belts, she assessed the spectators, but none met her low but reasonable expectations. Perchance her intended had no penchant for punctuality.

"Now then, as both parties art present, let us begin the ceremony." Archbishop Winchelsea held up a leather bound tome and cleared his throat. "Prithee, join hands."

When the tallest, most colossal giant stepped to the fore, a harsh realization dawned, and Isolde emitted a whimper. Uttering a silent entreaty for mercy, as she would never survive one of his lashings, she retreated in panic, but Father shoved her forward, into the enormous arms of her future husband.

"My lady Isolde, art thou unwell?" With tenderness of which she had not thought him capable, her soon-to-be-spouse held her upright. "Dost thou require a moment of rest, as thither is a small bench around the corner, whither thou might take thy ease?"

"What my daughter needs is strict authority to reinforce obedience." Sneering, Father adjusted his cloak. "Heed my advice, Sir Arucard. Spare not the strap, as she is a willful sort."

With that she teetered, but the knight extended unshakeable support.

"How very kind of thee to offer sage counsel, Lord Rochester. But whither I come from, we shield our women." So her new master was called Arucard, and she favored his judgment and his name, as well as his rich baritone. "We do not batter them."

"That may be, but thou art in England, now." A telltale red hue spread across Father's face, as he stuttered and stammered, and she was grateful she no longer shared his house, but she worried about the servants who often bore the brunt of his ire in Isolde's stead. "And thou must honor our traditions."

"Allow me to assure thee, I am aware of my locale, Lord Rochester." Twining his fingers in hers, Sir Arucard peered at her and smiled. "But I would argue thither is little honor in such barbarity."

"Thank thee for thy concern, my lord Arucard." In that instant, she decided, were she given a choice between the two, she rather preferred her knight, despite his immensity, as his proclamation did much to soothe her frazzled nerves. And in light of her father's reliable temper, she opted to hope for a new and better future. "We may commence the service."

Without further ado, the archbishop flipped through the parchment, until he found his mark. "Dearly beloved friends…"

And in the next hour, Isolde became a wife to a creature she knew not.

In true English tradition, the actual nuptials took place outside the Chapter House. Listening with determination, she made her vows, repeating the archbishop's pronouncements with care and nary a misstep. With the King in attendance, her husband lifted her veil. For a few minutes, he simply scrutinized her. Then he bent and pressed his lips to hers.

Theirs was not the most romantic kiss, as they were, for all intents and purposes, utter strangers. But she viewed the simple formality as the beginning, of sorts, to a long journey; the destination of which she pledged would end in friendship. Again, she kept her presumptions modest, as never would he love her, and she was not so naïve to set such lofty aspirations that would only result in desolation and disappointment. If they could form an abiding connubial bond based on mutual respect, she would be content.

After the marriage mass ended, Arucard escorted her to his carriage. "Well, it is done."

"Indeed." As she grasped for something to say, or a bit of courtesy to impart, her mind wandered, and she started when he rested his hands at her waist to lift her to the seat. "My lord, I am quite capable of negotiating the step, and I would not burden thee."

"Thou art displeased with me?" He chuckled, as he perched beside her, and the entire bench shifted, which sent her lurching into him. "Easy, my lady."

"Nay, my lord. I am not displeased, as a dutiful wife would never object to her husband's inclinations." Brushing the wrinkles from her skirt, she scooted to the right. "But I would not encumber thee, when it is unnecessary, as I am no fragile waif."

"I find it rather intriguing that thou dost profess an unimpeachable allegiance with my proclivities, even as thou dost express opposition to my noble actions, which were motivated by naught more than a sincere desire to attend to thy welfare, Lady Isolde." Stunned by his reproach and her unforgivable breach in decorum, she almost swallowed her tongue, until Arucard glanced at her and winked. "I tease thee, my lady. But it is nice to see some sign of life."

"Often my mouth has provoked trouble and brought shame to my door." She bowed her head, as she had been married for all of five minutes and already erred. "I apologize, my lord."

"No apologies necessary, and may I call thee Isolde?" With a finger, he tipped her chin and brought her gaze to his. "Thou art charming when thou dost blush, and I prefer thee look at me, when we speak."

"Thou mayest address me however thou dost wish, as thou art my master." Goodness, how had she neglected to note the clarity and compassion invested in his blue eyes? "And I wonder if thither is a pet name thou would rather I employ?"

"A pet name?" With unmasked confusion, he arched a brow, and she laughed. "I must confess I have none."

"Then I shall have to compose one, just for thee, as a sign of endearment." When he grimaced, her confidence flagged, and she remembered her proper place. "That is— if thou dost not protest."

"Wherefore would I protest, unless thou dost plan to mock me?" With his elbow, he gave her a gentle nudge and narrowed his stare. "Wilt thou make me thy fool?"

"Oh, no." As they neared Westminster Palace, the site of the wedding feast, she bit her lip. "Never would I— thou dost bait me, sir."

"Aye." In his booming chortle, she found refuge and solace. "And I should compose a special term of address, just for thee, but I would ask thee to confine use of such informalities to our private conversations, otherwise my men would taunt me without mercy."

"That seems a very wise request, and I shall defer to thy judgment." When he handed her to the walk, she demurred. "So we dine with His Majesty?"

"I am afraid we have little choice in the matter, as he insisted." As before, he settled her palm in the crook of his elbow. "And now that we art wed, may I inquire after thy age, Isolde?"

"Of course." Yet, as she acquiesced, she wondered if he would regret taking her to wife, given her advanced years. "I am eight and ten. And thou?"

"Two and thirty." Having anticipated an exclamation of shock, given her declaration, his unimpaired composure rendered her giddy. "I hope the difference in our years does not trouble thee."

"Not at all." She lied, as his youth and handsome features inspired myriad fantasies and possibilities she dared not covet. "Must confess I supposed I might disappoint thee, as most brides celebrate their nuptials at four and ten. Dost thou feel slighted?"

"By thee?" When she nodded once, he frowned. "Never." Then he did something that surprised her. Cupping her chin, he trailed his thumb along her jawline. "Thy skin is like alabaster, and thy lips lush and ripe as a pomegranate. Thou art quite lovely, and I count myself fortunate to be thy husband."

For as long as she could recall, Isolde had considered herself something of a wit. Forever garnering rebukes from her father, she could always be relied upon to formulate clever repartee, without notice. But in that instant, her dependable faculties abandoned her, as no one had ever proclaimed her attractive.

"Ah, hither is the happy couple." Standing large in Westminster Hall, the King took her hands in his. "And Lord Rochester never told us his daughter was so beautiful. Wherefore have we not seen the Lady Isolde at court?"

Because he never permitted such luxuries, she longed

to reply, but she would not admit the truth and embarrass herself and her father. "I prefer the country life, Majesty. But hadst thou commanded otherwise, I would have obeyed."

Elegantly dressed lords and ladies filled the chasmal hall, which boasted opulent tapestries, resplendent paintings of kings past, marble-topped tables decorated with bird and lion figurines molded from jelly or pastry, and a massive dais at one end, beneath an intricate hammerbeam roof. The tempting aroma of roasted beef hung in the air, but a splendid fountain that produced wine and spiced pimento manifested an extravagant masterpiece unlike any she had ever seen.

Seated beside her husband, at a place of honor, Isolde devoured generous portions of miniature pastries filled with cod liver, brewets, broth with bacon, meat tiles, capon crisps, frumenty, lampreys with hot sauce, and venison. And Arucard consumed his fair share, which brought a query to mind, as she sought to win his approval and affinity via his stomach.

"The feast is delicious, is it not?" She scooted a bite of beef across her plate.

"It is outstanding." As she discovered was his habit, he paused and gave his full attention, which she found a bit discomfiting. "And I see thou hast a robust appetite."

"Art thou vexed?" Mayhap she should forgo the final course of sweets.

"Not at all, Isolde." When he pronounced her name in his velvety deep tone, he carried out the 'o' and gave her delightful shivers. "I prefer a woman with a healthy palate."

"Lucky for me." She forced a laugh. "My lord, if I may, thither is any particular dish thou dost favor?"

"Thither is." Leaning to the side, he whispered, "My mother made a most excellent blancmange, and I have never sampled its equal."

"What a fortuitous coincidence." At that minute,

Isolde could have jumped for joy. "As that is my specialty, and more than once it hath been declared the best in England."

"Then thou shalt cook it for me." In close proximity, she admired his chiseled cheekbones and the thick lashes she could study for the better part of an hour, if given the chance. "And I will be the judge."

How she wanted to believe in him. "Arucard, thou art—"

"We would ask the ladies to perform a carol for us, to commemorate the wedding of our esteemed knight." His Majesty stood and raised high his goblet. "And we bid the Lady Isolde adieu, as she must prepare to fulfill her duties. Guards, escort the new bride to her chambers."

#

The hour was late when Arucard, surrounded by royal sentries, returned to his private apartments in the palace. After several hearty backslaps and bellowing guffaws from his fellow Nautionnier Knights, and an unequivocal order from the King, Arucard surrendered his tankard of beer and mulled the monumental task, which neared with each successive second he counted as a death knell.

Although he posited himself no expert in such affairs, he considered the day a triumph of cooperation, and his wife bespoke a naïve charm he found unutterably arresting. To her credit, she struck him as possessed of uncommon good sense, so he approached her with a single objective, fostering and maintaining honesty, which had driven his conversation, at times, to his embarrassment, because he thought her the most striking creature of his acquaintance. Of course, he had no one with whom to compare, given Isolde ranked as the first and the last woman he would ever know beyond mere polite exchanges. Thus the prospect of marital familiarity had led him to seek advice from an unusual source—His Majesty.

According to the Sovereign, the female sex lacked the physical strength to pose any real threat, and they were singularly deficient in their ability to reason. Incapable of surviving alone, ladies relied upon men to persevere in a harsh world, and as such had been relegated to chattel, for their own protection. The lone weapon in their arsenal, and it posed a perilous hazard unlike any other, which could drive a sane man mad as a March hare, given it could consume the most ruthless warrior, rested between their legs.

It was with that thought swirling in his brain he entered the solar of his rooms. A fire in the hearth warmed the space, and the double doors to the bedchamber stood open. Then he spied Isolde, wearing a simple linen night rail, with her long hair, black as a raven's feather, cascading over her shoulders.

"Hello." Wringing her fingers, she shuffled her bare feet and then curled her toes. "I turned down the bed. Shall I help thee disrobe?"

"Uh—no." In a flash, below his belt any signs of life vanished from the most necessary part of his anatomy for consummating his vows, and he sought an escape or, at the very least, a delay. "Wilt thou take a drink with me?"

"If that is thy wish." When he stepped aside, she strolled into the solar, and he tried but failed to ignore the cleft of her bottom, just visible through the gossamer fabric. With an enviable air of calm, she picked up a pitcher and poured two goblets of wine. Facing him, she smiled, and the blaze from the fireplace reflected in her green eyes, transforming them into something altogether ethereal. "Shall we toast to our future?"

Whatever he had planned to impart suddenly eluded him. In search of distraction, he downed the contents of his glass in a single gulp. "So art thou originally from London?"

"Nay." Sitting at the large table, Isolde shifted and tucked her legs beneath her. "I was born in Rochester, the site of my family's ancestral pile. And from whither dost thou hail, as thy accent suggests thou art not English?"

"Thou art very perceptive." Entranced by her beauty and the aureoles of her rose-tipped breasts, Arucard averted his stare. "And I am from Nivernais, which is north of Bourbon. Dost thou know it?"

"I cannot say so, as I have never traveled beyond our shores." She cleared her throat. "But I should like, very much, to know how thou didst come to be in service to the Crown, if thou art amenable to sharing the details of thy history."

"Thither is much I would share with thee, Isolde." But could he trust her with his most intimate secrets and his dubious affiliation as a Templar? "Yet the night grows old, and we depart for Chichester with the dawn." With that, he stood and unbuckled his belt.

A cry of alarm signaled his wife's distress, though he knew not what caused her anxiety, and she toppled her goblet. In the next second, she flew from her seat, glanced left and then right, seized upon his halberd, which perched in the corner, and she assumed a provocative stance. "What have I done? Did I insult thee, however unintended? Wherefore would thou treat me thus, when I yielded without compunction?" With wild and jerky movements, she thrust the pointed end in his direction. "And thou didst seem so nice."

"Calm thyself, Isolde." Palms splayed, he lowered his chin. "Thou dost misunderstand my actions, as I plan to sleep in the solar."

"What?" Inclining her head, she narrowed her stare. "Wherefore should I believe thee, when the King commands we consummate our vows?"

"But His Majesty is not hither, and what he doth not know will not hurt him." What spirit she displayed, and how he admired her courage. Recalling her father's harsh words, he realized his mistake. Moving slow and steady, he set the belt on the table and retreated. "Put down the weapon, before thou dost injure thyself, as I only seek to make myself comfortable enough to retire. Please, Isolde.

I would never harm thee."

"So thou dost not want me." Squared off as two opponents, he drew upon the patience of a saint, as she compressed her lips. At last, she sighed and returned the long-handled, combined spear and battle-axe to its previous innocuous position. "And I suppose now I have given thee reason to spank me."

At her sullen admission, he laughed. "Methinks not."

"Is this pity?" With an adorable pout, she sniffed. "Dost thou grant mercy?"

"Never have I known anyone less in need of mercy." One after the other, Arucard tugged off his boots, under her wary gaze. "And as I have never shared a bed with a woman, I thought it best to allow for a period of adjustment, for both our sakes. When the time is right, we will secure our vows in obeisance of the Crown's dictates—but not tonight."

"Wait." With an expression of confusion, she blinked. "Art thou telling me that thou art a virgin?"

"Aye." He knew not what he expected in her reaction to his revelation, but she neither snickered nor laughed. "My faith is such that I will join my body with whom I have taken the sacrament and no one else. To do otherwise is an abomination."

"Dost thou speak in truth—not in jest?" She opened her mouth and then closed it. "Dost thou mock me?"

"My dear Isolde, I know naught but the truth, and never would I treat thee with such condescension." Arucard walked into the inner chamber and retrieved a blanket and a pillow. Then he opened his trunk and located a particular item of importance. In the solar, he handed his bride the canvas bundle. "A wedding gift for thee."

"Thou hast brought me a present?" She tugged on the twine. "But I have naught for thee."

"At the risk of again ending up on the wrong end of the halberd, I must confess the King proclaimed thee my gift." When she unwrapped the illustrated book of Psalms, he situated a rudimentary pallet on the floor. "I hope thou art pleased, as it belonged to my mother."

"It is a psalter." With reverence in concert with a mix of hushed gasps, she fingered the parchment. "The pictures art so colorful, and never have I owned anything so grand." When she glanced at him, she started. "Prithee, thou art not going to sleep thither."

"Indeed, I am, and I will be fine." To his chagrin, she hugged the family heirloom to her chest and marched straight toward him. "Isolde, I have endured far worse conditions."

"Not in my presence, and thither is no need for thee to do so now, because the accommodations art generous." A hint of a feminine smile graced her lips, as she bent, snatched the cushion, and returned it to the large four-poster. "Let us divide the mattress, as thou mayest take one side, and I will recline on the other, unless thou art incapable of controlling thyself."

"I beg thy pardon." Wounded by her insult, he leaped to his feet and dragged the blanket behind him, determined to prove her wrong as he stomped to the bed. "I am no godless heathen to molest thee." Then he noted her impish grin, as she slipped beneath the covers. "Now thou dost bait me."

"Yea." She peered over her shoulder. "Art thou vexed?"

"I am verily so." In play, he wrinkled his nose and scowled. "Mayhap I should spank thee, after all." The abrupt change in her demeanor, the sheer horror in her once appealing gaze had him cursing as he eased beside her. "I am sorry, Isolde. I quipped in haste, but I can see from thy countenance I failed. Please know that I would sooner cut off my arm than strike thee."

"Would that all men were so chivalrous." Inhaling a shaky breath, she flinched when he cupped her cheek. "And I have known little kindness in this world, so I pray thou wilt forgive me."

"Thither is naught to forgive, as I should not have frightened thee." Whereas he had prepared to experience ardor, passion, or even base lust on his wedding night, he had not anticipated the altogether different sensations waging war within him, at that moment. The urge to protect her, to comfort her, to hold her in his arms, and to defend her to his death burned as an unquenchable flame in his chest, and he longed to reassure her. "Sleep, sweet Isolde. And I shall guard thy slumber with my life."

#

A sharp pounding on the door brought Isolde abruptly awake and alert. Warm and cozy, she yawned, cuddled closer to the unfamiliar heat source, and relaxed—until she realized she rested against her husband. With his chiseled features softened in repose, at some point during the night he had draped an arm about her waist, and she had curled to his side. Curiosity beckoned, and she availed herself of the opportunity to admire his magnificent profile. Another loud rap brought a frown to his full lips, and Arucard opened his eyes.

"Good morrow, Isolde." With a finger, he tapped the tip of her chin. "It appears we have an unwelcomed intruder. If thou wilt remove thyself from my person, I will answer the summons."

"Of course." Embarrassment burned in her cheeks, and she scooted to the opposite end of the bed. "I should apologize for impinging on thy territory, in breach of our arrangement."

"Thither wilt come a time when thou wilt not apologize for everything thou dost perceive hast irritated me?" Still fully clothed save his boots, her husband stood, raked his hair, walked to the washstand, splashed water on his face, dried himself with a towel, and then strolled into the solar. He took two steps, paused, and then closed the doors.

Alone, she flew from the four-poster. After tugging on her hose and garters, she exchanged the nightgown for a chemise and then pulled a cotehardie over her head, just as Arucard returned. "Who was it?"

"The King's guard." His harsh expression gave her cause for concern. "His Majesty demands proof I have claimed thy maidenhead. God's bones, what art we to do?"

To Isolde, the answer seemed simple, yet she trembled at the prospect. "Then thou must do the deed."

"My dear, I shall abide the Crown's request, soon enough." With a heavy sigh, he peered toward the floor, or so she thought. "But as of this instant, it is a physical impossibility, and the additional pressure does not help matters."

"Oh." Despite her virginal state, she understood his meaning, given the ribald behavior of her brother William, who seduced every pretty maid in their home in Rochester, producing more than one by-blow, which was wherefore Father hired either older or younger servants, thereafter. Then a brilliant idea shot to the fore. "We need blood presumably on the bedclothes?"

"So it seems." Arucard nodded in agreement.

"All right." Quickly, she yanked the sheet from the mattress. "If thou wilt stoke the blaze in the hearth, please."

"As thou dost wish." Arching a brow, he scratched his temple and then stomped to the fireplace.

Before she lost her nerve, she rolled up her sleeve and then retrieved and unsheathed his sword. The heavy weapon presented quite a conundrum, as she could not wield it, so she ran her forearm along the blade. As crimson oozed from the small wound, she staunched the flow with the linen, achieving the necessary stain. "Thither, it is perfect."

"What is thy—what hast thou done?" Her knight yanked hard on her wrist. "Thou hast injured thyself."

"How else can we fulfill our duty, if not by the usual activity?" When he tore a scrap of cloth and bandaged what she considered a mere scratch, she laughed but treasured his show of disquietude. "Now drape the sheet over the chair near the fire, so it will dry, and then we should ready ourselves to depart."

"But I would have taken care of it, hadst thou told me what thee planned." While she buttoned the front of her cotehardie, he pulled on his boots. "And it is my responsibility, as thy husband, to preserve thy welfare and to sacrifice when such action is needed."

"Thou art most chivalrous, sir." And she remained unaccustomed to such concern, as her father cared not for her well-being. "My lord, if the Sovereign wants my blood, then he will have it."

"Whilst I commend thy courage and resourcefulness, I would argue the King would not know mine from thine, and I will not permit thee to harm thyself for my sake." To her surprise, he brought her knuckles to his lips and pressed on her a chaste kiss, which gave her a strange sensation, neither flirtatious nor serious, but nonetheless potent, in the pit of her belly. For several seconds, Arucard did naught but gaze into her eyes, and he managed to touch her without touching her. Then he cupped her cheek, bent his head, and set his mouth to hers. Just as fast, he retreated. "I am sorry, Isolde. But thou art quite honestly the most beauteous creature I have ever beheld, and thou art mine, thus thou dost present temptation as I have never known, yet I will try to restrain myself until we art better acquainted as I would not frighten thee."

"Husband, I hope thou art not displeased, and I mean no offense, but methinks thou art the last man I would ever fear, after thy solicitous behavior on our wedding night. And I would ask thee to cease thy apologies, in the same spirit, as we art married." And she would never forget his kindness, when Margery had imparted horrid tales of all manner of dreadful possibilities, given their unfamiliarity prior to their nuptials, so she had anticipated the worst. "Know that when thou dost choose to demand thy matrimonial rights, I will bear it without complaint."

"How romantic thou dost make it sound." Again, to her amazement, he drew her into his arms, and she fought rising panic, as Margery ranked as the lone person to ever hug Isolde. To her delight, she found her husband strong and comforting, in spite of his size. Although his hands were twice the breadth of hers, he was gentle with his caresses, and she sank into his tender embrace. "I prefer we enjoy the consummation of our vows, and that is wherefore I delay the inevitable, as I would celebrate the portentous occasion—not simply tolerate it."

"A very noble gesture, my lord." Without thought, she clutched him at the waist and pressed even closer, until he ran his palms over her back, which irritated her injuries, yet she reveled in the solace he offered. When he flinched, she withdrew. "Did I hurt thee?"

"Er—no." Yet a telltale hue spread from his neck to his face, and she suspected otherwise. "Now we should garb ourselves for an audience with His Majesty, as our presence is requested in the great hall, along with the proof of bedding, which should be sufficiently dry."

"Pray, a moment, as I must braid my hair." In haste, she completed her morning ritual, as Arucard shaved. "Dost thou groom thyself every day?"

"Aye, as it is a sign of discipline." He brushed his short hair.

"Hast thou never pondered growing a beard?" She tugged on her leather slippers and smoothed her skirts. "As it is the fashion, and thou would wear it well, my lord."

"I am not partial to such frivolous embellishments." In that instant, she decided she rather preferred his austerity. When he stripped to trade his lawn shirt for a fresh garment, she could not stop herself from ogling his muscled back and broad shoulders.

"Perchance a mustache?" she inquired, with a grin, as

he seemed so virtuous she could not resist teasing him.

"Nay." He wrenched on a blue tunic, which bore an unusual insignia with a wind-star design at center. "Art thou trying to tell me thou dost not like the way I look?"

"On the contrary." After repacking her meager belongings, she waited in the solar for her husband. Anon, she checked the sheet, and the stain had dried, so she folded the linen. When the escort arrived, Arucard joined her.

"I wish I could spare thee the spectacle, Isolde. And I do not approve of such vulgar practices." In the passage, he took her by the elbow. "Remain at my side, and say naught unless thou art addressed. If the King questions thee, give short and direct answers, and if thou art unsure how to respond, defer to me."

"Yea, my lord." Something in his demeanor changed, and palpable tension invested her nerves, given his cryptic warning was the first sign of unrest since their wedding.

In the great hall, they neared the dais. As customary, she curtseyed, and her husband bowed.

"Sir Arucard, we trust thou passed a pleasant night?" A guard carried the sheet to the Sovereign. "And thou hast fulfilled our edict, though I suspect thou should thank us, as the Lady Isolde blushes."

"Thou hast my eternal gratitude, Majesty." In a bold display of affection, Arucard kissed her hand. "And never have I slept so little."

A chorus of laughter filled the cavernous chamber, and various nobles gathered at the table, shared whispers, and traded hearty guffaws at her expense, but she cared not.

"And is Lady Isolde happy with our choice?" the Crown asked, with a snicker.

Gazing at the plush red carpet, she dipped her chin. "I am exceedingly happy, Sire."

"We art delighted to hear it," the King replied. "And now thou art to depart for Chichester, as we have signed a bill of attainder, and we bestow upon Sir Arucard the earldom of Sussex, whereupon thou shalt establish the garrison we require."

"Gramercy, Majesty." Arucard squeezed her arm, and she followed his lead. "By thy leave."

"Wait." To her chagrin and trepidation, her father rounded the buffet. "I would bid my daughter farewell."

Reluctant to relinquish her husband's protection, she held tight to him, until her father drew her into an awkward embrace. "Take care, Father."

"Read this missive when thou art alone, and do as I instruct." He slipped her a sealed envelope, which she promptly tucked in the fitchet of her cotehardie. With that, he patted her back, as if to remind her of the consequences should she defy him, and she emitted a bare whimper. "Never forget I will be watching thee."

"I will miss thee, too, Father." She gritted her teeth against the pain, as he knew well the damage from his last beating had yet to heal.

"Come, Isolde." Then Arucard did not speak until they entered the palace yard. "Wilt thou long for thy family and London?"

Pondering the contents of the mysterious message, which portended nefarious enterprises if she knew well her father, she could not put the city behind her soon enough. "Nay."

CHAPTER THREE

With his hands at her waist, Arucard lifted Isolde into the four-wheeled wagon, which had been outfitted with substantial comforts. And for the second time that day, he struggled with unfamiliar and discomposing activity below his belt. As a virgin unaccustomed to physical enthusiasms, he knew not how to control the strange, but not altogether unpleasant, sensations emanating from his unusually active crotch region.

"Art thou settled, my lady?" Just a glimpse of her shapely hose-covered calves elicited an uncanny tension in his muscles, and he bit back a groan. "As I prefer thee enjoy our journey."

"Brother, the Lady Isolde has a visitor." Averting his stare, Demetrius shuffled his feet and frowned, as his fellow Brethren of the Coast had yet to adjust to a woman in their midst.

"Margery?" With a gasp, Isolde descended from her perch. "And Anne? What art thou doing hither?"

Lingering in his wife's wake, Arucard peered at Demetrius. "Is everyone prepared to depart?"

"Aye, sirrah." Demetrius rubbed the back of his neck. "Well, did the mountain stag stir her waters?"

"I knew thee would ask." As his bride conversed with her acquaintants, he admired her swanlike neck, imagined running his tongue along the gentle curve, and a vicious erection roared to life in his braies. How would he manage a long ride on horseback with a loaded trebuchet? "Art the soldiers assembled?"

"Thou dost avoid the question." And knowing Demetrius, the interrogation would not end until he was satisfied. "So how was it?"

"Have I not told thee that thou dost talk too much?" In that instant, Isolde glanced over her shoulder, and he spied distress in her expression. "Something is wrong."

"Thou dost seek an escape." Demetrius chuckled, as Arucard approached the three women.

"Shall I beg an introduction?" Then he noted the tears. "Wherefore dost thou weep, my lady?"

"Oh, Arucard, I have such dire news." Her chin quivered as she clutched his hand. "My father terminated the employment of two of the most faithful servants from his household, and I cannot abandon them. If thou wilt not—"

"Then let us take them with us to Chichester." It seemed the obvious solution, and they could use the additional attendants. "In fact, thou mayest consider them another wedding gift."

"Wilt thou do that for me?" she inquired in a small voice, as if he had just handed her the world. In that moment, he realized she had not exaggerated when she stated she had known little if any kindness in her life, and he vowed to correct the injustice. "When I have given thee naught in return for thy generosity?"

"Would it make thee happy?" Without thought, Arucard traced the edge of her jaw in a shocking demonstration of familiarity. "Because I do so wish to make thee happy."

"Thou hast, my lord." For the glow in her countenance, he would purchase a thousand such luxuries, if only to see her shimmering smile. "Mayest Margery and Anne ride in my wagon?"

"They art thine to do with as thou wilt." The knowledge that his pleasure inextricably intertwined with hers perplexed him, even though it was right, given they had taken the sacrament. And their nuptials forever fixed her as his property, which both repelled and fascinated him, and he had yet to reconcile the two. "I charge thee with their supervision, my lady wife."

"By thy command, my lord. Margery, Anne, wilt thou stow thy belongings, as Sir Arucard requires we set out, with undue haste." As she spoke, Isolde never broke their contact. To him, she said, "And might I impose upon thy assistance, again?"

"Thou art no imposition." In a repeat of his earlier moves, he made to heft her to the bench, but she stayed him when she wrapped her arms about his neck.

"Given I have no money or property, as my dowry is thine, I have but a single meager offering to bestow upon my valorous knight." And then she did something he never would have predicted. She kissed him.

The taste of her lips, sweeter than any confection, posed an alluring enticement doubled by the knowledge that she initiated the diverting interlude, and his man's yard grew hard as stone, while the ground seemed to pitch and roll beneath his feet. But when she parted her sumptuous flesh, mingled her tongue with his, and moaned, he well nigh spilt his seed in his braies. A hunger like no other charged his nerves, and uncharted heat simmered in his muscles. Somewhere in the deep recesses of his mind, a jolting understanding occurred to him then—he desired his wife.

On the heels of the thought, he lifted his head. "It appears we have reversed positions, and I am now in thy debt, as thither was naught meager in that incomparable reward."

"What a lovely thing to say." With an adorable giggle, she rubbed her nose to his, and instinctively he pressed his hips to hers. As she gave vent to a gasp, she peered between them and favored him with an expression of wonder. Had she noted his aroused state? Had he shocked her? "My lord, fear not, as I will not wait too long to come to thee."

And how he suddenly looked forward to the exceptional event, which represented a drastic shift in his perspective in a short span of time.

At first when they slipped between the sheets the previous night, whilst they cuddled abed, his lower territories had remained stubbornly dormant and impervious to her influence. But at some point throughout the wee hours, when she cuddled close, and her warm soft body caressed his frame, he decided the marital condition posited unforeseen benefits, chief among them his bride's beauty, which he savored in the dim light from a single taper. Thither, beneath the clear blue sky, the sun's bright rays, and amid a throng of servants, soldiers, and knights, Arucard could have taken his wife in the wagon, with all present as witnesses to the deflowering. However, he had no intention of baring his backside to a mixed audience.

"As I said, I will not pressure thee." With care, he planted her safely on the bench and winked, as he squeezed her ankle. "But at this moment, I am infinitely grateful to the King."

"Oh, so am I." A rosy hue about her face bespoke the truth of her much-cherished declaration, and she brushed the back of her knuckles to his cheek. "May I confess, when we took our vows, I knew not what to expect, but I am not so afraid, anymore, and I have thee to thank for that?"

"Then let us away, as our new home awaits." And the future seemed bright, indeed. Humming a flirty little ditty,

Arucard turned—and halted.

Standing in a half-circle, with rigid postures, arms folded, and impressive scowls, his brethren formed a formidable line of resistance and disapproval, and he guessed at their objection. Their long-held beliefs proscribed overt displays of affection, yet their credence had not accounted for a papal betrayal, a hasty exile, an impromptu commission under a new monarch, and an unplanned union. Not to mention, he had yet to divulge the fact that the Nautionnier Knights had been commanded to take brides chosen by His Majesty, on a date to be named. But he would fight that battle at the appropriate time.

"Not a word, brothers." In a few steps, he climbed into the saddle of his destrier and grasped the reins. "Now gain thy mounts, as we have much to achieve, and the day grows old."

#

The evening sun danced on the horizon, and a cool wind lashed the cover of her wagon, as the procession pulled into an open field for the night. A copse of trees formed an informal border, of sorts, and from her bench seat, Isolde peered at her knight and smiled, which he returned in equal measure. For the better part of the journey, thus far, she had passed the time in idle reflection, admiring her husband's glorious physique and patrician profile. Instead of riding at the front of the line, in a position of prominence, Arucard remained near; casting haphazard glances, always accompanied by a grin, which she found infectious, in her direction, as though he guarded a most precious cargo.

"My lady, thou hast not said much, but I would ascertain thy condition that I might serve thee." With her head bowed, Margery averted her gaze. "I have soothing bath oils and an acopon for the pain, should thou need to recover from thy consummation."

"Thither is no need for such potions and balms, old

45

friend." Mulling her restful night, Isolde chuckled. "My husband is a thoughtful and considerate man, and he granted a deferment until we art better acquainted."

"What?" Panic invested her tone, as Margery wrenched Isolde's arm. "Dost thou mean ye hast not sealed thy vows?"

"Wherefore dost thou worry?" Given her husband's patience and noble nature, Isolde covered the housekeeper's hand, as thither was no cause for alarm. "Really, thou must calm thyself, else thou wilt give thyself a terrible megrim. And Arucard is the kindest and gentlest spouse. What have I to fear?"

"Dost thou not see the danger of thy position, child?" With a half-sob, Margery bit her bottom lip. "My lady, what the archbishop hath done, thy father can have undone, on a whim. Until thou dost surrender thy maidenhead to Sir Arucard, he owns thee not. And though I hesitate to speak of it, as the earl employed me, I suspect Lord Rochester doth conspire against the Crown."

"Nonsense." Then Isolde recalled the letter, which she had yet to read, that her father had passed during their awkward farewell, and she pulled the envelope from her fitchet. "I am positive thou dost misunderstand the situation, as Father is a complicated man."

"My lady, I beg thy indulgence." Inhaling a shaky breath, Margery stared at Anne. "Wherefore dost thou not set up a fire, so we may prepare dinner?"

"But thou art about to discuss something of interest." Pouting and grumbling her protest, Anne shuffled to the bench and jumped from the wagon. "I always have to do the dirty work."

"Because that is thy occupation." Margery wagged a finger. "Now mind thy manners, cease thy complaints, and tarry not, else thou mayest walk back to London."

"Do not be so hard on her, as she hath had her life upended." Then again, Isolde had confronted similar chaos in her circumstances, yet fate smiled upon her, as

Arucard seemed more a blessing than a curse, and she counted herself fortunate. "And as for my stalwart spouse, he is not what he appears. Regardless of his formidable stature and somewhat abrupt demeanor, Sir Arucard is a soul of compassion."

"My dear, at the end of the day, he is the King's servant, His Majesty ordered the marriage, and all men desire political advances. Dost thou not fathom the reality of thy situation?" With desperation in her visage, the housekeeper grabbed Isolde's wrist. "As long as thou dost remain a virgin, thy nuptials can be annulled. Whilst thy faith in Sir Arucard is commendable, thou dost hardly know him. He can, at this very instant, sue for dissolution of the marriage on the grounds that thou hast failed to perform thy wifely duty, and no one will argue otherwise. Given Lord Rochester's disposition, and his propensity for violence whither thou art concerned, dost thou believe thou wilt survive his wrath should thee shame the family?"

The confidence Isolde coveted had just vanished.

"If what thou dost say is true, and I suspect thou art correct, as thy instincts have always been infallible, then I should make myself available to him—tonight." At the prospect, she gulped but then ticked off an imaginary list. "Margery, pluck two chickens, and locate the stores of rice and honey, while I mash the almonds. And have Anne set up the small table from Sir Arucard's wagon."

"What art thou going to do?" The steward furrowed her brow.

"Just as thou dost suggest, but I would soften him with my blancmange." Again, Isolde remembered the correspondence in her fitchet, and she withdrew the missive. "Go, worrisome friend, and do as I ask, as I would not serve my husband a maw-wallop on our special night."

Alone, Isolde fingered the wax seal and then cracked it. As she unfolded the parchment, a chill of dread, which augured doom, shivered down her spine, and she clenched her teeth. The opening salutation foretold disaster, and she knew not what to make of the details the note contained, but she did not, for a brief second, trust her father.

My darling Isolde,

By now thou art wedded and bedded to a foul animal with immoderate inclinations, and thy only hope for survival is to remain loyal to thy family. Please know I had no choice in the matter of thy betrothal, as I serve the King. As thy father, I claim thy allegiance that I might save thy soul and enact thy eventual rescue. Whilst the consummation of thy vows could not be avoided, and we shall seek absolution from the archbishop once thou art free from the monster thou hast married, know that my heart weeps for thee. Watch Sir Arucard closely, and report to me any revelations, however thou mayest deem insignificant, as thou art incapable of discerning important facts from trivial details. If possible, try to learn of his background and connection to the Crown. And what is the origin and location of Sir Arucard's fortune? I expect a response from thee, posthaste.

Thy loving father, Lord Rochester

Her *loving* father? Had he been drunk when he composed the letter, because never had he made such a declaration? At once, everything inside her railed against her father's claims, and a wave of nausea rocked her belly, as Isolde believed the worst of him. And despite her brief association with Arucard, she doubted him not. Yet Father presented a threat she could neither ignore nor suppress.

Searching the area, as her first instinct was to inform her husband of the dubious request, she frowned when she could not locate her knight. Soldiers and servants scattered in all directions, setting up tents and lighting fires to service the encampment. Then she spotted her spouse standing amid his friends, and she steered for him, determined to disclose the entire contents of the malevolent message and seek counsel.

"My lady, I found the ingredients thou dost require, and the chickens art almost ready." Stepping into Isolde's path, Margery wiped her hands on a cloth. "For the best flavor, thou should pound the breasts whilst they art fresh. After all, thou dost not want to give thy husband any reason to regret wedding thee."

When the significance of Margery's hapless warning struck Isolde, she halted and reconsidered her course of action. Father's correspondence marked her as a collaborator of the worst sort, and thither was no guarantee Arucard would believe her an innocent, given their brief association, despite sincere protestations of blamelessness. A wise woman would soften her husband's mood before relaying bad news.

"Help me, Margery." Isolde thrust the offensive dispatch into her fitchet, grabbed an apron, laced it behind her, and snatched a heavy dowel, which she used to mash the meat. "Tonight, it is imperative I serve the best blancmange Sir Arucard hath ever tasted. And send one of the manservants to station a barrel of ale, as my husband prefers it to wine."

"Yes, my lady." The housekeeper half-curtseyed as Isolde poured milk into a pan. "Shall I set the special table for the two of thee, mayhap, in thy tent?"

"What a wonderful idea—wait." Then Isolde snapped her fingers. "Disregard that order, as I would do something else, entirely. I want a position of distinction, but not for us, and not in private. Rather, I would have thee situate enough seating for Sir Arucard and his knights, in a place of honor and prominence, as I would have him know I esteem him and his men. And I will dine with thee and Anne."

"But thy place is at Sir Arucard's side." In the makeshift outdoor kitchen, Margery untied a bag, which she handed to Isolde. "Careful not to burn the milk, my lady."

"I will take care of this, and thou should secure additional assistance, as we must feed everyone in our traveling party." She added rice to the pan and stirred the contents with a wooden spoon. "And can thou find Anne and have her search out the bread?"

"Now whither did I pack the trenchers?" With arms folded, Margery furrowed her brow and inspected the various trunks filled with cooking implements. "Oh, never mind. Let me see to the dining area, and then I will return to forage for the utensils."

The despicable petition weighed heavy on her heart and mind, as Isolde tarried, and while her thoughts raced, she could seize upon no clear solution to her quandary. No matter how she sliced it, the ignoble entreaty put her at odds with her new spouse, when she sought accord. Wherefore could Father not leave her in peace?

Closing her eyes, she slipped beyond the present and traveled back to her last day at home. Amid lash after brutal lash, Father made no secret of his utter contempt for her. Bereft of breath from the exertion necessary to deliver the blows, he sputtered and laughed at her sharp inhalations, which kept rhythm with his beating as she braced for the strike and accompanying pain. At one point, he professed a deep-seated hatred of Isolde, and she bore his ire to spite him, which seemed to further incite his fury and abuse.

Yea, she could have relented, could have collapsed in a heap of tears and begged him to stop, but she refused to grant him the satisfaction of victory. Instead, she persevered as she always had, and he thrashed her until he buckled, presumably from exhaustion, and could deliver no more punishment. And should Sir Arucard develop the same penchant for her flesh and blood, she would respond in similar fashion, even if it killed her, because she knew no other way.

After the small army of servants set up camp, Isolde's pudding firmed, and Anne assisted in making enough food for everyone else, Margery summoned the group to supper. As was tradition, the women in the party distributed ample portions to the men and then served themselves. It was only when Isolde perched on a bench that she chanced a glance at her husband.

Chuckling with his knights, he scooped a bite with his fingers and brought the fare to his mouth. To her amusement, he paused, sniffed the morsel, and sampled the dish. When he snapped to attention, peered left and then right, spied her, and waved, she gulped. Just as quick, he elbowed Demetrius, who scooted to one end, and then Arucard again motioned for her to join him.

Nervous, her hands shook as she collected her meal and goblet of wine. With cautious strides, she navigated the sea of travelers until she loomed before her mate and curtseyed. "My lord."

"My lady." He stood, rounded the table, took her trencher, grasped her wrist, and led her to a spot at his side. "Wherefore dost thou hide with the maids?"

"I did no such thing." Too late, she reminded herself not to argue with him, as the husband was always right. And she had yet to share Father's diabolical letter. "I merely show deference, as a good and dutiful wife."

The knight called Aristide snorted, and Demetrius snickered, but the remaining warriors all but ignored her.

"As a good and dutiful wife, thou should know thy place is with me." For a scarce second, Arucard appeared vexed, and then he smiled, which put her at ease, as he settled himself. "This blancmange is outstanding. And I must beg my mother's forbearance, as never have I tasted its equal. Is that not right, brothers?"

"The pudding is sufficient—*ouch*." Aristide flinched and grimaced. "I mean, yea. By God's bones, the food is delicious."

"The lady Isolde is a fine cook." Shifting his weight,

Demetrius shot a wicked scowl at Arucard. "So thou mayest spare my shins, brother."

"I know not of what thou speak." Pounding his fist atop the table, which gave her a start, Arucard narrowed his stare. "And is that the sum of adulation and gratitude my bride earned for her labors?"

In unison, Geoffrey and Morgan muttered almost incomprehensible compliments.

"Praise, indeed." Bowing her head, she bit her tongue to stave off laughter. To Arucard, she whispered, "Dost thou verily like it?"

To wit he leaned close, winked, and replied, "I would have married thee for thy blancmange, alone."

#

It was late when Arucard shuffled into the tent he would share with Isolde. When he drew back the interior panel, he discovered Pellier sitting on a stool near the huge ancere, a wedding present from the King, created to accommodate Arucard's large frame.

"Whither is Lady Isolde?" Glancing about the sizable temporary abode, Arucard suspected she remained with the servants, because it had not taken long to discern his wife possessed an admirable work ethic. "Has she returned from the night's feast?"

"I would not know, sir." The marshalsea carried a towel from the washstand. "Shall I help thee disrobe and bathe?"

"Do not take insult, old friend." After unfastening his belt and stripping off his tunic, Arucard sat on the hastily erected bed and doffed his boots, as he selected his words with care, because he would not incite discord between his bride and his manservant. "Methinks, mayhap, now I am married, thou should no longer tend my personal needs. At least, not until I negotiate such details with Lady Isolde. In future, we shall confine thy services to battle preparation and maintenance of my armor and weapons, unless I command otherwise."

"A very shrewd decision, my lord. And I would not ruffle that haughty maid Margery, given her quick temper." With a grin, Pellier bowed. "By thy leave, I wish thee a pleasant rest."

"And I bid thee the same." Heaving a sigh, Arucard stood, walked to the back corner, and opened his trunk. In pursuit of fresh braies and a clean linen shirt, he flipped through his belongings, secured the necessary items, and then removed his remaining clothing. Naked, he eased into the ancere, reclined, sank beneath the surface of the hot water, and closed his lids.

In a flash, visions of a green-eyed angel with lush black hair danced in his thoughts. He had known her for two days, yet she was his woman, and that singular realization inspired all manner of naughty notions and foreign sensations. Then again, as she was his bride, was it not natural to desire her?

Minutes later, a frolicsome hum snared his attention, and he peeked through his lashes just as Isolde entered the tent. In the faint light of a single brazier, she had not noticed him, and he sat mesmerized as she stepped from her shoes, lifted her skirts, removed her garters and hosiery, and unbuttoned her cotehardie. Without warning, his unusually exuberant nether dragon breathed fire. When she turned, she gazed straight at him and shrieked.

"My lord Arucard, I did not see thee when first I entered our tent." In an instant, she averted her stare, and he would wager she blushed, which amused him for some odd reason. "Let me restore my clothing, and I will wait outside whilst thou dost wash."

"Do not be foolish." In a show of modesty, he shielded his crotch with a small cloth. "Thou need not—"

"Actually, it is my duty to assist thee." Contrary to her outward behavior, which bespoke internal discomfit, the quick alteration in her manner caught him unaware, but when she dropped her outer garment, leaving naught more than her sheer chemise to cover her enthralling female curves, he came alert. "As thy wife, I should scrub thy back and whatever else thou dost require. And if it is no inconvenience, I would use the ancere once thou art finished."

Whatever he had expected her to say, that was not it, and he sloshed water as he sat upright. It occurred to him then that he had no real concept of the matrimonial state, and they had yet to determine the rules of engagement. "Isolde, cleanliness is part of my discipline, it is ingrained in my character, and I do not demand such habits of thee. But if thou dost wish to share my daily ritual, I would have thee bathe first."

"Art thou always so gallant?" She knelt beside the ancere, took the soap from his grasp, lathered his chest, and splayed her sudsy palms across his flesh, which again woke his one-eyed dragon. "How didst thou get this scar?"

"In battle." Painfully aroused, he hunkered forward in an attempt to conceal his affliction and vowed to master the volatile protuberance, which had grown evermore unpredictable since Isolde entered his life. "But the wound has long since healed."

"Wherefore were thou fighting, and who were thee defending?" The answers to her seemingly harmless questions revealed more than he dared share, until they consummated their union. She leaned near to scrub his hair. "And who won the engagement?"

"We safeguarded our beliefs and stood for those who could not protect themselves." At that instant, he noticed the front of her slip had dampened, and the wet fabric hid naught from his scrutiny. Never had he found female breasts so beguiling, as he had no experience with them, but never had he contemplated the singular womanly feature in such close proximity. The twin crimson-tipped peaks lured him as a bee to honey, and he ached to caress her. "And we prevailed, my brothers and I." Anticipating additional queries, he ceased ogling her body only to find her studying him.

"Wilt thou not touch me?" Slowly, she clutched his wrist and brought his hand to her mound of firm flesh. "Art thou not pleased with me? Dost thou not want me?"

"Isolde, thou dost please me more than thou dost know, and I long to take thee." As he cupped, stroked, and explored her oh-so-mesmerizing endowments, her nipple hardened, and she inhaled a rush of breath. "Did I injure thee?"

"No." She licked her lips. "It is just that never have I been thus affected, and if thou would claim that which is thine by law and the sacrament, I will not oppose thee."

"A generous offer from a benevolent lady—*my* lady." Through the fine linen undergarment, he teased her taut pebble with the pad of his thumb. Yea, his anatomy could satisfy her, yet his body had not allied with his mind, and he wanted to know more about her prior to negotiating intimacy. "But I am unprepared for what thou dost ask of me."

"Wilt thou not send me away?" The fear in her countenance altered his stance, as it was clear she required validation, of a sort. "Wilt thou return me to my father for failure to comply with thy wishes?"

"Ah, thou dost not trust me, when I refuse to take thee as a poxy-cheeked strumpet. And I would allay thy doubts in regard to the constancy of my devotion in advance of our consummation." So what could Arucard do, without violating his promise and her maidenhead, as some barbarian boothaler? Then he recalled her gift in exchange for the servant wenches. "Come hither, Isolde."

Cupping her chin, he tilted her head and set his lips to hers.

As before, molten heat poured through his veins, and she flicked her tongue at his. When she speared her fingers through his hair and moaned; he teetered on the precipice of some odd strength of sentiment he had not experienced since his youth. His gut tensed, and he clenched his teeth. Well nigh dizzy from the force of her enthusiasm, he massaged her pliant breast one more time and then retreated.

"Thither now." Resting her forehead to his, she rubbed her nose to his and smiled. "I am appeased, sir. And I should complete my chore, as the water grows cold, and I do wish to clean myself without catching a chill."

Just then, she peered into the tub and snatched the cloth. To his everlasting shame, his healthy and erect man's yard caught her attention. For a minute, she held his stare, then glanced at his mouth, and again met his gaze.

"Dost thou understand what that means?" Anticipating shock and reproach, he choked when she closed her hand about his length. "Isolde, thou should not tempt me thus."

"Yea, I understand, as my brother doth lack discretion in his conquests." Then she tugged gently and said, "Thou dost want me."

A violent shudder seized him, and his seed shot forth as though launched from an imposing carro-ballista. Groaning as wave upon wave of release wracked his frame, Arucard rested his head on the edge of the ancere and closed his eyes. A repetitive spasm drew out the blissful release, and he shifted his hips and savored what he had not enjoyed since joining the Templars and mastering his base desires, as the Lord's men revered austerity in all things.

Anon, he recovered enough to muster a chuckle and discern his wife's distress. "What is wrong? Have I frightened thee?"

"Perchance, as I know not what happened." With an expression of horror, she blinked. "Did I wound something of importance?"

"Nay, my sweet Isolde." Given that gem of logic, he surrendered to a full belly laugh. When she frowned and sat on her heels, he stood, snatched a towel from the stool, and wrapped the square of linen about his waist to mitigate his nudity. Dripping wet, he bent, slipped his arms about her waist, and lifted her. "Thou hast bestowed upon me another treasure, and thou art most kind." He claimed another kiss and set her on her feet. "Now I must don my garb and fetch fresh water for thy bath."

"Prithee, only a pail, and I shall make do with that." Unaware that the entire front of her slip had been rendered sheer by his damp hug, she shielded naught from him, and he took advantage of the moment to look his fill as he dressed.

"As thou dost wish." With that, Arucard nodded once and stepped into the chilly night air, which he hoped might cool his blood. Beneath the silver light of the moon, he glanced at the starry sky and smiled. Yea, the lady Isolde had cast a spell, and he ached to yield to her demands, but he would linger and win her fealty. Then he would claim her body.

CHAPTER FOUR

Four days later, Isolde descended from the traveling wagon, after the procession pulled into an expansive glade for the night. The distinct keen of sea gulls declared they neared the coast and Chichester, but the weather had turned, the roads had deteriorated, and the sun had set, so Arucard commanded they halt their progress, rather than risk a broken wheel or an injured horse due to the muddy ruts.

"So thou hast not consummated thy vows?" Margery arched a brow and snorted. "Thou hast always been stubborn to a fault, and this instance mayest be thy worst yet."

"But my husband hath been most supportive." With a groan of exertion, Isolde dragged the trunk containing the cooking utensils to the place that would serve as the temporary kitchen. Given the length of their journey, she had organized the necessities to ensure rapid setup and packing. "And he shows his affection with greater frequency."

Not to mention, he had become far more amorous.

Ever since that glorious interlude in their tent, when she had accidentally brought him to completion with her hand, Arucard had increased their intimacy in small but effective strides. The previous eventide, after supper, they took to their bed and explored their bodies beneath the animal pelts they shared to keep warm, and just thinking of it gave her a shiver of delight, because he touched her as he had never touched her.

As they kissed, she caressed his man's yard, and he eased his hand between her legs. At his first brush of her most sensitive flesh, Isolde knew not how to respond to the experience, but his whispers of praise and encouragement had soothed her nerves and calmed her fears, and she allowed him free rein. The end result, a rather quick affair, required a change of braies for her knight, and she could not stifle a giggle at the thought.

"Then thou would do well to surrender thy maidenhead before telling him of the letter." The irascible steward hefted additional items and followed in Isolde's wake. "Else Sir Arucard could accuse thee of betrayal and ship thee home."

"Must thou always sing the same tune?" The relative euphoria vanished, as she pondered the possibility. In a short span of time, she had grown fond of her husband and their fledgling routine. "And Arucard is my champion, so he would never do such a thing. Set up the spit, so we can serve a hot meal, as the rain has stopped."

With that, Isolde abandoned the task at hand and sought her knight for inspiration and confidence. As was his way, he supervised the preparation of their tent, their ancere, and their bed, so she could situate their belongings and hasten their rendezvous after dinner. When she found him, she smiled.

"Place the rug at center, as the ground is damp, and I would ensure my wife's comfort." As he directed the servants, Arucard fluffed the straw-filled mattress and placed it on the ropes of the bed frame. "And fetch the large brazier, as the wind is strong, and it will be a cold night."

The servants scrambled to fulfill his commands, and she pressed a finger to her lips as she entered their temporary quarters. Alone with her husband, she slipped her arms about his waist and hugged him from behind. "Wherefore dost thou require a brazier, when thou shalt keep me warm?"

"My lady." Covering her hands with his, he squeezed her fingers. "Am I not thy champion? Thy health and welfare art of great importance, and I would not fail thee."

"When shall we arrive at Chichester, as I long to have thee to myself?" The attendant returned, carrying the requisite item, and Isolde released her knight. "Perchance, I should move the small table into our tent, and we could dine in privacy. Thou hast never finished thy story last eventide, and I do so wish to know more of thy family history."

"Mayhap tomorrow, mayhap the day after, our journey will end." Quick as a flash, he turned and pulled her into a more intimate embrace. "And perchance thou shalt take thy sup in my lap, if thy meal is pleasing."

"I am making cameline meat brewets, as my lord declared them another favorite." How she adored his smile, which featured the hint of a dimple on his left cheek. "Will that suffice?"

"Sounds delicious, and Demetrius will be happy, as they art his favorite." Then he bent his head and kissed her. As she suckled and laved his full lips, a bewitching aspect of marital life she had mastered, she relished the taste of him. All too soon, he ceased the interlude but kept her close. "Isolde, thy mouth is far more tempting than thy fare, although thou art an excellent cook."

"Praise, indeed." For a scarce second, she pondered Margery's warning and considering revealing the letter to Arucard. But they had yet to consummate their vows, and Isolde feared he might return her to London and her father. And she viewed that as a fate worse than death. With a wicked shudder, she rubbed her arms and laughed. "Allow me to be of use and gather the skins for our bedding. Mayhap thou should place clean braies beneath thy pillow, in anticipation of our nightly games."

"Mayhap thou should keep thy hands to thyself, thus I would have no need of clean braies." When she pouted, he winked. "Perchance I should forgo braies, altogether, when we retire."

"Art thou complaining? And I didst naught more than thee instructed." Isolde spread the hides, as he positioned the ancere and carried in the table. Then she checked the pillows, as her husband preferred the firmer cushion. "Thither, it is done. Now I should return to the kitchen, as Margery and Anne might have need of me."

"Prithee, a moment." Ah, how well she knew his playful side. She lowered her chin, he arched a brow, she veered left, and he caught her. "Dost thou run from me?"

"Never." With a squeal of joy, she wrapped her arms about his neck. "But thou hast quite an appetite, and supper will not cook itself."

"Anon, might I persuade thee to forgo a night rail?" He nuzzled her temple, and she well nigh melted. "As never have I seen thee without benefit of clothing."

"Thou dost wish me to sleep nude?" At the prospect, she gulped, as she had kept her scarred back hidden from view, given she feared he would use her marked body as an excuse to end their marriage. Until they consummated their vows, she wanted to maintain that secret, along with Father's correspondence. "Dost thou intend to claim my maidenhead?"

And that singular query interrupted his mischievous diversion.

"Isolde, as I told thee, it will happen when it happens." To her regret, he frowned and put her on her feet. "I had thought we could advance our forays between the covers, and thou dost not know whither that mayest lead us."

"Until then, my lord." In a rare display of confidence, she jumped up, kissed him hard and fast, and ran from their tent, and his chuckle rang clear behind her. As she marched for the makeshift kitchen, she thrust her hands in her fitchet and came to an abrupt halt. For several seconds, she dug and searched, as her heart pounded, her ears rang, and her breath came in fits and starts. When reality set in, a chill of dread settled in her chest.

Father's letter was gone.

Ever since she read the missive, she kept it on her person, as she could not risk her husband finding it, hadst she hid it amongst her belongings. The earth seemed to pitch and roll beneath her leather slippers, as she hiked the skirts of her cotehardie and ran to the tent.

Standing with his back to her, Arucard loomed large but appeared fine, as he dismissed the help.

She exhaled in relief and dipped her chin to the servants, as they exited. "My lord, I was just—"

Slowly, her knight faced her. In his grasp, he held her downfall, the telltale parchment. "Is this what thou dost seek?"

#

"Wherefore art thou so determined to consummate our nuptials?" Raw rage charged the field, as Isolde's treachery cut like a knife, and Arucard crumpled the damning correspondence. "Dost thou intend to seduce me into thy web before thou dost betray me to thy father? And is that the reason thou dost seem so interested in my history?"

"Nay." As he expected she wept, but her tears moved him not. "Pray, thou must believe me. Never would I disclose the information Father demands, as I owe him naught. Thou dost own my allegiance, and never would I break my vow."

"Thou dost speak pretty words, but thy letter reveals the truth of thy character and motives." And pain cut to his core, as he contemplated her deception, given his stated intent to foster marital accord and trust. "I should hie thee back to London and the earl."

"*Nay.*" With a wild-eyed expression, she threw herself at his feet. "Prithee, *nay*. I beseech thee to have mercy, sir." Clutching his shins, she bowed her head. "I hid the missive because I feared thou would send me away, and I was wrong. By my troth, I am thine to command."

How he longed to believe her, as he revisited brief but cherished moments of their journey. But the truth was she had wounded him, and he had not prepared for that injury, which hurt worse than any he had suffered in battle.

"Arucard, come hither." Morgan charged into the tent. "We art under attack by an unknown enemy."

Operating on instinct, Arucard grabbed his sword and shield. "Lady Isolde, thou wilt remain hither, as I am not done with thee. And if thou art not present when I return, I will search for thee, and when I find thee, thou wilt not enjoy the outcome. Dost thou understand?"

Sitting on her heels, she wiped her nose and whimpered. "Aye, my lord."

Riding a wave of righteous fury mixed with bone-chilling disappointment, he ran into the field, whither he found hooded bandits engaging soldiers in combat. As the men had been setting up the encampment, and none had anticipated an assault, the raiders had met little resistance—until Arucard and the Brethren entered the fray.

Forming a formidable line of defense, the Brethren of the Coast waged war with a rallying cry. Bereft of heavy armor, Arucard moved swift and sure, thrusting and swinging, and taking down various adversaries with his weapon. With a single graceful flourish, he severed the head of a marauder and impaled another. Standing shoulder to shoulder with Demetrius, Arucard's faithful comrade in arms, they plowed a wide path through the boothalers.

To his right, Arucard noticed Pellier struggling to subdue a large assailant. "Step aside, old friend." Arucard pushed his marshalsea clear. "Let us see how the ornery giant handles an evenly matched opponent."

"Thou dost not intimidate me, silk-snatcher." The flaxen-haired oaf rushed Arucard, and steel clashed with steel. "If thou hast come hither to steal more lands on behalf of the King, thou art mistaken, as we rebuke thy authority."

"I know naught of what thou speaks." As his opponent swung wide, Arucard landed a fist to the rival's chin, and the young man dropped to his arse. With the pointed end of his sword leveled at the combatant's throat, Arucard lowered his chin. "If thou wilt call off thy forces, I shall hear thy complaints, as I am the newly commissioned guardian of Chichester."

"I care not for fancy titles." The provoking challenger spat blood and wiped his mouth. "And wherefore should I believe anything thou dost say?"

"Because I will spare thy companions, good sirrah." Arucard stretched to full height. "Otherwise, if thou dost prefer a warrior's death, I shall indulge thee. And my knights and I will slaughter thy men. The choice is thine."

"Wherefore should I take thee at thy word?" He frowned. "The Crown spreads lies, denying the rape of our property, while we endure the thefts and the accompanying humiliation."

"I am Arucard de Villiers, the King's emissary, and on my honor, I shall deal with thee honestly and fairly." He retreated a step and extended a hand in a gesture of faith. "What is thy name?"

"I am called Aeduuard de Cadby." The gadling stood, and his scowl deepened. "Wherefore should I trust thee, when I know thee not? Thou could renege and run me through, as lies know no boundaries, rank, or sworn oaths, sir. And a few pretty words cannot undo years of ill treatment, thus I have had little reason to confide in anyone."

The statement, stark in its meaning, jolted Arucard.

In an instant, he recalled Isolde and her tragic relationship with her father and brother, which she shared in bits and pieces over the past few days. Like de Cadby, she had been cautious and suspicious of Arucard's motives, and he had considered her misgivings a barrier he had yet to breach. Given the dissension in her family, the letter should have struck Arucard as odd. Instead, unchecked ire blinded him, and he leapt to unsupported conclusions, when he should have permitted his wife to explain her situation. Despite the urgency of the conflict, he needed to return to his bride.

Regardless of their short acquaintance, Isolde would never betray him, and he knew that now as he sure as he knew the origins of his birth. Pain of a different sort settled in his chest, and he rubbed the back of his neck. Around him, the fighting ceased, as the Brethren bested the ill-skilled raiders.

"Stand down thy men, and I shall see to their welfare." Arucard signaled Demetrius. "We have plenty of stores and a physic. If thou hast knowledge of a particular complication in Chichester, then I should know it, so that I may deal with it."

"And how shalt thou deal with it?" Aeduuard sheathed his sword. "As we will tolerate no more."

"What is thy command, brother?" Holding three fighters at bay, Demetrius neared. "What would thou have me do with these whelps, as they do not appear old enough to grow a beard?"

"Treat them with respect, and see to their comfort." Arucard glanced at his fellow knight of the realm. "Give Aeduuard accommodations fitting his stature, and comprise a list of injuries and losses. I shall be in my tent."

With that, Arucard turned on a heel and navigated the crowd. Driven by the urge to reconcile with Isolde, he broke into a sprint. Anon, he ducked beneath the flap, entered his quarters, and breathed a sigh of relief to find her thither still. When she spied him, she choked on a sob.

"My lord, art thou wounded?" In silence, he cursed, as he noted her swollen eyes and tear-stained cheeks.

"Nay." He tossed aside his sword and shield. "Wherefore dost thou ask?"

"Thou art covered in blood." It was then he noticed she shivered violently.

"It is not mine." At the small washstand, he scrubbed his face. "But I struck a tenuous accord, and the battle is ended."

"I am grateful my prayers were answered, so I might beg thy forgiveness. I was wrong to conceal Father's letter, but I did so because I feared thou might send me to London, and I did not want to be parted from thee. While I disappointed thee, I am thy wife, and I owe thee my loyalty. Thou must know I trust not my father." It was just as he suspected, but he had not anticipated her next move. To his shock and amazement, Isolde neared and presented his belt, which he accepted. Then she unbuttoned her cotehardie, loosened the ribbon of her chemise, and inched the garments to her hips. Without hesitation, she turned and knelt on the ground. "Thou art justified in thy anger, and I have earned thy discipline, which I pledge to take in the spirit of recompense, if thou would mete it and be satisfied."

It had to be a nightmare of the worst sort, as he blinked and winced. Suddenly, everything made sense, as he recalled her reaction on their wedding night, when he attempted to disrobe, and she armed herself with his halberd. Frozen in some hell on earth, Arucard bent and studied her back. Mottled scars declared years of brutal abuse, and fresh injuries marred her creamy flesh. As he pondered the cruelty she had survived, he swallowed hard. Then he stomped forth, grasped her by the shoulders, drew her to stand, turned her about, and shook her.

"Who is responsible for this travesty?" Again, he

rocked her. "Who did this to thee?"

"Who dost thou think?" He caught his breath when he glimpsed the terror in her expression. "My father."

"Wherefore?" Arucard narrowed his stare. "What could thou possibly have done to merit such barbarity?"

"As I already told thee, my mother died giving birth to me." Now Isolde wept without restraint. "I took the love of his life, and I must pay just penance for my crime."

"By Christ's fingernails. What manner of people art thine, that they doth commit such heinous atrocities on a vulnerable lady? Whither I hail, we shield our women." In frustration, he flung the leather strap into the brazier. Then he sighed. "That was my favorite belt."

Isolde opened and then closed her mouth. And then she bestowed upon him a watery gaze and a lopsided grin. "I can work another and soften the hide for thee."

"I am so sorry, Isolde." In a flash, he wrapped his arms about her waist, drew her close, and cradled her head. So many emotions, none of which he could identify, flooded his senses, and all Arucard could do was hold his wife and savor the warmth that was uniquely hers. "In haste, I mistreated thee, and I beg thy forgiveness."

"But the error is mine." She sniffed and burrowed closer. "I should have told thee of the note when first it arrived."

"Wherefore didst thou hide the letter?" When he shifted and cupped her cheek, she pressed her lips to his palm. "Hast thou so little faith in me?"

"It is not a question of faith." Gripping his tunic, she furrowed her brow. "Didst thou not read the missive? Father threatens to take me away from thee, even after we have consummated our vows. But without the surrender of my maidenhead, thou dost own me not. And as I told thee, I cannot be parted from thee. I cannot bear to think it."

"Sweet Isolde, thou became my wife when we stood before the archbishop and pledged the sacrament." He bent and kissed her. "Thou art mine."

"But the law says—"

"I care not what the law says. What God hath joined thy father shall not break." It occurred to him then that he had to make her understand his logic, and thither was only one way to relay the depth of his commitment. As a man with a purpose, Arucard released Isolde and dropped to a knee. With a clenched fist to his chest, he said, "On my honor, I am thy champion to my death. And if thy father again wishes to threaten thee, he must first go through me."

"Oh, my lord." With a shriek, his bride lunged, toppled him, framed his jaw with her hands, and showered his face in precious kisses. "Thou art wonderful, and I vow to confess any future correspondence with my father, upon receipt. Perchance, thou might help me pen a response, as I have yet to fulfill his request for information."

"We will address that, anon." Without conscious intent, he squeezed her round bottom. "Right now, I fret for thee. Art thou truly well?"

"Indeed." She nodded. "Margery hath rubbed one of her yarrow salves on my lash marks, so I shall heal, and thou art kind to inquire. Wilt thou not tell me the source of thy noble nature, as I do so wish to know thee."

"In light of thy candor, I owe thee the same." He whisked a stray tendril and tucked it behind her ear. "My brothers and I belonged to the once great knighthood known as the Templars."

"I know of them, as I have heard stories." She rubbed her nose to his. "The Templars were arrested and prosecuted for unspeakable acts of depravity, but thou wilt never convince me that is thy character."

"We were innocent warriors falsely accused by a greedy king bent on pilfering our amassed wealth. We served with distinction, and that was our reward." In brief, Arucard revisited painful memories of the past. "So many died for naught more than lust for power. I sailed for England and spent the last five years in a small stone cell at White Tower, until the Crown had use for me."

"My champion—locked in some horrid dungeon? I bleed for thee." Isolde nuzzled his temple. "In bestowing upon me thy confidence, thou dost me a great honor, and by my troth, I shall bear thy secrets to my grave."

"I am not worried about that, my lady." In that moment, he realized his bride, naked from the waist up, sprawled atop him, and his thoughts veered in a different direction. Standing, he carried her with him and then conveyed her to their bed. Sitting on the edge, he shuffled her in his lap. As he brushed his knuckles to her pert nipple, she licked her lips and set her mouth to his. The initial taste of her honey kisses in the wake of their first argument well nigh slayed him, and she leveled his personal restraint.

Fire burned beneath his flesh, and a familiar hunger gnawed at his belly and below. Instinctively, he supported her shoulders, reclined her, and suckled her breasts. When she wove her fingers into his hair, she moaned, and Arucard slipped his hand beneath her skirts and sought the supple flesh between her thighs, which he ached to know on a more intimate basis.

A thousand times more intense than the heat of battle, her passion could vanquish untold armies, and the enchanting wiggle of her hips could conquer the will of the mightiest knight. How he desired her. And then he realized he had no reason to delay. He could take what she so readily offered and feed his hunger. He could—

"Brother, we have—" Demetrius averted his gaze. "Forgive my intrusion, but thou didst order me to report on the outcome of our brief skirmish."

"Wait outside, and I shall join thee." Cursing, Arucard shielded Isolde and situated her garments to cover her nudity. To his wife, he said, "Thou could tempt a favored toy from a babe, sweet Isolde. But duty calls, and thou dost require attention of a different sort. I shall send Margery to tend thy needs, and I expect thee to rest abed when I return, else I shall be quite vexed."

"Prithee, good sir. I shall defer to thy charge." Isolde stood but held him fast. "Dost thou regret our union, as I am damaged?"

"On the contrary." He patted her bottom. "I count myself most fortunate, as never hast thou been more beauteous."

#

Anon, with Margery's aid, Isolde stepped from the ancere after a long relaxing soak. "How bad doth it look?"

"Better than I hoped." The housekeeper dried Isolde's legs. "But hadst thou permitted me to treat thy wounds, as usual, thy injuries might have healed faster. Now lie down, my lady."

Situated on her belly, Isolde hugged a pillow, sighed, and sank into the mattress. "My lord Arucard thinks me beauteous."

"Sounds like a man of excellent judgment, as thou art quite fair." Margery smeared salve onto Isolde's scarred back. "Hold still, my lady. I would cover thy wounds with boiled linen to protect thy tender flesh from re-injury."

"Didst thou see him fight?" Isolde recalled the terrifying sight of her husband charging the field of combat in naught more than his woolen garments, with his sword and shield. "Though he demanded I remain in the tent, I could not resist peeking outside, as I worried for his safety. Hast thou ever witnessed such graceful violence?"

"Never." Margery peered over her shoulder and then leaned forward. "Sir Arucard fought as a man possessed, and I fear for thee."

"What?" Astonished, she propped on her elbows. "Wherefore art thou fearful? Surely thou dost not think my husband would subject me to such savagery."

Although the steward said naught, her silence spoke volumes, and Isolde mulled the pleasurable interlude she shared with her knight, after their clash. Despite the enormity of his frame, and the size of his hands, he had been gentle—almost loving, if she could call it that, as she had naught with which to compare. But she nurtured hope for something more than she had ever dared fathom, and no one would convince her otherwise.

"Art thou decent?" Holding a steaming bowl and a trencher of bread, Arucard strolled into the tent and smiled as he met her gaze. "How art thee, my lady wife?"

"Much improved, thanks to Margery's skills." And a tempting aroma teased her nose. "That smells delicious."

As he gazed at her body, he arched a brow. "I presume thou hast not supped?"

"Nay. And I could not prepare the brewets, as I remained here, at thy request." She blushed, as Margery settled the pelts to cover Isolde's nudity. "But I am hungry."

"Margery, thou art dismissed, as I shall care for my bride." Then Arucard gave Isolde his full attention. "Remain abed. Whither thou art, I shall come to thee."

"Wilt thou?" She swallowed her laughter, as he wrangled a chair and located it at bedside. However, when he placed the meal on the seat and then plopped to the ground, she fought happy tears. "Hast thou bathed?"

"Aye." He blew on the soup. "This is broth with bacon, which Anne cooked. And I ate with the men, as I did not want to hurry Margery."

"How thoughtful is my champion." With care, he positioned the dish, and she scooted to the edge of the mattress and drank from the bowl. "What of the bandits?"

"They art locals with a serious problem, and I must send notice to the King when I have collected additional information." He tore off a small piece of bread and fed it to her. "Hast thou ever heard of Juraj de Mravec?"

"Aye." Before she could answer, he kissed her. "De Mravec is my father's friend. But thou should question Margery, as she has information related to the letter. She

71

claims my father conspires against the Crown."

"She said that?" He lifted the vessel, and she took another sip. "Perchance, I should—"

"Sir Arucard, I beg thy indulgence, as I brought some hot tea with thyme to help Lady Isolde sleep." With her mouth agape, Margery blinked. She paused and then stepped forward. "Shall I leave it with thee, my lord?"

"Yea." He indicated the chair, and the steward set the cup on the seat. "And I would like to speak with thee in the morrow."

"Have I done something to offend thee, my lord?" Margery wrung her fingers.

"Nay, Margery." Isolde perched on an elbow. "Sir Arucard would know the facts surrounding thy suspicions regarding Father. And mayhap thou hast details to support thy beliefs."

"My lady, thou should not have repeated my notions." Margery shuffled her feet. "And I am no herald."

"Dost thou know of Juraj de Mravec?" Arucard queried.

Margery snapped to attention. She glanced at Arucard, then Isolde, and then to Arucard. "My lord, thou hast been good to my lady, and for that I shall confide in thee. Aye, I know of him."

"Then let us break our fast together." Isolde dreaded the possibility that her family engaged in nefarious deeds, but naught surprised her when it came to her sire. "Until then, I bid thee a pleasant night."

Margery curtseyed and exited the tent.

It was then Isolde noted the stillness investing her husband. For a long while, he simply gazed into her eyes. Then he traced the curve of her cheek and touched his lips to hers. "Art thou truly well? I have not done irreparable harm to our marriage?"

"Nay, my champion. And that is thy pet name, known only to us." After emptying the cup, she passed it to him and teased his shoulder with a light caress. "Now come to bed, as I need thee to keep me warm."

"I had thought to sleep on the ground, as I would not risk hurting thee." Gooseflesh covered him, as she speared her fingers through his rich brown hair. "Prithee, if thou would, pass my pillow and a hide."

"I will not, unless thou dost wish I recline with thee on the earth." She made to sit upright. "And I could suffer a cold, as it is damp and chilly. Now take off thy tunic and hose, and come hither."

"Isolde, thou art the most stubborn woman of my acquaintance." His playful grin and wink belied the seriousness of his rebuke, as he stripped bare save his braies.

"Thou hast claimed I am the only woman of thy acquaintance, so thou dost not say much." She drew back the hides as he eased to the mattress. "And hast thou composed my pet name?"

"Given thy singular topic of conversation, I had pondered something akin to an old horse." Beneath the skins, he pinched her bottom.

"Ooh, thou art the villain, sir, as I am no nag." She pouted even as he burst into laughter. "Mayhap thou should sleep on the ground or with thy soldiers, if thou dost find me so offensive."

"Thou art not offensive." Whither she had moved to the furthest edge of the bed, he slipped an arm beneath her and pulled her to his side. "Thou art my beauteous Isolde."

"And thou art my champion." She cuddled close, as the thyme worked on her, and fought to stay awake. When she yawned, Arucard kissed her forehead.

"Sleep, my lady wife." Then he suckled her lips. "In the morrow, we complete our journey to Chichester. And once thy wounds have healed sufficiently, I shall take thy most intimate gift."

CHAPTER FIVE

"Lord Rochester hath been corresponding with Juraj de Mravec for the past few years, Sir Arucard." Frowning, Margery sat across the table from Isolde. "To my dismay, their letters became more frequent about six months ago, and I feared thy marriage had something to do with the awful business."

As Margery related more information, Isolde's heart raced. Could it be true? Was her father a traitor? And what of her brother? Then she wondered whether or not the scandal could threaten her husband, and she fretted for his welfare, given he had recently spent five years in White Tower.

"An understandable conclusion, but how dost thou know they conspire to commit nefarious deeds?" Arucard rubbed his chin and ignored the insult, to Isolde's relief. "Mayhap they art naught more than friends sharing harmless banter."

"Nay, because his lordship bade me take the alley and deliver the letters to a masked courier, after dark, and a good distance from the house, to evade suspicion. And on three separate occasions, when I had the misfortune to read a portion, his lordship wrote of stealing lands and blaming the Crown to undermine the realm." The housekeeper peered at Pellier, who sat beside her. "And just before he terminated my employ, the earl threatened to cut my throat should I ever betray his confidence."

For Isolde, the revelations were too much, and she bowed her head in shame. But Arucard lent support, as he covered her hand with his and squeezed her fingers.

"Worry not, fair Margery." Pellier lifted his chin and compressed his lips. "I will protect thee, as Sir Arucard guards Lady Isolde."

"Humph." Margery snorted. "How can thou protect me, when thou cannot take care of thyself, little man?"

"Careful, woman." Pellier snickered. "Thou didst not think me so little last eventide."

At the shocking declaration, Isolde gasped and glanced at Arucard. In unison, they blinked.

"Foul creature, thou dost tell wild tales." The maid folded her arms. "Ask someone else to boil the elecampane for thy cough."

"What?" Pellier shrugged. "Thither art no virgin ears at this table, as Sir Arucard and Lady Isolde art newly wed and, therefore, I presume art becoming quite practiced at grooming the one-eyed horse. Wherefore should I conceal that which is obvious to everyone but thee?"

Arucard winked at Isolde, and she cursed the burn of a blush.

"And that would be—what?" With a huff of breath, Margery gazed at the sky and shook her head.

"Thou art taken with me." With a hearty guffaw, Pellier poked Margery in the ribs. "Admit it, thou art mad for me."

"I must be mad to involve myself with the likes of thee, and I have wasted enough time on this conversation. Sir Arucard, if thou dost require additional details, I am at thy service." Standing, Margery tossed her napkin in Pellier's face. "My lady, if thou hast no further need of me, I would pack the wagon."

"Thou art dismissed." Reeling from the events that had transpired, Isolde pushed from the table. "I should stow our personal items and close our trunks, so we may depart."

"Allow me to help thee." Her husband chucked Pellier on the shoulder and said, "Thou hast dug a deep pit for thyself. Perchance, thou should seek out Margery and apologize for thy ill manners, thou sad sack of ignorance."

In their tent, Isolde faced her knight, covered her mouth, and together they burst into laughter. After a few minutes, she wiped a stray tear from her cheek. "Dost thou believe it?"

"Pellier and Margery? Nay." Pressing a clenched fist to his belly, he chuckled. "And never would I have guessed, as those two art as night and day."

"And they have—what did he call it?" She searched her memory and giggled. "Groomed the one-eyed horse. Doth that mean what I think it means?"

"Aye." Slipping his arms about her waist, he pulled her close. "It would appear our stewards have beat us to the consummation, but I will see to that once we arrive at Chichester."

"Is that a promise?" Of course, her maidenhead seemed insignificant, in light of the morrow's developments. "Arucard, what will we do about de Cadby and the questionable burgage plots? If my father and de Mravec have stolen lands under the Crown's seal, the King will want my father's head on a pike. And when it comes to His Majesty, often the entire family bears responsibility for the crime. Whither will that leave us, as I am frightened?"

"Wherefore that I should meet with the locals, hear their complaints, gather evidence, and deliver everything to the King for his judgment." How could he remain so calm? "Now give me a kiss to see me through the day's ride, as young Aeduuard insists we shall arrive in Chichester by the eventide, and I suspect we shall be right busy."

Knowing a mere kiss would not satisfy him, she did as he bade, the usual accompanying ache blossomed in the pit of her belly, and her gut clenched. As she moved her mouth over his, something grew between them, a foreign but mystical power she tried but failed to identify, and it spun its delicate web, enfolding them in a gossamer cocoon of comforting warmth. When he squeezed her bottom, he suckled her lips, and she relished his taste and scent. And, as always, he ended the sweet moment with a hug.

"Dost thou feel it?" She shivered, as he caught the crest of her ear with his teeth.

"Aye. I desire thee." Grasping her wrist, he settled her palm to a telltale bulge. "Never doubt me."

"Oh, my champion." She gazed into his eyes, as he cupped her cheek. "I desire thee, too. And I am so glad we waited, as I feared thee on our wedding night."

"And now, my beauteous Isolde?" Arucard arched a brow and grinned. "Art thou still afraid?"

"Nay, my lord." As she caressed his hard length, she trailed her tongue along his jawline. "I yearn for thee."

"I understand." He massaged her breast and teased her nipple through her wool cotehardie, and she moaned. "As I shared thy consternation, but not so anymore. And once we art unpacked in our new home, and thy wounds art healed to my appeasement, my first order of business is to consummate our nuptials, as I burn for thee."

#

The sun rested low on the horizon, when the procession approached the north gates of Chichester Castle. A wide moat surrounded the square structure, which boasted crenellation and balistraria fortifications about the exterior curtain wall and towers, along with a spectacular view of the coastline. A narrow bridge accommodated only a wagon or two horsemen riding side by side, to negotiate the expanse, which attached to an outer causeway.

With a tight grip on his sword, Arucard steered right and crossed the first drawbridge, which led to the main gatehouse and an impressive barbican marked by a vaulted ceiling filled with murder-holes and three wooden portcullises. But an overwhelming stench left him gagging, and he searched for and discovered the source, an uncovered garderobe in dire need of cleaning, which he would have flushed before posting soldiers in the gatehouse.

The second drawbridge presented a hazard, as damaged timbers rendered the traverse unstable in places, but the group successfully navigated to the twin-towered, machicolated inner gatehouse, which connected to the lesser curtain wall. The strategic entry opened to a large courtyard, as the castle had no keep, and all manner of refuse littered the yard.

"What a bit of good fortune." He dismounted his destrier and then handed Isolde to the ground. "It appears our new home is in excellent condition."

"Art thou blind?" With a wide-eyed gaze of incredulity, she scoffed. "This place is a filthy tragedy of the worst sort. Just look at that pile of trash, as it must be at least as tall as thee, and I insist thou burn it, at once. Lord knows how many little creatures dwell thither, and I shudder to think of what I may find in the private rooms."

"Demetrius, organize a search of the entire premises." Arucard signaled his brothers. "And if thou would—"

"Prithee, have Morgan stock the kitchen with wood and start a fire, as Margery and I must prepare thy supper." His wife ticked off an imaginary list on her fingers. "I need Aristide to assemble some men to convey the food stores to the undercroft, provided we have an undercroft, and Geoffrey must locate my cleaning supplies. And if thou would bear our personal trunks to our chamber, which I have yet to establish, I shall make some attempt to settle our lodging."

Palpable silence fell on the group, as his fellow Nautionnier knights cast him a harsh stare, and Arucard tugged on the collar of his tunic. How he responded to his wife's request could either reinforce or destroy his authority, so he pondered the situation and composed a polite but unmistakable reprove.

"Isolde, I command His Majesty's servants." Checking his tone, as he had no wish to frighten her, he folded his arms. "Thy entreaties must perforce yield to mine."

"Dost thou wish to eat?" She tapped her foot in an impatient rhythm. "Dost thou wish to bathe? Dost thou wish to sleep in a warm, comfortable bed? Mayhap thou would prefer the stables."

At the thought, he swallowed hard, stretched to full height, and glared at the Brethren. "Thou didst hear the lady. Wherefore dost thou linger?" After a few grumbles in protest, the knights hurried about their tasks, and then he winked at his wife and smiled.

"Well, I would ask the same of thee." Narrowing her stare, she lifted her chin, and he adored her fiery spirit. "Else I am certain thy stallion would love to share its stall with thee."

"Banishing me from our marital bed?" In an instant, he swooped, flung her over his shoulder, and smacked her bottom. "I think not."

"Oh, Arucard." Pounding his back with her fists, she attempted to wriggle free. "Put me down."

"Apologize."

"Nay."

"Apologize."

"*Nay.*"

"Then thou wilt spend the eventide thus, and I quite enjoy the arrangement." To impress upon her the seriousness of his proclamation, he hefted her trunk and carried her into the living areas, which lined the interior curtain wall. "It appears I have found the great hall."

"And it is dirty." Isolde shifted and propped herself on her elbows. "The dais is serviceable, but the tables and chairs art in disarray, so thou should release me to be about my work. And I should remind Margery to inspect the chimney before lighting a blaze, as she could fill the castle with smoke."

"I am sure Margery can survive without thee, and she seems competent enough." Arucard spied a narrow passage, which led to a stairway, and he ascended to the second floor, whither he discovered a dusty solar and what he suspected were the main accommodations. "Home, at last, my lady."

"And thither is much to be done, if we art to retire after supper." Again, she squirmed, and he tightened his hold. "Pray, let me go."

"What hast thou to say?" He pinched her round arse, and she shrieked.

"Now." In response, she attempted to kick free.

"Wrong answer, my lady." In play, he rotated in circles, until she begged him to stop. "Art thou prepared to offer thy words of regret?"

"Art thou truly annoyed?" she asked in a small voice, and he altered his grasp, letting her slide down the front of him, but her feet dangled as he hugged her about the waist. "I am sorry if I disappointed thee."

"On the contrary, thou hast neither annoyed nor disappointed me." Resting forehead to forehead, he sighed. "But thou must remember thy station and mine, else I cannot maintain discipline, as the men will not respect me."

"I had not thought of that." To his delight, she brushed her lips to his and wrapped her arms about his neck. "The bedframe and ropes art rotted. We should move ours hither; else we may end up on the floor. And I should sweep and scrub everything."

"Isolde, I would caution thee to take care of thy

person, as I would prefer thy injuries heal that we might consummate our vows." Given the depth of their regard, which had grown in so short a space of time, he anticipated a magical night. "Or would thou delay the singular event?"

"Oh, no." And now she favored him with her shy smile, which never failed to stir his blood. "But I would do my duty as chatelaine."

"Precisely." He rocked on his heels. "Thou art no scullion, and we have servants. Thou dost need only to direct them."

"But I have strict standards, sir. As thou dost well know." Then, to his surprise, she kissed him, his ears rang, his blood stirred, and the one-eyed stallion reared its head. Some day soon, he promised himself the simple expression of affection would no longer startle him, but at that moment she captivated him.

"Margery bade me clean the fireplace and—" Turning to the side, Pellier cleared his throat. "Beg thy pardon, Sir Arucard. Should I come back anon?"

"Nay." To his chagrin, Arucard set his bride on the floor. "Lady Isolde and I were just assessing our rooms."

"That is precisely what I thought." Pellier's sly smile declared otherwise, and Arucard ignored his marshalsea. "Permit me to build a fire, and thou may continue inspecting the fertile surroundings and, perchance, spark another blaze."

"Very funny." Arucard grimaced.

"My lord, look." Aglow with joy, and attempting to hide her charming pink cheeks, his wife jumped and pointed to the rear wall. "We have glazed windows. Is that not wonderful?"

"I suppose." He shrugged. "Does it make thee happy?"

"Yea." As she admired the glass inserts, she trailed her finger along the casement. "I should wash them, but they art in fine form, and we will be grateful for them when winter arrives."

"Art thou always so practical?" Baring his teeth, Arucard distracted his shy bride, as Pellier waggled his brows and thrust his hips in a crude gesture. "And what lovely tapestries hang in the solar."

"Indeed, they art exquisite and very heavy, which will shield us from the cold. Mayhap thou could help me take them down, as I must beat them." How quickly she changed purpose, when all Arucard could think of was what would eventually occur in the inner chamber. "Canst thou unfasten the frame?"

"Of course." As she perched on tiptoes, he reached above her and unhooked the mount. Then he rolled the heavy wall hanging and set it on the table in the solar. "I suppose thou would clean the other two, as well?"

"Yea, as I would not unpack our belongings until everything is scrubbed." With Isolde's supervision, he retrieved the other coverings. "If thou would carry the tapestries into the courtyard, I will ask Anne to beat them, if that will satisfy thee."

"It will." When Pellier snickered, Arucard groaned. "But I would ask thee to take care of thy person, as thou art precious to me."

In the hall, Isolde spun about and faced him, and her hopeful expression touched him beyond words. "Am I?"

"Aye." Adjusting the load on his shoulder, he eased an arm about her waist and drew her near. "I understand it not, as our situation is still quite new to me, but I speak the truth."

"No one has ever manifested such sentiments for me, and I treasure thy declaration." Given her tear-filled gaze, he doubted her not, and in silence he cursed her father for the cruelty she suffered at his hands. "My lord, thou art precious to me, too. And like thee, I am confused in relation to my feelings, but do not let that diminish the depth of my regard for thee."

A small army of servants scurried about, and with great

reluctance he released his bride. Together, they strolled into the courtyard; whither Aristide had set fire to several piles of trash, per Isolde's request.

"Brother, we found a postern gate on the south wall." Geoffrey wiped his brow. "The drawbridge ropes art in disrepair, so we must replace them, and we could use thy assistance."

"Thither I will be, anon." Arucard glanced at his wife. "Whither shall I deposit the tapestries?"

"In the corner." She pointed. "I shall ask Anne to erect temporary frames, so we can beat the fabrics free of dust and dirt."

"All right." He did as she bade and then caught her chin. "Remember what I said. Thou art no scullery maid. Thou art the lady of the castle, and I would have thee behave as such, if for no other reason than to preserve thy health, which is dear to me."

"Aye, my lord." Grinning, she sketched a half-curtsey.

And so he ventured to the battlements, to aid his men as they reinforced the barbican and the postern gate. With new twine in place, the rear bridge was raised to protect against a surprise assault. Then he assisted Morgan, as the soldiers cleared the garrison quarters, so the maids could sweep and wash. Next, he labored in the stable, as drains were cleared, fresh straw was spread in the stalls, and horses were settled.

The castle drew water from three wells conveniently situated near the kitchen, the stable, and the garrison. Twice, as Arucard worked, he caught Isolde bearing a shoulder yoke, and he had but to arch a brow, and she surrendered the task to a nearby servant. At last, the primary living spaces had been rendered fit for occupation, and it was late when he retired to his private accommodation.

After a quick bath, he pulled on clean braies and a robe. In the solar Isolde set out their meal of a savory roasted bream with darioles and her signature fresh herb bread. At one moment while they dined in quiet, as they were too exhausted to share conversation, he discovered she dozed with her chin propped in her palm, and he could not help but laugh. So he lifted her into his lap, held her close when she stirred, and fed her a good portion.

"My lord, I fear I am too tired to eat." As proof of her claim, she yawned, and he carried her to their bed.

In mere seconds, he doffed his robe, blew out the candles, stoked the blaze in the earth, and slid between the covers. As always, his wife shifted and draped herself alongside him. He slipped his arm beneath her, and she nestled ever closer, with her head resting on his shoulder. In the flickering light from the fire in the hearth, he studied her pert nose, apple cheeks, and heart-shaped face, so elegant in repose.

She manifested an odd combination; delicate yet strong, shy yet confident, and reserved yet bold. And with each passing day, he found her far more fascinating and difficult to resist. How strange it was that what he once had viewed as a curse he now considered a blessing, and he kissed her forehead. "Soon, Isolde, thou wilt be mine."

#

"My lord, if thou dost wish to dine, thou must first clean thy muddy boots, hands, and face." Five days after arriving at Chichester Castle, Isolde stood guard at the main entry to the great hall, clutched a large wooden spoon, assumed a formidable posture, and folded her arms. "Now."

"My lady, the men have labored for hours, clearing and restocking the undercroft, at thy behest." Arucard adopted an equally imposing stance, and she gulped but did not falter. "And we art hungry. Step aside, so we may eat."

"Not until thou dost doff thy shoes." Somehow, she had to make him understand her perspective, so she tapped her foot and held firm in the righteousness of her cause. "As the women have wasted valuable time picking up after thy men, again and again. Wherefore should we tarry, when thy knights will destroy what we have worked so hard to achieve?"

"Arucard, wilt thou remind thy lady of her place?" With a narrow stare, Demetrius rested fists to hips. "As my belly grumbles, and I grow impatient."

"Mayhap a good spanking will soften her mood." When Aristide reached for her, she rapped his knuckles with the spoon. "*Ouch.*"

"If thou dost try it, thou should sleep with one eye open, good sir." Not for a minute did the knight frighten her, as her husband would never let anyone hurt her. "And what I ask is no great burden, given the fare the cook hath prepared. What say thee to cameline meat brewets, to which Sir Demetrius is partial, hot flampoyntes, loach in green sauce, stewed beef, and capon crisps? We also have fresh herb bread, jellies, and a lovely apple muse. And for Sir Arucard, I made my special blancmange. Such a pity, that it should go to waste over a simple entreaty."

For several seconds, the group appeared on the verge of a siege, and no one relented. As she pondered her request, which she judged reasonable, she thought she might have to cede her fight. All of a sudden, a commotion stirred at the back, and the crowd parted.

"Make way." Morgan, the youngest and most audacious of her husband's friends, marched to the fore. At the entrance, he kicked off his boots, extended his hands for inspection, and winked. "What say thee, fair Isolde? Dost thou approve?"

"Traitor." Geoffrey scowled.

"Brother, were I not about to faint from starvation, I might take offense to thy insult." Just as she feared she might have incited a riot, Morgan grinned and bowed with an exaggerated flourish. "But I have been invited to dine with a beauteous lady, so I dare not linger, as the food grows cold."

"Welcome, Sir Morgan." In fine humor, she curtseyed. "Thou mayest sit whither thou dost wish, as thither art plenty of empty chairs." With renewed confidence, she leveled her stare on the remaining opposition. "Well?"

"Ought to lock her in her room." With a mighty scowl, Aristide relented.

"Never will I take a wife." Kicking a rock, Demetrius made for the well.

Soon, the angry crowd followed suit, with a single exception.

"Isolde, thou should not challenge the men, as it is not proper behavior for a wife." Her greatest ally stretched tall, and just as she wavered beneath his scrutiny, he smiled. "Dost thou know that when thy temper is engaged thine eyes sparkle?"

"Art thou trifling with me?" She inclined her head. "As I quite enjoy thy playful conversation, my lord Arucard. And I missed thee this morrow."

"Thy burgundy cotehardie brings out the blush in thy cheeks." He checked the immediate vicinity, swooped, and claimed a quick kiss. "I missed thee, too. But thither is much to be done, if we art to be ready for the winter. And I cannot hold assemblies until the castle is adequately fortified, but I assigned my men to thy cause, for thee—and thee, alone. Dost thou understand the urgency?"

"Aye, my lord." It was all she could do to manage her excitement, as he expressed affection in so many ways, great and small, and he never failed to thrill her. "And I cooked my blancmange for thee—and thee, alone, in grateful appreciation of thy efforts in the undercroft. At last, the kitchen, the spicery, the saucery, the pantry, the buttery, and the scullery art fully repaired and operant. And when thou dost hold thy first feast as lord of Chichester, thy staff stands at the ready to fulfill thy commands, as fit for a king."

"Owed in large part to thy hard work, despite my commands to rest easy." As soldiers from the garrison, washed in obeisance of her demands, strolled into the great hall, Arucard lowered his voice. "But I am so proud of thee."

"I apologize for disobeying thy directives, but I am unaccustomed to being idle." Grasping his wrist, she led him to the well. When she picked up a bar of soap, he retrieved a bucket of fresh water. As a dutiful wife, she lathered his hands and then scrubbed his face. After he rinsed, she pulled a towel from her fitchet, daubed him dry, and bestowed upon him a whisper of a kiss. "Thither, thou art presentable."

"Now may I dine?" He arched a brow.

"Aye." She nodded once.

As they returned to the great hall, he removed his boots and set them in a long line of shoes. "Shall I escort thee to the dais?"

"Prithee, most gallant knight." Arm in arm, they navigated the crowd, which took note of the late arrivals, as conveyed in a lull of boisterous mirth. As she settled in her seat, she waved to the servants, who brought food and drink. "Eat thy fill, my lord. And on the eventide, I shall prepare thy bath with mint, to soothe thy aches and pains."

"And wilt thou join me?" As he lifted his tankard of ale, he cast her a side-glance.

Isolde almost choked on her wine, but she recovered before she embarrassed herself. "Dost thou truly wish it?"

"We have tried many things since we wed." With his fingers, he scooped a morsel of blancmange. "I have yet to see thee completely nude."

"And thou would have me know thee?" The prospect gave her gooseflesh, as he requested something they had never before attempted. "Wilt thou consummate our vows?"

"Margery tells me thy wounds could benefit from another few days to heal." To the left, the Brethren roared, and Arucard nodded. "She suggested a fortnight from the time of injury would suffice to avoid further damage to thy back."

"Thou didst speak with Margery about our situation?" Despite her close relationship with the steward, his candor shocked Isolde. "Thou didst share the private details of our marital life?"

"Nay, as I could never be so indelicate." Atop the table, he covered her hand with his and squeezed her fingers. "I merely inquired after thy health, as a concerned husband. She knows not the motivation for my query."

"Well I should hope not." Just then, Sir Aristide approached the dais, and she dipped her chin in acknowledgement. "Is the loach to thy liking, as I had it made at thy request?"

"It is superb, my lady." The most temperamental of the Brethren shuffled his feet. "I made thee a new tapestry frame to replace the broken one, and Pellier had a servant install the mount, so thou wilt have no more trouble."

"How thoughtful of thee, Sir Aristide." Was it her imagination, or did he blush? "And how is thy back?"

"Much improved, thanks to thy services." He rubbed his neck and leaned forward. "The henbane worked a miracle, and I thank ye."

"Thou art most welcome, Sir Aristide." And then Sir Morgan neared. "Good sirrah, how dost thou favor the capon crisps?"

"Lady Isolde, thou hast outdone the eels, which I once considered my primary partiality." Morgan cast a sly grin, waggled his brows, grasped her hand, and pressed his lips to her knuckles. "Were thou not wed, I should take thee to wife."

"That is a lovely offer, Sir Morgan." She could not help but giggle, until her husband wrenched her chair closer to his.

"Let go my bride, brother." Not for a minute did she take Arucard's warning serious, even when he bared his teeth. "Thou hast lingered long enough to express thy appreciation of my lady's talents."

"My apologies." Again, with a wild exhibition, the gadling bowed and chuckled as he returned to his seat.

With a grimace, Arucard huffed a breath. "Isolde—"

"Excuse us, brother." With unveiled pride, Demetrius, with Geoffrey in tow, conveyed a small wooden bench. "Lady Isolde, I am most grateful for thy delicious meat brewets."

"I am right glad I could serve thee well, Sir Demetrius." Beneath the unanticipated praise, she could have wept tears of joy, as never had her father or brother ever expressed recognition of her efforts.

"And the tunics thou didst sew for me art incomparable, my lady." For some reason she had yet to discern, Geoffrey never met her gaze, but he blushed crimson whenever he addressed her. "As thy original furnishing was damaged beyond repair in the journey from London, Demetrius and I built a new one for thee."

Now she cried.

"Er, leave the gift, brothers." With his napkin, Arucard wiped her damp cheeks. "On behalf of Lady Isolde, I thank ye." Then her husband flagged a passing servant. "Carry the bench to my chamber."

"Aye, sir." The young man bowed.

Then, to her surprise, Arucard stood, flagon in hand, and the great hall quieted. "My friends, it hath been a difficult journey, but we hath persevered, thanks in no small part to the women in our midst." A chorus of concurrence erupted. "So I ask thee to raise thy glass in toast." Her husband turned and faced her. "To my Lady Isolde of Chichester Castle."

"To Lady Isolde." The singular rally echoed in the cavernous hall, and the crowd rapped their fists atop the tables.

For as long as she could remember, she had yearned for acceptance—for validation of any kind, however minuscule, but never had she dreamed it would actually happen in her lifetime. And she vowed, thither and then, to merit the cherished accolade until she breathed her last.

Powerful emotions cascaded over her, and she tried but failed to muster a response. Then she realized thither was only one thing she wanted, and with that in mind she addressed the gathering. "Words cannot express the value of thy approbation, and I shall endeavor to deserve thy praise, every day. For now, Sir Arucard and I bid thee a pleasant eventide, as we take our leave."

Confusion invested his handsome features, as her husband escorted her into the hallway, which led to their private rooms. "Isolde, art thou upset with me?"

"Nay." She paused, and he faced her. "I cannot tell thee what I feel, as I know it not, but I am conquered." As something between euphoria and pain assailed her senses, she clutched her throat. "I can only say that I wish to be alone with thee. Nay—I need to be alone with thee, as I require the warmth and comfort of thy body. I need thee."

In a flash, Arucard bent, lifted her into his arms, and carried her to their sanctuary.

CHAPTER SIX

Two days anon, wearing a mail coif and hauberk over his garments, Arucard strolled into the courtyard a tad late for weapons practice, after lingering in bed with his bride. As had become a most agreeable habit, his wife tarried to solve what he had considered the new bane of his existence. In short, every dawn since his wedding, he woke with a stout and stubborn man's yard, and it often took hours to calm his dragon, as he suffered in silence.

However, in light of the spectacular night in their room, when they shared the ancere for the first time, and she noted his affliction as he soaped and bathed her breasts, she labored to ease his discomfit. And in Isolde's delicate but firm grasp, she never failed to drain his moat and appease the beast in a matter of minutes, much to his relief and everlasting gratitude.

"Wherefore art thou grinning like a giddy virgin?" Demetrius snickered. "As thou didst surrender that distinction a fortnight ago."

"And thou dost appear to have shrunk since then." Aristide elbowed Morgan. "Mayhap the lady wields the longsword better than our good sirrah."

"Mayhap we have no need of arms, as thy wife hath evacuated the castle." Geoffrey peered at his fellow brethren, and the knights burst into laughter.

"Art thou not the wit?" Naught could ruin Arucard's mood, as memories of Isolde's tender touch proved a powerful shield. "Perchance, thou missed thy calling, and thou should compose a comedy. And thou should not gainsay what thou hast yet to sample." Then he seized upon the one proclamation guaranteed to quell the jests. "Of course, thou wilt learn, in time."

The ensuing quietude was deafening.

When Pellier emerged from the servant's hall, he glanced in their direction and came to an abrupt halt. "Did I miss something?"

"Nay." Chuckling, Arucard waved at his friend, and they gathered near the stable, because it was past due to launch his plan. "My brothers art a curious cadre, as am I."

"Oh?" The marshalsea unsheathed his sword, in preparation to train. "I am interested, my lord. Hast thou a question for me?"

"Actually, I have several." He assumed the proper stance, and they engaged in a bit of play. "First, I would have thee know that I am not entirely ignorant of the marital bed."

"Ah, I see." Pellier smirked. "Young Arucard wishes to know how to seduce thy wife."

"Wilt thou keep thy voice down?" He winced, as never would he hear the end of it, were his fellow knights to discover the truth. "I know whither goes what, but I would not terrorize the poor girl."

"Hast thou considered a bath for two?" Metal clashed with metal.

"Aye, we have tried that." Arucard deflected Pellier's lunge.

"Hast thou taught her to rub the Franciscan monk's

bald head?" The second-in-command guffawed.

Arucard frowned. "Dost thou reference choking the fire-breathing dragon?"

"Is that what thou dost call knighting thyself these days?" Pellier grimaced, as Arucard charged.

"Aye." Arucard nodded. "She hath done that, several times, in fact."

"And yet thou still hast not consummated thy vows?" Pellier scratched his temple and narrowed his stare. "Wherefore not?"

"Because I would not frighten Isolde." And he struggled with another reason, which he had steadfastly refused to examine in the light of day. "She is a fine lady, and I would foster an abiding devotion."

"And thou would not injure her." Signaling a pause in their activity, Pellier walked to the well, dipped a ladle in a bucket, and took a drink of water. "Sorry, my lord. But Margery told me how Lord Rochester treated his daughter, and it grieves me more than thou dost know, as Lady Isolde is a gentle soul."

"Hear me well, sirrah." Studying the sharp edge of his sword, Arucard clenched his jaw and pictured her torn flesh. "What the earl hath wrought upon Isolde, he shall reap."

"I do not doubt thee for an instant." Pellier gazed at the sky and sighed. "Margery says thy wife is partial to lavender in her baths. And Lady Isolde favors mylates of pork for supper and a sweet of gyngerbrede. Mayhap thou should make a special request of the cook. Have the maids light candles, instead of the braziers, and romance thy lady with pretty words and praise."

"And what of the deed?" He braced for all manner of mirth at his expense. "As I would be a considerate husband."

"With thy fingers, prepare her nether eye until she is moist. Then set thy hips to hers to mount her, and be gentle, as thou dost part her thighs. Teach her to lift her ankles and hug thy waist with her legs. Ask if thou art too heavy, and prop thyself on thy elbows to ease her burden." The marshalsea's crude instruction sufficiently startled Arucard, but he listened with intent. "When thou dost breach her, restrain thyself, as thy instincts will tell thee to ride hard, but thou must resist. And use passionate kisses to distract her. Take her slow, and heed her warnings, else thou mayest hurt her. If she is distressed, thou must retreat, even if it kills thee, and it might." When a soldier passed within earshot, Pellier lowered his voice. "Use her but a single time, as her untried flesh will be sore in the morrow. Perchance, thou might arrange for one of Margery's soothing soaks to ease any lingering aches, as the second coupling often proves far more enjoyable than the first. Trust me, if thou dost desire her now, thou wilt crave her body doubly so after the deflowering, especially as thou art a virgin, too."

"While I am grateful for thy wisdom, I am not entirely comfortable with the breadth of thy knowledge of such intimate matters." With his course set, Arucard made a momentous decision. "And I shudder to think on thy exploits and thy soul's ascendance to the glorious hereafter, but it is not for me to judge thee."

"Worry not about my soul, Sir Arucard." Pellier chuckled. "Thou art the Templar Knight, and I always thought thy abstinence born of lunacy. I am but thy not-so-humble servant, and I caution thee not to place thy tenets upon my conscience. When I meet my fate, I shall make my own way."

"Somehow, I know thou wilt be fine." With renewed vigor, Arucard picked up his weapon and swung wide. In a matter of seconds, he backed Pellier into the curtain wall. After a few more rounds, which resulted in similar outcomes, the marshalsea surrendered.

"My lord, we both know thy heart and mind art otherwise engaged." Pellier sheathed his sword and bowed. "And before thou dost sever something I need, I suggest thou dost heed my advice."

"Deliver these to my chambers." He ceded his arms and mail coif. "And whither might I find Margery at this hour?"

"Mayhap, in the spicery." Pellier grinned. "And I shall drink to thy success in the great hall, but thou must take my word for it, as thou wilt be otherwise occupied."

And so Arucard went in search of Margery to make plans. To Pellier's credit, Arucard found the steward and made arrangements to woo his wife. As he walked through the screen passage to the great hall, he spied his lady in conversation with a trio of maids.

Gowned in vivid emerald velvet, with her hair plaited, she embodied elegance. After a few minutes, she dismissed the servants and turned in his direction. When she spotted him, she bestowed upon him a brilliant smile, and he nodded an acknowledgement. Under his breath, he said, "This eventide, Isolde, thou wilt be mine."

#

It was late in the afternoon, when Isolde ventured into the kitchen to finalize the menu, and she was surprised to find the cook had employed Margery in the preparations, as Chichester Castle was fully staffed. But the servants assured Isolde thither was no cause for concern, as they labored to produce a special meal, which they preferred not to discuss.

As she neared the fire, a distinct aroma caught her attention, and she halted and sniffed the air. "Is that gyngerbrede I smell?"

"Lady Isolde, thou art no scullion." Frowning, Margery wiped her hands on an apron and then ushered Isolde into the great hall. "And, mayhap, thou might do me a favor. Hast thou checked on the between maids? As Pellier informed me they lingered about, whilst the soldiers washed for supper, and I object to their questionable behavior. They should have finished their chores long before the men returned to the garrison, so thou canst guess at their motives."

The steward spoke so fast that Isolde could get nary a word edgewise. "Of course, but—"

"And then thou should return to thy chambers, as Anne guards the set pot, and thy bath should be ready, anon." Then Margery gave Isolde a gentle push. "Hurry along, my lady."

Amused by the steward's unusually abrupt demeanor, Isolde walked to the servant's rooms, whither she observed the young maids in conversation. When one servant struck the other with a pillow, the work yielded to play, amid a chorus of giggles and shrieks, which she loathed to interrupt, as theirs seemed a harmless game.

"Oh, didst thou see Sir Demetrius in the communal bath?"

"Yea." A particularly lovely domestic clasped her hands beneath her chin and sighed. "And what a large sword he doth brandish."

"How I would love to polish his helmet."

"Well, I prefer Sir Morgan." Another maid arched a brow and grinned. "Hast thou admired his one-eyed horse?"

"Mm." A brunette rocked on her heels. "What I would give to ride him."

"I like Sir Geoffrey and his flaxen hair."

"I favor Sir Aristide, as he is quiet." A blonde bit her lip. "And the quiet ones art always the most adventurous."

"Indeed, the knights art giants, and Lady Isolde hath married the biggest, of all," declared the redhead.

"But I imagine her ladyship doth not complain."

"Who would, with that in thy bed?"

The women collapsed into a fit of hilarity, and Isolde retreated to the courtyard. Never had it occurred to her that another female would admire Arucard, as he was Isolde's husband, and the revelation disturbed her for some reason she could not quite understand. But she would caution her man to guard his habits, as she would neither tolerate nor permit unsanctioned observation of Arucard, as his man's yard was hers. As her mood grew sour, she stomped toward her chambers, but a soldier flagged her.

"Lady Isolde, a message is just arrived for thee." He handed her correspondence, which bore familiar script.

"Thank ye." A wave of nausea swirled in her belly, as Isolde noted her father's seal. Clutching the letter to her chest, she ran through the great hall and navigated the passage to her quarters. When she strolled through the solar and entered her room, she started. "*Oh*—Margery. What art thou doing hither?"

"As thou hast hired no lady's maid, I shall continue to perform the services thou dost require." The steward glanced at Isolde and frowned. "What is wrong, my lady? Thou art white as a sheet."

Seized by fear neither frivolous nor acute, Isolde could not manage a reply, so she merely thrust the envelope at her friend. When Margery did not immediately respond, Isolde flicked her wrist.

"What is it?" Margery took a single step, her expression sobered, and she flinched. "Nay, not again."

"Help me, Margery." Shivering with uncontrollable terror, Isolde dropped the parchment, fell to her knees on the stone floor, and clutched her throat, as all manner of nefarious enterprises assailed her. "What am I to do if Father comes for me? His first missive declared his unmistakable intent to take me from Arucard, and I cannot allow that. I must act with expediency, so how can I stop him?"

"Stop—who?" Arucard loomed in the solar, and Isolde gulped as she pondered his reaction to her dire news. "And wherefore art thou on the ground? Art thou ill?" Then he peered at Margery and narrowed his stare. "Hast thou revealed my surprise?"

"Nay, my lord." With a shrug, Margery folded and unfolded her arms, and then she glanced at Isolde. "I was just preparing thy wife's bath, as usual."

"What surprise?" Isolde inquired, as he grasped her by the elbows and lifted her to her feet. "Have I displeased thee? Art thou vexed?"

"Thou art on the verge of tears, when I bring glad tidings." He framed her chin and turned her left and then right. "Wherefore art thou distressed?"

Given the grim backlash from the first letter, which still possessed the power to cause her alarm upon reflection, and her promise to apprise him of future correspondence, Isolde pointed to the disconcerting item. "Father hath written again, and I dread reading his entreaty, which I suspect contains evil intentions, given his last demands, and I have yet to fulfill his petition."

"That is thy worry?" In play, he tapped her cheek and then bent to retrieve the envelope. Without hesitation, he broke the seal and unfolded the note, which he scanned. "Margery, thou art dismissed, as I shall see to Lady Isolde's bath. And I trust everything is in order for our supper?"

"Aye, sir. I shall convey thy meal to the solar at the requested hour." After a quick curtsey, Margery scurried from the lord's apartment.

It was then she noticed his damp hair. "Hast thou already washed?"

"Aye." He grimaced, and her belly twisted and turned. "I joined my men in the communal quarters, as I did not wish to disturb thee."

That revelation did little to improve her state of unrest, as she imagined the maids admiring Arucard's sword.

"Husband, take pity on my gentle spirit, as it withers beneath the weight of my father's unscrupulous scheme." In that instant, Isolde could tolerate no more suspense, and she tugged on his sleeve. "Pray, what does it say?"

"More of the same nonsense, which does not signify at this moment. As it stands, I have arranged a meeting with the locals, with the assistance of de Cadby, and I shall gather information regarding the contentious burgage plots and inform His Majesty of the developments." He set the parchment on his bedside table and then faced her. "Now about thy bath, shall I help thee disrobe?"

"Thou cannot be serious." Venting a half-smothered sob, she flung herself at her husband and wrenched his tunic, as the tension investing her burst forth. "Do not let him take me from thee. Give me thy solemn vow, else I shall go mad, as I cannot be parted from thee."

"Sweet Isolde, if thou dost require it, allow me to allay thy fears, as I will never surrender thee to thy father, or anyone else, as long as I draw breath." Then he unbuttoned her cotehardie. "Is that lavender I smell?"

"Yea, it is my favorite." But she could not believe how calm he remained, when all she wanted to do was scream. "My lord, dost thou not perceive the danger? Dost thou not comprehend the threat my father presents? As we have yet to consummate our nuptials, our marriage—"

"—Shall at last be unimpeachable, once I claim thy maidenhead this eventide." With that, he kissed her silent, nibbled gently on her flesh, but he could not quiet her thoughts, which ran amok in light of his statement. When he lifted his head and met her gaze, he smiled. "Better?"

"Dost thou speak the truth, or dost thou jest?" After kicking off her leather slippers, she shed the heavy wool outer garment and then turned, so he could unlace her gown. Then she untied her chemise, and he whisked the slip from her body. Naked, she accepted his escort, as he led her to the ancere. Nudity bothered her not in his presence, as they had engaged in various intimate diversions since they journeyed to Chichester. "Prithee, do not tease me, as I cannot bear it."

"My lady, I would think thou dost know me well enough by now to know I would never jest on the matter." As she eased into the warm water, he grabbed a barilla of soap. "And I know of no other way to ensure thy father cannot annul our marriage. But the real reason I wish to seal our vows is far simpler." With great care, he scrubbed her back. "The fact is I want to make thee mine, and I can delay no longer."

"Oh, my lord." How her heart sang in accompaniment to her amazement, as she would shout from the rooftops that she was Arucard's wife in every way. "I want that, too." Reaching up, she cupped his cheek and drew him to her. Emboldened by newfound courage, she licked his lips, and then took his mouth, as she speared her fingers through his thick hair. At once, he dropped the cloth and caressed her breasts.

"Isolde, thou art a sorceress, and thou has cast a spell over me." He tickled her navel, and then touched her between her legs, and she gasped. "I am thy grateful servant."

"Art thou?" She adored his warm and flirty side, which he reserved for their private hours, and she caught his earlobe with her teeth. "And what would thou do for me?"

"Whatever thou dost require." He nipped the tip of her nose. "As I am thine to command."

"Thou dost know what I want." As he eased a finger inside her, she nuzzled his chest. "What I have always wanted."

When she spread her thighs further apart, he groaned. "Then permit me to tend thy needs, that we might hasten to our bed."

#

At the table in the solar, Arucard sat across from Isolde, both wearing naught but robes, and shoveled a healthy portion of pork into his mouth. In painful silence, he mulled the situation, which had grown ever more contentious after her bath, and he was at a loss to explain what happened and whither he had lost control.

What began as a pleasant interlude had devolved into an awkward series of clumsy moves on his part, after he spilled her wine and knocked over his tankard of ale. As he sipped his beer, he cast his wife a furtive glance, and she peered at him and blushed. And he returned his attention to his trencher, as the tension built.

"So how was thy day?" Isolde inquired in a small voice.

"Fine." Like an idiot, he searched for something to say but could seize upon naught of interest or significance, so he settled for the obvious. "And how was thy day?"

"Fine." With her elbow propped atop the table, she rested her cheek to her knuckles and huffed a breath.

Again, the room grew quiet as a tomb, while they ate. Then Arucard snapped his fingers. "How is thy meal?"

"Delicious." With a hopeful expression, Isolde sat upright. "Mylates of pork art my favorite."

"Yes, I know." Wherefore had the heretofore-pedestrian act of conversing with his bride become so difficult? "I asked Margery for information regarding thy preferences, as I would please thee on our special occasion."

"Thou art very thoughtful." For a brief moment, she smiled—until she gazed at their bed.

"I would be a good husband to thee." What an imbecile he had been, planning the singular event as a staged production, when he could have taken her after they retired, as they always engaged in a bit of intimate play before they slept. It would have been a natural progression on their nocturnal games. Instead, he quivered like the virgin he was and cursed himself a fool.

"My lord, may I ask a question?" Shifting her weight, she bit her lip. "If it is no trouble."

"Thou mayest ask whatever thou dost wish." He reached across the table and covered her hand with his. "What would thou know of me, as I have naught to hide from thee?"

"Art thou nervous?" After a strained lull, she inclined her head. "About tonight, I mean. As I cannot stop shaking."

"I hope this doth not lessen thy opinion of me, but I am nervous, too." Yes, he had bungled the entire affair, but how could he set it right? "In fact, I quiver as a green lad on the eve of his first battle."

"Oh, I am so glad to hear thee say it." To his surprise, she jumped from her seat and walked to his side. "Wilt thou hold me, as I am never afraid in thy embrace?"

"Of course." Without hesitation, he tossed his napkin atop the table, eased back his chair, and stood. When he splayed his hands wide, she all but ran into his waiting arms, which he closed about her. "Isolde, thou art shivering." He tightened his grip and posited a proposal that might render him insane if she agreed. "If thou dost prefer to postpone the consummation, I will not protest."

"Art thou mad? I cannot bear to delay another second." With a violent flinch, she grasped fistfuls of his robe. "I demand thee take me now."

Given her haughty demeanor, he could not stave off laughter, which did much to abate the tension currently investing his shoulders. But her innocent request also had another effect he had not foreseen, as his man's yard grew hard as stone, upon which he could bounce a thousand groats should he choose to do so.

"But what of thy sweet?" No, Arucard had no intention of denying his wife, but he could not resist baiting her. "I had Margery prepare the gyngerbrede just for thee."

"We could enjoy it, anon." With a half-sob, she wrested free, grabbed his wrist, and led him to their inner chamber. "Perchance, thou might feed me, as a treat, after the deflowering."

"An excellent suggestion." So he stoked the blaze in the hearth and wondered whither to begin, as Pellier had provided no specifics, in that respect. Again at a loss, Arucard rubbed the back of his neck. "Art thou warm enough?"

"Aye, my lord." Wringing her fingers, Isolde shuffled her feet. "May I ask another question?"

"My dear, thou mayest ask whatever thee dost wish."

Painfully aroused, he feared he might spill his seed before they ever made it to bed, but her trembling chin gave him pause. Summoning the patience of a saint, he sighed. "What dost thou want to know?"

"What if I fail to please thee?" Wide-eyed, and her distress apparent, she hugged herself. "What if thou dost find no satisfaction?"

"Thou must be joking." At the irony of her worry, he chuckled. "Allow me to assure thee that thy anxiety is ill-founded, as what concerns thee is not possible."

"I do not follow." In light of her naïveté, she furrowed her brow. "Of the marital relations I know naught, and I have no idea how to inspire thee. But another woman of experience could service thee to my detriment."

"As I told thee on our wedding night, I will join only with whom I have taken the sacrament, and that is thee." How could make her understand his predicament, when he possessed no direct knowledge, either? "Dost thou trust me?"

"Aye." She nodded once.

"Take off thy robe." She did as he bade, untying the belt and letting the garment slip to the floor, and he smiled. "I am inspired."

"Art thou truly?" Telltale fidgeting declared her skepticism.

Without a word, he doffed his garb and shrugged. As he anticipated, her gaze lit upon his most prominent protuberance, which, at the moment, provided substantial and indubitable proof of his desire. "Dost thou still doubt me?"

"No." With an arresting grin, she shook her head.

"Then come hither." While his petition seemed rather pedestrian, his current state proved tricky, until she situated his length to rest against her belly. As she nestled close, he kissed her hair. "I am sorry, Isolde. Thou dost deserve a man familiar with the mysteries of intercourse."

"I prefer thee." Then she met his stare. "So how

should we initiate the deed?"

"The natural progression would be to lie abed." His gut clenched at the mere suggestion. "Shall we adjourn to our respective places?"

It struck him as ridiculous that he should suffer uncanny nervousness at the prospect, when he and Isolde had shared the tent, the mattress, and even the ancere since their wedding a fortnight ago. So he bolstered his resolve as he slide between the sheets, reclined, and exhaled. After adjusting his pillow, he studied the dancing shadows on the intricate wood ceiling, as the flames flickered in the fireplace.

"Now what should we do," Isolde inquired.

"Mayhap we could indulge in our usual fare." Just as he turned on his side, she faced him, and her ill-situated knee almost ended the evening on a sour note. He jumped and groaned, as he shielded his most male member. "Careful, my lady."

"Sorry, my lord." She reached for him, just as he drew her near, and her forehead collided with his chin. "*Ouch.*"

"No apologies necessary, as I am but a sad sack of ignorance." Given the information Pellier had imparted, and Arucard had committed to memory, he mulled the most reliable path to his goal. "Perchance, we should kiss."

"All right." To his unutterable astonishment, she charged as if running the gauntlet and bit his lip in the process. Wild and wanton, she yanked his hair and darted her tongue at his, as she pressed her pelvis to his.

It occurred to him that he was supposed to direct their movements, and in that he had failed. Recalling Pellier's sage counsel, Arucard nudged her legs apart and settled his palm to her thatch of sweet curls, as he always gave her the opportunity to adjust to his caress. Isolde shuddered and moaned, and he well nigh lost himself in the moment.

Slow and steady, he slipped a finger into her moist and tight sheath, and she bucked as an unbroken horse. He had touched her thus on previous occasions, but each contact had been brief, as he had spilled his seed and brought their nightly forays to an abrupt end. In a scarce second, he promised himself to persist in his goal.

To advance his cause, he rolled his wife onto her back, and she gasped as he loomed above her. With his mental notes ordered, he lowered his hips to hers and gently spread her thighs to accommodate him. Propped on his elbows, he framed her face. "Art thou comfortable?"

"Is that of great importance?" Her expression did not inspire confidence.

"It is to me." Shifting, he brought his man's yard to her slick passage. "Art thou ready?"

"Aye." She nodded and clutched his shoulders. "What should I do?"

"Lift thy ankles." As she abided his request, he flexed his spine and inched the tip of his arousal inside her. Everything Pellier recommended flooded Arucard's consciousness, and he pressed forward. As she took him into her body, bathing him in succulent heat, he clenched his jaw and gritted his teeth. Resistance halted his path, and he paused. "Kiss me, Isolde." When she set her mouth to his, he proceeded until he had fully seated himself deep within her pliant flesh, and she tensed beneath him. Against his better judgment and Pellier's warning, Arucard retreated and then repeated the sumptuous attack—and he fired his seed in a vicious volley that left him huffing and wheezing for breath. "Oh, holy mother."

As the world spun beyond his control, a powerful euphoria simmered in his veins, and bursts of light flashed before his eyes, he relished each successive spasm of pure, unadulterated pleasure, such as he had never known possible. Tremor after spectacular tremor rocked his frame until he was spent, and then he collapsed. For a long while, he simply languished and savored the intimate bond with his bride.

"My lord, is it done?" she asked in a whisper. "Art thou all right?"

"Aye." With insufficient energy to lift his head, he merely sagged atop her and grunted. "I have claimed thy maidenhead."

"So I am, at last, thine." Then she wept and curled about him. "And our marriage is irreproachable."

"Wherefore dost thou cry?" Summoning the strength to shift and gain a view of her much-cherished visage, he frowned. "Have I hurt thee?"

"Nay." Favoring him with her shy smile, she brushed aside a lock of hair. "I am happy, my lord. In fact, I have never been so happy. And should my father attempt to take me from thee, I would fight to my death to stop him."

"That will never happen, Isolde." When she hugged him tight with her arms and legs, a primitive hunger, raw and insatiable, flourished in the pit of his belly, and he struggled with a potent possessiveness he could neither understand nor contain. "Never will I surrender thee, as thou art mine per the sacrament and His Majesty. And I would slay an army to defend thee."

"Thou art my champion." As she bestowed upon him another oh-so-tempting kiss, which stirred the dragon, she wiggled her hips, and that was all Arucard needed to resume the exquisite dance. When she closed her eyes and compressed her lips, he thrust. "*Oh*, my lord."

"Ah, thou dost entice me, beauteous Isolde." Now he comprehended Pellier's fascination with the female sex, as Isolde posited an allure he could not and would not resist. In silence, he swore an oath to sustain their conjugal activities beyond the meager two thrusts that marked their first coupling and injured his pride, and somewhere in the recesses of his mind, he vaguely recalled a recommendation to abstain from further enterprises in deference to his wife's delicacy. As she voiced no complaints, he saw no reason to deny them the rapturous diversion he found so enthralling.

But enchanting completion beckoned with the third drive of his hips, and he counted that a small yet significant improvement.

Now he comprehended His Majesty's caution, as Arucard would be content to spend the remains of his days between his bride's supple thighs, and he counted himself a most fortunate husband—until Isolde tapped his shoulder and inquired, "So, is that all thither is to it?"

CHAPTER SEVEN

The sun cast its brilliant rays through the glazed windows, as Isolde stirred. At her side, Arucard slept, and she smiled as she revisited memories of the previous night. After the initial much prayed for consummation of their vows, her husband had taken her three more times in the wee hours, once following the tender relaxation wherein he fed her the gyngerbrede she loved, and she would treasure the memory until her death. And yet she remained oddly discomfited.

While he declared his satisfaction in startling grunts and groans, she had been left oddly cold and empty by the experience, which she had not anticipated. The gentle caresses and long, intimate kisses, coupled with the joining of their bodies, had awakened something within her that she tried but failed to identify; yet she could not escape the pervasive intuition that something was missing.

For a barely ex-virgin, the connubial games proved a mystery, as a foreign tension twisted her insides, pressure built in the now sensitive flesh between her thighs, and then—naught. As he found his prize, she ached for what she knew not. In short, she lacked.

"Art thou awake?" With a chuckle, he poked her with a telltale aspect of his anatomy, and she giggled.

"Aye, and it appears thou art aroused again." Without prompting, she rolled onto her back and spread her legs in welcome, as she knew what he wanted. "So take thy ease, my lord. As I am thy most willing servant."

"Isolde, thou art irresistible when thou art so accommodating." In mere seconds, Arucard lowered himself atop her and situated his sword, and she lifted her ankles and hugged him with her limbs. In a single fluid flex of his spine, he entered her, and she winced. Pausing, he kissed her forehead. "Did I hurt thee?"

"Nay, my lord." Despite her faults, and of that thither were many, he desired her, and that was all that mattered, so never would she refuse him. "Given thy appetite, which seems endless, I am a tad sore, but if thou would but move, I will adjust to thy gratifying invasion."

"Sweet Isolde, thy body intones a bewitching siren song to which I am incapable of contravening." As he rose on his arms and towered above her, Arucard closed his eyes, grimaced, and pumped in a now familiar rhythm. When she splayed her fingers across his beauteous chest, he groaned. "Yea, I crave thy touch."

For some strange reason, she suspected he counted his drives, which struck her as absurd, so she dismissed the thought. But then the oh-so-tempting heat swirled and soared within her, providing fortuitous distraction, and she yielded to the sensations he incited, as he set his lips to hers. And just as she gained momentum, and her muscles tensed, Arucard threw back his head, contorted his face, and emitted another dramatic roar, which well nigh terrified her. Then, huffing and puffing in time with tempered thrusts, his pleasure evident, he draped atop her.

Thirsting for something as yet unknown to her, she remained strangely unfulfilled by their coupling. But she would not apprise him of that fact, as she feared the fault rested with her.

"I am late for weapons practice." He trailed his tongue along the curve of her neck. "But thou art a sorceress, and thou hast cast a spell over me, so I am thy most obliging prisoner." As he shifted and withdrew, she vented a plaintive cry. "And I have used thee without compunction, when I should have moderated our first union. Forgive me, Isolde."

"Thither is naught to forgive, as I am thy wife, and it is my duty to please thee." He could not possibly know what his declaration meant to her, as no one ever cared whether or not she was injured, much less expressed remorse for her pain. As she slipped from their bed, she took a single step, flinched, and toppled to the mattress. "*Oh*. I ache in places I did not know I could ache."

"God's blood." In seconds, her husband came to her aid. He flung back the covers and halted, as his gaze lit upon the small but distinct crimson stain that sealed their bond for all eternity. When he stared at her and brushed his knuckles to her cheek, she spied regret in his countenance. "I should be horsewhipped for abusing thee on our special occasion."

"Nay, my champion." As he tucked her in with care, he kissed her forehead, and the customary yearning blossomed anew, in spite of her discomfort, which rendered her confused. "If thou would send for Margery, I will soak in a soothing bath and regain my strength for my lord's taking, this eventide, as I would not disappoint thee."

"Thou dost employ my pet name, which I have yet to compose for thee, as it must be perfect, just like thee. And given our consummation, thou dost know that is not possible." How she adored his blush and boyish grin. "But I would grant another deferment until thou hast recovered, before I take thee again, if thou art amenable."

"Nay, I do not accept, as I am not amenable to any further deferment." To her relief, his man's yard grew hard, offering irrefutable proof of his passion, and she worked his length, as she yearned to discover what she had yet to experience. "And thy body agrees with me."

He studied the ceiling. "Isolde, I must partake of weapons practice."

"Indeed, I concur." A drop of moisture seeped from the tip. "As thy primary weapon beckons."

"Thou dost know what I mean." He closed his eyes.

"As doth thee." She yelped when he jumped her.

And so they ended up right whither they started—back in bed.

The next thing Isolde knew, she woke just as Arucard bent and kissed her.

"I have sent for Margery, and I have given orders that thou art to remain in our chambers and rest." Again he claimed her mouth in a lengthy and thorough affirmation of his regard, and Isolde wrapped her arms about his neck and held him close. "Thou dost make it difficult to leave thee, but I shall return in time to sup with thee."

"But thou wilt not stay away too long." As he made to withdraw, she tightened her grip. "Promise."

With nary a word, he seized her lips in a searing demonstration of his ardor, which left her breathless and in no doubt of his affection. Then he marched into the solar, closed the doors behind him, and she sighed and stretched. Almost immediately, visions of a heretofore-impossible future sprang to life, and she clutched the sheet to her chest, but a knock intruded on her fanciful thoughts.

"Come." She burrowed into the pillow and laughed.

"My lady, how art thou this fine morrow?" Carrying her usual bag of potions, Margery perched on the edge of the mattress. "Thy bath is ready, and I had cook prepare a light meal."

"Trust me, after last night, I could eat a heavy meal." Scooting to the side of the bed, Isolde accepted Margery's proffered hand and stood. "Oh, dear friend, I am not certain I can make it to the ancere."

"I would have had it placed in thy inner chamber, but I did not wish to disturb thee, given Sir Arucard had not yet appeared in the courtyard." The steward wrapped an arm about Isolde's waist for support. "Take it slow, my lady. Thither is no rush."

"Tell me the truth, is this normal?" At the tub, Isolde moaned as she lifted one foot and then the other and sank into the unusually hot water. "I can hardly walk, and I feel as though I have been run over by Arucard's destrier."

"I know not if I can describe it as normal." Situated at the rear, Margery chuckled and used a basin to wash Isolde's hair. "But it is a very good sign. And thy husband's commands show concern for thee, which is God's work, as thou art finally safe from thy father's schemes."

"That reminds me, I have yet to read his latest letter." Isolde peered over her shoulder. "It rests on Arucard's bedside table. Wilt thou fetch it for me?"

"Of course." Margery dried her hands and returned seconds later with the correspondence. "How I wish he would leave thee alone."

Sitting upright, Isolde scanned the contents.

Isolde,

Wherefore hast thou not written in accordance with my commands? Dost thou willfully disobey me? Must I remind thee of thy obligations? As thy father, thou dost owe me thy allegiance. I must know the origin and location of Sir Arucard's fortune, and how is he connected to His Majesty? I expect a response from thee, posthaste. If thou dost continue to disobey me, thou wilt live to regret it.

Thy father, Lord Rochester

"What does it say?" Margery massaged Isolde's scalp.

"If I may inquire."

"Arucard was correct." Isolde dropped the parchment to the floor, reclined, and resumed her soak. "Father repeats his demands, though he hath abandoned the false endearments that never fooled me."

"Dost thou intend to respond?" With a towel, Margery dried Isolde's hair. "Hath Sir Arucard instructed thee on a proper reply?"

"Nay." Savoring the bath, Isolde closed her eyes, revisited the glorious morrow, and savored the memory of her knight's ardent attention. "My husband will deal with it, so what have I to fear?"

#

It was well past noon when Arucard, garbed in his mail coif and hauberk, and sword secured in his grasp, sauntered into the courtyard. Three days after the memorable consummation of his vows, wherein he surrendered his virginity in the very same moment he claimed Isolde's innocence, and he had yet to report for weapons practice on time. As his marshalsea had correctly predicted, Arucard could not keep his hands off his wife.

The hour mattered not, as he sought her company and took her without compunction. That should have satisfied him, yet he craved her body the instant they parted, which always drove him back to her arms. And while she never turned him away, he could not elude the unsettling suspicion that Isolde did not derive as much pleasure from their interludes as did he. It was a disconcerting deficiency he intended to amend, without delay.

"Someone is distracted." Waggling his brows, Morgan assumed a provoking stance. "Mayhap I can help thee focus."

"And it appears that very same someone hath trouble abandoning his bed." To Morgan's left, Demetrius brandished his sword and adopted a goading pose. "Perchance a sound defeat will improve thy commitment to duty."

"Thou dost challenge my dedication and abilities?" It was to their misfortune that Arucard was in no mood to play—unless his partner was his delectable bride. So the sooner he dispatched his antagonists, the sooner he could broach the topic foremost on his mind with his chief advisor in matters of the flesh. Planting his feet wide, he bent his knees, squared his shoulders, and lowered his chin. "Gird thy defenses, brothers."

Metal clashed with metal, as Arucard engaged his fellow Nautionnier knights in spirited combat neither facetious nor serious. When Demetrius charged, Morgan attempted a flanking maneuver, but Arucard deflected the gadling with a wide swing and then followed with a vicious molinetto, which caught Demetrius by surprise.

As Arucard was briefly distracted, Morgan moved in with a wicked riverso, but Arucard spied the oncoming assault from the corner of his eye and turned aside the attack with a brutal taglio, which wrenched the weapon from the youngest brother's grasp, and he splayed his palms in submission. "I yield."

In a flash, Arucard whirled about and discovered Demetrius with his sword leveled in preparation to strike, but just as he initiated his advance, his fingers tensed, which signaled Arucard. Lightning quick Arucard shifted to the right, inverted his sword, stomped his brother's foot, and clipped his chin with the hilt. Demetrius dropped to the ground, and Arucard rested the pointed end of his blade to his friend's throat.

"Capitulate." Arucard bared his teeth. "Now."

With a mighty scowl, Demetrius nodded once. "I concede."

"That did not take long." With fists on hips, Geoffrey frowned. "Mayhap thou should concentrate thy efforts on thy own skills, and allow our fearless leader to tend his affairs."

"Indeed." The voice of reason, Aristide rolled his eyes and clucked his tongue. "Demetrius, see to thy injury, and be grateful Arucard only toyed with thee, as the last time someone challenged his prowess on the field of honor, the ignorant soul lost his head."

"I thought we were merely exercising." As he stood, Demetrius dusted off himself and then rubbed his jaw. "And we meant no offense."

"Perchance the Lady Isolde keeps thee busy in thy bed." With an exaggerated strut, Morgan thrust his hips. "And Arucard doth not sleep much, which hath fouled his mood."

"Do not gainsay what thou hast not tried." And that otherwise unremarkable comment brought Arucard full circle, as the pithy battle heated his blood, which pooled in a particular part of his anatomy, and he pondered a swift return to his chambers and his wife. Just then Pellier appeared in the courtyard. "Marshalsea, I require thy services, as Demetrius and Morgan have surrendered the fight."

"That is because they do not know thy weakness, as do I. And from what I hear from my fetching Margery, thy enthusiasm is possessed of black hair, green eyes, and tender flesh." Pellier guffawed and waved at the four other knights. "Entertain thyself near the stables, as Sir Arucard and I have important matters to discuss." As soon as the men were beyond earshot, Pellier scowled. "Hast thou lost thy mind? Art thou no better than a boothaler that thou would treat thy gentle wife with such callous indifference, as if she is naught more than a poxy-cheeked strumpet?"

"I beg thy pardon?" Arucard scratched his temple and slumped, as he recalled her wince and grimace when he took her in the faint dawn light. "I have shown great deference to my bride." Even as he voiced the claim, he knew he did not speak the entire truth.

"Of course, thou hast." The marshalsea slapped the flat of his blade to Arucard's arse. "That is wherefore Margery tends Lady Isolde every morrow, and thy wife cannot walk to the great hall without a noticeable teeter. Thou hast used her roughly."

Arucard opened his mouth and then closed it.

"Well?" Pellier folded his arms. "After I offered thee my best counsel, what is thy excuse?"

Denial danced on the tip of his tongue, but Arucard was no liar, and his friend had correctly assessed the situation. "I am a terrible husband."

"Nay, thou art fallible, as art we all." The second in command sat on a bench near the well. "And it appears the great Templar is but a man with the usual inclinations, and thither is no shame in that."

"Thou art correct in thy assumptions, as I ache for her, Pellier. Isolde is the most fascinating creature of my existence." In his mind, Arucard envisioned her as she looked at sunrise, with her raven locks splayed across her pillow and her luscious breasts jostling in time with his thrusts, as he claimed her. "I burn for her, and it is as thee didst warn. I cannot defend against her charms, and she hath not once denied me."

"That is because thy lady is a good and dutiful woman." The marshalsea narrowed his stare. "But thou art her caretaker, her owner, responsible for her health and welfare. Thou must learn to control thy lustful appetites."

"In that respect, I am an abyss of unknowing, but I would argue she owns me." Disheartened, Arucard plopped beside his friend. "While I have killed untold numbers in battle, and I have maintained an austere and faithful life, when it comes to Isolde, I am her devoted servant. Regardless of my intent, I am but clay in her hands, and I am powerless to resist her. Nay, I do not wish to resist her."

"Well, if she celebrates thy union, then who am I to argue otherwise?" In that instant, Pellier smacked Arucard on the shoulder, stood, and then furrowed his brow. "What is it? What bothers thee?"

"Thither is something I need to ask thee." The nagging

question, the original source of his quandary shot to the fore, and he shuffled his feet to ease the awkwardness. "How dost thou know whether or not thy mate enjoys the pinnacle of thy coupling? Not that I am unsure."

"Oh, my poor friend." With a snort of mirth, Pellier wiped his face. "Trust me, if thou must ask, thy lady hath not enjoyed it." Then he burst into a fit of chuckles.

"I find naught funny about thy observation." And Arucard's confidence flagged, but he cared not for his pride when it came to Isolde's satisfaction, or lack thereof. "And as thou art a trove of information on the subject, I would avail myself of thy recommendation."

"What hast thou tried?" Pellier inquired with a grin. "Owing to discretion and my respect for thy wife, know I shall never betray thy confidence, so thou mayest speak with frankness."

"I did as thee instructed." Arucard shrugged. "Naught more."

"Art thou joking?" When Arucard indicated otherwise, Pellier sighed and rested his forehead in his palm. "Dost thou mean to tell me thou hast spent a fortnight in thy wife's bed, thou hast claimed her maidenhead, and thou hast not explored her body?"

"I have touched her." In haste, he searched his memory. "We have kissed, we have engaged in intercourse, as thou didst dictate, and I followed thy instructions to the letter."

"And that is it?" Pellier furrowed his brow. "My friend, my directions were intended as a start on thy quest for carnal knowledge, the journey of which thou hast yet to complete. Hast thou not surveyed the paradise between her thighs? Hast thou not kissed her nether eye, spelt thy name in her most succulent flesh, suckled the pearl of her desire, or taught her to lick and nurse thy one-eyed horse?"

At the prospect of such arousing activity, Arucard stammered in disbelief, but his thoughts quickly turned to seductive strategy, with Isolde at the center of his erotic plans.

"What?" The marshalsea elbowed Arucard. "Art thou shocked?"

"I know not how to respond." He swallowed hard. "Is such behavior permissible?"

"Noble sirrah, what happens in thy connubial quarters stays in thy connubial quarters." Now Pellier collapsed in a full belly laugh. When at last he quieted, the marshalsea wiped a tear from his cheek. "Arucard, Isolde is thy mate, as charged by the sacrament. Thou hast promised to love and honor thy lady. How thou dost achieve that is up to thee. But if thou canst bring her sweet release and make her scream, the rest is simple."

#

It was an unusually sunny and warm fall afternoon, when Isolde ventured from her chambers in search of food to quiet her grumbling belly. Something about Arucard's lustful jousting between the sheets spurred a furious appetite. Just as she entered the great hall, she almost collided with her husband.

"My lady, thou art awake." With a smile, he whisked a stray tendril from her face. "I had thought, mayhap, we might partake of a ride, as the weather is fine, and I desire thy unreserved company."

"My lord, I would love to indulge thee, but I am famished and near wasting." At that very moment, her tummy emitted thunderous proof of her hunger, and she rolled her eyes as he laughed. "It is thy fault, as thou didst exercise me quite thoroughly this morrow."

All levity ceased, and he narrowed his stare, cupped her chin, and gifted her a whisper of a kiss. "Yea, I did, and I right enjoyed myself. But I have a solution that meets both our needs, if thou art amenable to my suggestion."

"Oh?" When he took her by the arm and led her into the bailey, she started. "Do I have a choice?"

"Of course." In a flash, he lifted her to the saddle of his destrier. "Thou canst come with me." Then he seated himself behind her, pulled her close to rest against him, tucked his ermine collared cloak about her, grasped the reins, and nipped the crest of her ear. "Or thou canst *come* with me."

"Arucard." Biting her lip, she shivered, as his rich tone betrayed an underlying meaning she understood too well, and her gut clenched, as they navigated the barbican and then the outer gatehouse. "Thou cannot intend to engage in...that is to say...we cannot possibly...out in the open...oh, thou dost know what I reference."

"My naughty wife, I like the way thou dost think." Once they cleared the castle battlements, he heeled the flanks of his stallion and galloped to the main road, whither he set a blazing pace. "Thither is a nice hilltop with an impressive view of the ocean, from which we might dine on a meal of boiled chicken, grapes, fresh bread, wine, and the gyngerbrede thee dost favor."

"What a wonderful idea." Reclining in his embrace, she squirmed when he nibbled her neck. "My lord, thou art brazen, but I favor that about ye."

"And thou art tantalizing beyond compare." He rounded a bend, steered for the verge, and then charged the hill. "The grass is tall, but hither it is dry, and I have a plan that should provide privacy for my shy bride."

"Thou art resourceful, my gallant knight." As they reached the top of the range, a spectacular vista spread wide before her, and Isolde turned and nuzzled him. "It is beauteous, Arucard. Thank ye, for bringing me hither."

"Mayhap we shall consider this our special place." He drew rein, dismounted, and then lifted her from the saddle. "And we might share this spot in milder seasons." With his sword, he cut a circular haven amid the thick foliage, which was dormant in the fall, and then untied a blanket from his horse, which he handed to her. "Spread the cover on the ground, whilst I retrieve the sack of food."

"Aye, my lord." She did as he bade and then sat. "This is cozy, just like our own little nest." As she glanced from left to right, she realized she could not see over the tips of the blades, but situated along the rise, she had an unimpeded outlook of the sea. Everything was perfect, and then she pondered his motives. "Hast thou discovered information relating to my father's letters and questionable activities? Wherefore dost thou require seclusion?"

"Aeduuard de Cadby will arrive this eventide to discuss the burgage plots, and he brings additional witnesses." Squatting beside her, he unpacked the fare. "I shall hear their complaints and seek His Majesty's counsel on a proper course of action."

"But what of my father?" While she had more to protest, he quieted her with a plump and juicy grape. "My lord, thou art distracting me."

"Nay, I am tending thy welfare, as a dutiful husband." As she made to argue, he shoved a portion of chicken into her mouth. "Eat."

"Arucard, that is too much," she said between chokes. "And I wish to know thy plan to deal with my father. He frightens me, as he is cruel, and he will punish me for not responding to his correspondence."

"Isolde, as I promised, I will handle thy father and protect thee, so thou dost worry for naught." Without ceremony, he stuffed a piece of bread between her lips. "And thy primary occupation, as of this moment, is to express thy appreciation my efforts. Art thou not pleased with my gesture of affection?"

"Is that thy aim?" Now he garnered her interest. "Thou dost wish to demonstrate devotion?"

"Aye." Then he shrugged, as he uncorked the wine and took a healthy gulp. "And I thought, perchance, thou mayest want to talk."

"About—what?" As he made it clear he had no desire to discuss the predicament with her father, she understood him not. "The castle is in order, we art fully staffed, with the exception of a lady's maid, and thou hast established the garrison, per the King's command. What else do we need to discuss?"

"Well, I wondered if thou art happy?" Exhaling, Arucard scratched his cheek. "As thy happiness is important to me."

"Yea, of course, more than ever." Thrilled by his boldly proclaimed interest in her contentment, she could have danced a jig. Taking his lead, she selected a large grape and fed it to him. "And what of thee?"

"Aye." And again he kissed her, but he lingered, and she sighed as a languorous calm settled her nervousness. "Thou art my treasure, Isolde."

And that statement inspired all manner of joy, as she relaxed. Peaceful quiet fell over their modest sanctuary, as they ate. And while the minutes ticked past, the gentle breeze rustled through the dry grass, the gulls keened in the distance, and the waves crashed ashore on the beach below, Isolde suspected her husband had not revealed the true motive to their special outing.

"One piece of gyngerbrede remains." She held up the tempting confection. "I will half it with thee."

"Thou art the soul of generosity." Despite his grin, she spied distress in his crystal blue eyes.

"What troubles thee?" After folding the cloths in which he stowed the food, she scooted closer to him, and, as she anticipated, he lifted her to his lap. Draping an arm about his shoulders, she hugged her husband. "Thou cannot keep secrets from me, as I share thy bed and thy body."

"Dost thou enjoy playing my fiddle?" With brows quirked, he grimaced. "Prithee, tell me the truth."

Well, she asked. And he most certainly answered.

"I beg thy pardon?" In her embarrassment, that was the only response Isolde could muster.

"My lady, thou art an uncommonly intelligent woman." Was it her imagination, or was he sweating? "Pray, I must know if thou dost find pleasure when I stir thy waters?"

Convinced thither was something inferior about her, given she had not celebrated their coupling in the demonstrative fashion as had her knight; she knew not how to reply without shaming herself. "Mayhap it is not the same for wives."

"I knew it." Smacking his forehead, he groaned. "This is all my fault."

"What?" Shock dispelled the tranquility of their interlude, as she digested his revelation. "Thou dost think thou art to blame?"

"I am thy husband." Arucard pressed a fist to his chest. "The responsibility for thy pleasure is mine, and I have failed thee."

"Nay, thou hast made too much of it, and I must explain." Never had Isolde fathomed confessing such embarrassing details, but she had to make him understand. Framing his jaw, she kissed him. "Do not overstate the issue, as it is not so great as thou dost believe. Yea, I cherish our intimacy, as thou dost inspire feelings I never knew existed, when we join our bodies." He rested his forehead to hers, and she drew strength to continue. "I ache for thee, but the balm doth not quite ease my pain, and wherefore I know not. Rather, it intensifies it, and I am left with a void I can scarcely bear. But I would never refuse thee, because I crave thy touch."

"Wherefore hast thou said naught?" In that moment, he settled his palm to her hose-covered calf.

"My lord, I would not hurt thee or thy pride for anything in the world." She met his gaze. "And I considered it my deficiency, as thou hast had no problem finding thy release. Thither must be something wrong with me."

"Well, thither is a way to find out, if thou art willing." With his fingers, he walked a path to the inside of her thigh, and she shuddered. "Dost thou trust me?"

"Always."

#

In a single tear, Arucard ripped the seam of Isolde's cotehardie. As she reclined on the blanket, with her eyes closed, he all but shredded her chemise and then spread her legs. Once again summoning Pellier's sage wisdom, he eased between her thighs and cupped her bottom with his hands. Slowly, he bent his head and expelled his breath to her triangle of soft curls, and she bit her fingers and emitted a muffled sob. That singular exhalation presented the greatest response he had ever garnered and did much to bolster his confidence, which he needed just then, so he trailed his tongue along her nether lips.

With an achingly sweet cry, his wife lauded his efforts, as he repeatedly spelled his name on her pliant folds, and he ventured further into her honey sheath, relishing the hint of lavender mingled with the tart essence that was uniquely hers. When he located what Pellier had referred to as the pearl of her desire, Arucard fastened his mouth about the tiny bud and suckled hard, and his bride bucked and squirmed. And with each successive murmur and wiggle, which he counted as a priceless treasure, he realized he had never felt more a man in his life.

"*Oh.*" Yanking his hair, Isolde rolled her head from side to side and then arched her back. "Prithee, Arucard. I can take no more."

Anchoring her firmly in his grasp, he licked and laved in a tempting rhythm, until his suddenly not-so-shy lady stretched her limbs, gazed at the sky, and heralded her release with an earsplitting shout of exultation, which echoed on the rocky cliffs. Never had he glimpsed anything so bewitching as his wife in the throes of passion, and a powerful hunger built in his chest and scored a path straight to his crotch.

In seconds, Arucard doffed his belt, hitched his tunic, untied his leather breeches and linen braies, and entered her in a single potent thrust. How he longed to savor her scorching wet heat, which branded him hers, but, as usual, he drove into her a mere five times before his seed burst forth deep within her.

Some day, he would linger and luxuriate in her body, but now was not that day.

Collapsing atop her, he reveled in her ready embrace, as she nestled close. But when he discovered her crying, he propped on an elbow.

"What is wrong, Isolde?" With care, he placed a kiss on the tip of her nose. "Did I hurt thee?"

"Nay." Tears streamed her temples as she smiled. "Never could I have imagined such sensations, and my emotions have run rampant, such that I cannot contain my joy. If I could describe it to thee, I would, but words fail me."

"Art thou trying to tell me I have, at last, pleasured thee?" With the pad of his thumb, he caressed her cheek. "And I did not frighten thee?"

"That is not possible." For a while, she stared at him. Then she clutched his wrist and pressed his palm to her lips, and his gut clenched. "At first, when I met thee outside the chapel in London, I pictured so many dreadful things, as thou art quite large and imposing. And when I witnessed thee fight the bandits and de Cadby, thou didst behead a man, and I was terrified of thee, as I suspected I might suffer thy violence. But despite thy incomparable size and strength, thou hast never harmed me." Then she drew him near and set her mouth to his. "In fact, thou art a most gentle husband."

Thither were many things Arucard wanted to tell his wife that afternoon, as she cradled him with her sumptuous thighs. He pondered declarations of devotion and trust, but none seemed sufficient to convey the depth of his regard and commitment. Instead, he took her again and said with his body what he could not voice.

Brethren of the Coast

Nulli Secundus

W   E

S

CHAPTER EIGHT

Chichester Castle came into view as Arucard steered his destrier to the south. Given the pleasant afternoon spent in his wife's company, his mood was light as he pondered the meeting with de Cadby and the locals. And while he should have focused his attention on the impending gathering, a series of memorable feminine screams echoed in his brain, and he hugged Isolde close.

"I believe I have composed an appropriate pet name for thee." In play, he rubbed his nose to crest of her ear. "And it is perfect, as art thou."

"Oh?" Wrapped in the blanket, because he had destroyed her cotehardie, and riding astride in his lap, she rested against his chest, turned her head, and lifted her chin in position to receive his kiss. "How would thee address me in private, my champion?"

"Well, thou art sweeter than any confection, which begs a comparison to honey, and I should know, as I sampled thy nectar more than once today." And then he chuckled, as he revisited recent activities and developments, which had surpassed his expectations.

"And it is said that a woman blossoms when she surrenders her maidenhead, but I would argue otherwise. I think ye blossomed when thee experienced thy first release, and I will endeavor to inspire thee in our bed, henceforth. So, combining the two, thou art my honey flower."

"Honey flower?" She giggled and then cast him a charming smile. "I like that."

"Then it is settled." And he would carry that bit of information to his grave, as he could only imagine how his brothers would react to that revelation. As he crossed the first drawbridge, he waved to the guards. "And this eventide, when we retire, I shall spread thy petals and make thee sing, honey flower."

"*Arucard*." Now she burrowed into his tunic. "Thou art shocking."

"What?" As he navigated the barbican, he pinched her bottom through the thick cover, and she yelped. "We art married, and the King demands I produce an heir, so I am but following orders." Then he whispered, "Mayhap I shall teach thee to pleasure my body as I satisfied thee."

"Is that permissible?" Was it wishful thinking, or did she seem interested as she peeked at him? "Thou hast been very naughty."

"My lady, what we do in our chambers is our affair." In his mind, he pictured her taking his man's yard into her mouth, and the dragon woke. "Wilt thou gainsay what thou hast not tried?"

"Dost thou truly wish it?" She sat upright and met his stare. "Thou would have me behave in such a manner, and thou dost encourage my adventurous nature?"

"Aye." As they entered the courtyard, he noted several horses tied neared the stable. "I adore thy adventurous nature, and I have scarcely wanted anything more."

"My lord." Pellier rushed forward. "Young de Cadby and his supporters have arrived. Margery hath installed them in the great hall."

"I should see to thy refreshments." Clutching the blanket, Isolde scooted forward, as Arucard dismounted and then handed her down. "But first I require a change of clothing in order to properly address our guests."

"And I shall inquire after their comfort." Disappointment sank into his bones as she strolled toward their quarters. But at the last second, she peered over her shoulder, and Arucard arched a brow in question.

"By thy command, I am at thy service." Then she stuck her tongue in her cheek. "And at thy earliest convenience, I shall fulfill thy humble request. Thou wilt be sure to let me know when that might be, as I would not wait too long."

And so it was with a spring in his step and wicked thoughts swirling in his mind that Arucard ventured to greet his visitors. When he strolled into the cavernous hall, Aeduuard stood from his chair, and Arucard extended his hand in friendship. "De Cadby, welcome to Chichester Castle."

"My lord." With an exaggerated bow, Aeduuard grinned and then rocked on his heels. "Or should I call thee Sir Arucard, as thou hast so many titles? Hast thou a preference?"

"I do not stand on formalities with friends, and I consider thee as much." Situated at a place of honor at the head of the table, Arucard paused to acknowledge the other wronged landowners. "Good eventide, and thank ye for coming on such short notice. As the new earl of Sussex, I am charged with dispensing His Majesty's justice and overseeing the garrison in this region, and it is my responsibility to determine the validity of the burgage plots, as well as the perpetrator of the scheme."

"I am Sewal Verley, my lord." An elderly figure with a regal bearing stood. "For almost a hundred years, my family farmed the pilfered acres, but with a single stroke of his quill, Juraj de Mravec executed the King's authority and stole our heritage. We art now but tenants on what we once owned."

"And I am in the same position," another man added. "Yet we were not compensated."

"We were robbed of our legacy," an unknown individual cried.

A murmur of concurrence built, slow at first, but erupted as an incoming tide. Each injured party nodded agreement, with revelatory parchment to support their assertions, which Arucard collected as evidence. As he perused the documents, he noted the Crown's seal and frowned. Naught made sense, given His Majesty had discussed his intentions and made no mention of the burgage plots. His instincts told him all was not as it appeared.

"This is puzzling." Stacking the papers, Arucard glanced at Aeduuard. "Wherefore didst the previous earl of Sussex not negotiate the deeds?"

"Mayhap because his head was rotting on a pike outside White Tower." De Cadby rubbed his chin. "Dost thou doubt our grievances?"

"Perchance thou art involved in the thefts." Verley narrowed his stare. "Wilt thou profit at our expense? Wilt thou continue our oppression?"

"Do not question my honor, sirrah." Arucard pounded his fist on the table. "The last man who doubted my sincerity met his demise at the rude end of my halberd. However, as our acquaintance is new, I shall indulge thee. But do not let it happen again."

The great hall fell silent as a tomb, and the tension mounted.

"A pleasant eventide, good gentles." Gowned in rich burgundy velvet, with her raven hair plaited in her usual style, Isolde inclined her head and curtseyed. "Am I interrupting anything of importance?"

In unison, the men stood and bowed.

"Allow me to present my wife, Lady Isolde, countess of Sussex." What perfect timing his bride possessed, as she had just diffused a rapidly deteriorating assemblage, and he considered her a heretofore-underutilized weapon in his arsenal. "Wilt thou join us?"

"Thank ye, for the invitation." With grace and elegance of which he was immensely proud, she waved to Pellier, who carried a chair, which he perched beside Arucard. "And permit me to offer refreshments, as supper will be served soon."

Isolde clapped her hands twice, and maids conveyed armfuls of mugs to the table. From a tray, his wife retrieved a pitcher and made the rounds, casting him shy glances and coy smiles, as if they shared a delicious secret. And then it dawned on him that they did, indeed, harbor a bit of confidential but mutual enlightenment, the extent of which had fueled his afternoon games. When he winked, he distracted her, and she spilt the ale.

"Oh, I am so sorry." Snatching a cloth from a passing servant, Isolde compressed her lips and then dried the unfortunate fellow's sleeve. "Margery, thou mayest deliver the meal."

"Yea, my lady." The steward rushed to perform Isolde's bidding.

Again and again, he shared furtive reflections with his lady, in unspoken summons, while she tended their guests, and in his brain he vowed to make his move in an altogether different direction, neglecting his chief duties, at the moment, if she issued another secretive invitation. When she steadfastly avoided his gaze, disappointment sparked in his chest, and he sank in his seat. Then he seized on an idea.

If his wife met his stare before he counted to ten, he would take her, thither and then.

As he advanced his cause, slow and steady, as he would not rush her, it occurred to him that the afternoon fostered new and enticing feelings he still could not quite comprehend, but one thing was certain—Arucard needed Isolde, and he needed no one.

Often the gentle curve of her swanlike neck held him spellbound, as he loved to suckle the shallow hallow just below her ear. And his wife was ticklish, which he discovered when he nibbled the succulent flesh of her round bottom and nipped at the indention above her hip.

Just then, she returned the ewer to the tray and looked him in the eye, and he lurched upright. Yea, she was his just as he was hers.

"If I may, how doth the Lady Isolde favor Chichester?" Verley inquired.

"It is quite beauteous. The seashore is rugged but breathtaking, and I find the hills rather stimulating." Her subtle reference did not escape him. After taking her seat, Isolde leaned to the side, offering him a delectable view of her bosom, and whispered, "My lord, I understand thy behavior, of late, as I crave thee, and I know not how to manage what threatens to consume me. Prithee, take pity, as I need thy assistance. Canst thou help me? Pray, what should I do?"

The raw hunger in her gaze, undeniable in its clarity, bespoke an unembellished truth and impressed upon him the urgency of their situation, as fiery desire simmered in his veins, capturing him to the detriment of all else. He could only imagine what she experienced, as an innocent. It was as though she had just punched him in the gut, because the force of her much prized confession rendered him almost giddy. And then his body responded, in kind.

"Meet me in the undercroft." Nay, he should not do what he planned to do, but he could not restrain himself when it came to Isolde, and he had to have her, else he feared he might degenerate into insanity, and she could run amok. "Go, now."

"Aye, my lord." To the gathering, Isolde said, "Forgive me, but I must check on the bread, as I ordered it fresh from the oven. By thy leave."

Deploying his earlier tactic, Arucard counted to ten and then vacated his chair. "My lady prefers wine with her sup."

Pellier stepped to the fore. "I can fetch it—"

"I will get it, myself." Driven by decadent determination, the potency of which he could not withstand, Arucard stormed into the kitchens, navigated the narrow passage, and all but ran into the storage cellar. "Isolde? Whither art thou?"

"Hither, my lord." From behind, she jumped him.

And the sumptuous battle commenced.

As Arucard turned and grabbed her, Isolde leaped, wrapped her arms about his neck, and set her mouth to his. The delicate taste of her, a thousand times more intoxicating than the finest liquor, rendered him drunk with passion, and his flesh burned for her. With his hands on her hips, he lifted her to sit atop a barrel. When he flicked up the skirt of her gown, she swept aside his tunic, fumbled with the ties of his breeches and braies, and freed his man's yard.

In implied surrender, she spread wide her supple thighs in welcome, and he could have cried in gratitude. Standing between her legs, he joined their bodies, and she sighed as he rested his forehead to hers and exhaled in relief. With his thumb, he massaged her pearl in rhythm with his thrusts, which became ever more frenetic. Riding her hard and fast, he savored the subtle gasps, each with its own unique pitch to laud his efforts, which she vented as he took her—until a servant interrupted their licentious liaison.

"Hello?" The maid cleared her throat. "Thither is someone in the undercroft?"

Furrowing her brow, Isolde tensed, and he stilled, yet an invisible but nonetheless powerful web spun a fragile swathe about them. Completion beckoned as a demanding lover, and Arucard ached to answer the call. Footfalls signaled the interloper's departure, so Arucard resumed the voluptuous assault. And when she stretched in telltale rigidity, he covered her lips with his palm and smothered her cry of release. Seconds later, he followed her into the bliss, gritting his teeth and clenching his jaw to stifle his groans of pleasure, as he bent over her and collapsed.

"My lord, I needed that." Giggling, Isolde kissed his ear. "Art thou disappointed with me?"

"Thou must be joking." Weak from their coupling, he mustered a half-hearted chuckle. "Admit it, thou art a witch in an angel's garb, and thou hast cast an incantation over me, as I am thine, body and soul. And while I should be entertaining our guests, all I want is to bury myself in thy sheath, honey flower."

"And I would hold thee in my arms until I pass from this life, my champion." How he loved it when she hugged him with her thighs and flexed her muscles, tempting him with a far more intimate embrace. "But what an ending. Shall we return to the great hall?"

"Aye." Against his wishes, he withdrew and secured his attire. Then he lifted her from the impromptu perch. As his thoughts centered on the land dilemma, something occurred to him. "Isolde, if thou dost ask thy father's opinion on the burgage plots, dost thou believe he will answer honestly?"

"Given my father thinks me ignorant, I suppose he will." Marching toward the kitchen, she paused when he tapped her shoulder. "Yea, my lord?"

"Pray, a moment." In good humor, he tugged the back of her skirt from her garter. "I would permit no one to look upon that which is mine."

"And shall I dine with thee and thy men?" The gentle sway of her hips held him mesmerized. "Or would thou charge me with another task?"

"I would have thee at my side, always." Plotting and strategizing in silence, he mulled the possibilities, in regard to the current problem. At the last minute, he snapped his fingers and swiped a pitcher of wine from the kitchen and then offered his escort. "And tonight, when we retire, I would have thee compose a letter to thy father."

#

"How is thy nose?" With a sheepish grin, Arucard shuffled his feet, and the poor man seemed so contrite, so she could not, in good conscience, tease him. "And I am sorry. If it makes thee feel any better, I will never forgive myself."

"It is much improved." Biting her lip, Isolde managed not to laugh, but she gave vent to a snort, and he groaned. "And it was an accident, so thither is no need to apologize."

"But I almost drowned thee." Prior to the day's events, his mighty scowl would have frightened her, but not so anymore. Instead, she could not help but notice his rippled muscles, broad shoulders, and thick hair. "We should not have attempted to...thou dost know what I reference. To my immense regret, I embarrassed myself."

After a spirited supper, wherein the guests consumed mass quantities of ale, and an odd contest ensued, regarding the length of their swords, which Isolde still didn't quite understand, she and Arucard had retired to their private quarters with like-minded intent.

As promised, she endeavored to pleasure her husband under his somewhat awkward tutelage, given neither had any personal experience with the maneuver she haphazardly employed. While the outcome went as planned, the path to release had been at her expense, because the instant she locked her lips about his length, he erupted with such force it had taken her by surprise, to the extent that she withdrew without warning, and he sprayed her face with his seed.

"Nonsense." How difficult he made it to focus on the task at hand, as he finally sat opposite her in the solar and pouted, and all she wanted to do was soothe his injured pride. "I am thy wife, and I should know thy body as intimately as thou dost know mine. I believe we achieved that, tonight."

"To my everlasting shame." With an adorable grimace,

he propped his elbow atop the table and rested his chin in his palm. "We will never do it again."

"Oh, yea, we will, my lord." Then she glanced at the parchment in her grasp. "Now what dost thou wish me to say in the letter?"

"Tell him thou dost not know the origin of my relationship with His Majesty." As he narrowed his stare, he scratched his cheek. "But thou dost suspect nefarious deeds in my history, which would render me vulnerable to attack. Pledge to uncover my secrets in thy father's service."

"Nay." She shook her head, as she found the mere suggestion repugnant. "I will not conspire with my father against thee. And I shudder to think what he might do, should he discover thy Templar associations, which I shall carry to my grave."

"But I am not asking thee to betray my confidence, as thou art incapable of treachery." On the precipice of conflict, the consequences of which could result in the separation of their heads from their necks, he remained calm, which kept her grounded. "However, if we art to appease thy father and divert his attention from thee, we must satisfy his curiosity."

"Is that thy only aim?" In accordance with her husband's directives, she scribbled a few sentences, even as his worry thrilled her. "As I would protect thee, too."

"Isolde, I can take care of myself. And I would have thee explain thy belief that my fortune is vast, but thou hast yet to locate it, although thou art searching, which should shield thee from thy father's wrath." Then he reached for and clutched her wrist. "Thy safety is my primary concern, as thy life is precious to me."

"Am I?" So many sensations rushed through her, as he leveled his gaze, and the truth of his statement shone clear in his blue eyes. In the brief term of their union, they had grown together beyond her wildest imaginings, and never would she doubt him. "As thou could always marry again, should I meet my fate. Most men take second wives in such cases."

"Mayhap that is true." When he stood, rounded the table, and came to a halt behind her, she gulped. Cupping her breasts through her robe, he trailed sweet but effective kisses along her neck. "But I am not most men, and, now and forever, thou art my only mate. So finish thy work, as I desire thee again, honey flower."

"Dost thou?" Tempted by his desire, and the mention of her pet name, which he had devised, she dropped back her head and cast him a side-glance. "I am hungry, too. But thou art distracting me, and I would fulfill thy request before I sup on thy flesh, as I would make a second attempt at thy favored exercise."

"Nay." And now he blushed, which charmed her to her toes. "We will abstain from that particular activity."

"We shall see about that." After composing a few more statements intended to mollify her father, she signed her name to the bottom of the correspondence. "Thither it is done." Quick as a flash, she spun about on the bench and grabbed his hips. Riding a crest of steely determination, and emboldened by his expression of affection, however moderate, she slipped her hand between the folds of his robe and found him hot and hard. "Now, whither were we?"

"Isolde—"

"Cease thy talking, my champion." Holding his gaze, she untied his belt, swept aside the cloth, and pressed a kiss on his plumb-shaped tip, and he hissed. Oh, yea, he was hers every bit as much as she was his. "Unless thou would impart thy words of passion, which I rather enjoy."

"Words of passion?" He tensed at her touch, and she found her rhythm as she worked him. "I know not of which thou dost speak."

"Thou dost know what I mean." Slowly, she drew him into her mouth and retreated, and again he groaned. "Ah, that will suffice."

As it turned out, naught else was said that night.

CHAPTER NINE

A fortnight later, well past the noon hour, Arucard strutted into the bailey. To his infinite satisfaction, Isolde remained tucked, safe and sound, in their bed, sleeping the sleep of the sated, which was just as he preferred her. In his mind, he pictured his wife, her raven hair splayed across her pillow, revisited sweet recollections of what he had done to tangle her thick locks, and he smiled.

Given he clutched a letter from her father, which had just arrived via a messenger wearing the earl of Rochester's colors, he would rather discuss the correspondence with his brothers, put a plan in place, and devise a written response before burdening his lady. Waving at Demetrius, he nodded at Aristide, and that was all that was necessary to clue the Brethren.

In the great hall, he selected a smaller table near the back wall and sat on a bench. Soon, his fellow knights joined him. Without a word, he passed the earl's missive to Demetrius.

"Surprised to see thee up and about so early, brother."

Geoffrey snickered.

"I cannot recall the last time thou hast attended weapons practice at sunrise." The telltale frown of disapproval signaled Aristide's disappointment. "Art thou no longer a warrior in service to the Crown?"

"Or hast thou misplaced thy dedication to duty?" Morgan inquired.

"Thou art mistaken, my friends." It would have been easy to take insult to their comments, but Arucard knew his aim was true. "As it stands, I labor every eventide at the Crown's direction, long after thou hast retired."

"Thou art not serious." Aristide scoffed. "Would thou make light of our reasonable concerns, as thou art the lord of Chichester Castle?"

"Not at all." Just then, Demetrius glanced at Arucard. "I am charged with begetting an heir, and I endeavor to fulfill my Sire's command, but it is strenuous work. Hence I have launched numerous initiatives to the task, yielding precious hours of sleep to the cause."

"Methinks thou dost complain in jest." Demetrius attempted to return the parchment, but Arucard indicated otherwise, so Demetrius handed it to Aristide. "I take it thither art more notes?"

"Aye." Arucard nodded and revealed the two previous dispatches. "The first was given to my wife on the day we departed London."

"The earl threatens his own daughter?" With an expression of unmistakable disgust, Aristide grimaced. "Dost thou believe he would hurt her? Although Lady Isolde is a fine woman, mayhap she is involved in the scheme, and the warning is intended to divert thee from the obvious."

"Nay, it is not possible." The mere suggestion incited anger, but Arucard took no offense, as Aristide knew not the depth of her suffering. "Her heart is pure."

"How dost thou know for certain?" Geoffrey scanned the original letter. "Thou hast known her but a short length of time."

"She fears her father," Arucard replied, as he pondered her wounds, which had at long last healed. Yet the invisible injuries plagued her still, and she often woke him with screams of terror, quieting only when he held her. "And with good reason."

"I saw her that night in thy tent, after the battle with de Cadby and his men. I apologize, brother, but she was unclothed, as she sat in thy lap, and I could not help but notice the scars." Rubbing his neck, Demetrius sighed. "Did the earl do that to her back?"

"Aye." How was it the simple acknowledgment of Isolde's hardship, the whole of which occurred prior to their acquaintance and nuptials, managed to hurt him? "He abused her for much of her life, and she is terrified of him. And despite what the earl hath done to her, she frets for my safety. Believe me, she owes him no allegiance."

Morgan arched a brow, and Demetrius said, "The man beat her to the extent she is forever marked, and it sickens my stomach to think any father could visit such brutality upon his child."

"Art thou talking a few lashes with a belt?" Geoffrey appeared skeptical. "Perchance the earl disciplined Lady Isolde and naught more."

"What I witnessed is not the result of discipline, as her flesh is disfigured from shoulder to shoulder and down to her waist." Demetrius wiped his forehead. "Conjure thy worst imagining and then double it. Never have I seen anything so hideous, and I find it a testament to her character and admirable she survived, given we discuss a gentlewoman, which makes it far worse in my humble estimation."

"Christ's bones." Morgan blinked. "What dost thou intend?"

"We must defend her, at all costs." Considering the options, Arucard formulated a strategy. "First, I would send word of the burgage plots and the earl's suspected involvement and conspiracy with Juraj de Mravec, which seems construed to implicate the Crown in the land thefts and undermine the King's authority in the region."

"And what of the earl's queries regarding thy background and fortune?" After a quick check of the vicinity, Aristide gathered the letters and stacked them in a pile at the center of the table. "We cannot permit anyone to know of our history, as we could still end up burning at the stake."

"Isolde is aware of my affiliations, and she would never betray my confidence." Arucard braced for their reaction, as his confession revealed their connections, too. "But she is my wife, and I could not keep it from her, after she shared her secrets."

"Arucard is right." The voice of reason, Demetrius stretched his arms. "Lady Isolde is our family, and we will sacrifice our lives to save hers, if necessary." Then he extended his hand, palm down. "For King and Country we stand."

Together, the men followed suit, one atop the other, forming their customary bond forged of flesh, blood, and bone. In unison, they stated, "For love and comradeship we live."

"Oh, my." Clutching a pile of folded cloth to her bosom, Isolde peered at Arucard. "My lord, have I interrupted something of significance?"

"Nay, my lady." With a smile, Arucard stood, as did the Brethren, and he walked to her side and slipped an arm about her waist. "We were just discussing thy brewets, as we can smell them from the kitchen."

"As Sir Demetrius and Sir Geoffrey favor them, I asked the cook to prepare a special batch. And for Sir Morgan, thither is bream and eel pasties." How she beamed beneath his praise, and the now familiar but unsettling sensation, which he had come to anticipate every time she entered the room, built in his chest. Then she dipped her chin. "And good morrow, to all."

Morgan furrowed his brow. "But it is past the—
oomph." The youngest Nautionnier knight winced, when
Demetrius elbowed Morgan in the ribs.

"Good morrow, my lady." Aristide bowed. "And
thank ye, for the excellent mend to my breeches. Thy
sewing skills art such that I cannot locate the original tear."

"That is because it was to thy arse." Geoffrey rolled
his eyes. "Must thou wear thy garb so tight?"

"Mayhap he hath not much to stow." Demetrius
smirked. "Else he might injure something of value."

"Art thou not the wit?" With a scowl, Aristide
smacked a fist to a palm. "Perchance I shall teach thee
some manners on the practice field."

"Prithee, do not argue." As they quieted, Isolde
approached Morgan. "I completed thy tunics, to thy
request." And then she addressed Geoffrey. "And thou
hast four new sets of hose and braies." To Demetrius, she
said, "Per thy charge, I fashioned a sack, of sorts, to hold
thy various small weapons and appurtenances, and thither
is five, one for each knight. Thou canst attach it to thy
saddle, using the ties on the back. I hope thee dost find it
serviceable."

"My lady, thou art too kind." When Demetrius met
Arucard's stare, he nodded and then dropped to a knee.
Together, the other Brethren knelt and pressed a clenched
fist over their heart. "On my honor, if called upon, I shall
give my life for thine."

With immense pride, Arucard studied his friends, as
they pledged fealty to his wife, which she had won in
honest trade.

"Sir Demetrius, they art but a few garments." She
opened her mouth and then closed it. "Never would I
exact so high a price in return."

"Because thou art a fine woman, thou would never take
advantage, but I would protect thee, nonetheless." After
regaining his feet, Demetrius bowed. "Come, brothers. I
am interested in the manners Aristide doth claim to

possess and would commence the instruction."

"Oh, thou art itching for a bruising, brother." Aristide chucked Demetrius in the shoulder. "And I am the man to deliver it."

The jokes continued until they exited the great hall. Alone with his bride, Arucard pondered how to reveal the most recent letter and its contents. Were it possible, he would spare her the details, as she had suffered enough.

"Thou hast heard from father." It was then he noticed she had retrieved the missive from the table. In minutes, she scanned the parchment and then glanced at him, her distress evident in her tear-filled gaze. "I will not do it. I will not aid my father's schemes, even in play. And I will never leave thee." Then she flung herself at him, hugging him tight at the waist. As the first drop of moisture coursed her cheek, she beckoned, and he kissed her. "Arucard, thou art...I am so...it is such that I cannot describe...oh, dost thou feel it, too?"

"Aye, I feel it." Without doubt, he knew to what she referred, and he could manage it no better. "Honey flower, thy safety is my chief concern."

"And thy neck is mine." Resting her head to his chest, she sobbed, and he cradled her in his grasp. "Wherefore will my father not let us live in peace? Wherefore must he ruin everything? Have I not paid his penance a thousand times over? Hath he not exacted his revenge upon me? Am I not absolved? Am I not entitled to a measure of happiness? Am I not permitted to dream?"

Her torment, raw in its intensity, cut to his core, and he could not bear it. In an instant, he silenced her the best way he knew how, with his lips. Summoning the patience of a saint, he tasted her slowly, savoring her soft flesh, until she joined the dance and relaxed in his embrace. "Come to our chambers, whither I shall feed thy desire, and we might take comfort in shared pleasure."

"But I should see to the midday meal." As he nibbled her ear, she gasped. "And what of thy weapons practice?"

"Sweet Isolde, it is well past the noon hour. Thither is only one sword I would wield with thee, to our mutual gratification." And then it struck him—the hunger he could neither control nor deny, as he still had not mastered it. It dawned on him in that precise moment he cared for her beyond the bonds of friendship, and the realization unnerved him. Before she could protest, he bent and scooped her into his arms. "Now let us seek solace in our bodies."

#

It was the first dawn of a new day, absent the sun, Isolde could recall enjoying in more than a month, as grey clouds blanketed the sky, and light snow dusted the courtyard below. Fluffing the pillows, she tucked the covers beneath the cushions and then strolled into the solar, just as Arucard, carrying a tray, returned to their chambers.

"Good morrow, honey flower." Every time he looked upon her, his gaze softened, and a shiver of delight traipsed her spine. "Wherefore art thou out of bed, as I rode thee hard, and thou dost require time to recover."

"But I am accustomed to thy naughty games, my champion." Then she noticed the subtle strain in his expression. "What is wrong? What troubles thee?"

"Am I that obvious?" As he set the tray on the table, he frowned. "I brought thee some tea, bread, and a sop, as thou hast worked up an appetite."

"Thou art thoughtful." When he sat, she strolled to a position beside him and arched her brow. Without a word, he scooted back, slapped his thigh, and steadied her as she eased to his lap. Cupping his cheek, she kissed him. For a long while, they indulged in the exquisite communion of flesh, and it never ceased to amaze her how gentle he handled her, when he could crush her like a twig. "Given I am thy mate, thou could never hide anything from me."

"Thou dost distract me, my lady." As was his way, he

caressed her bottom. "Shall I feed thee?"

"I would like that, very much." Again she could not escape the sense that something was amiss. "Wilt thou not share thy concerns with thy wife?"

"It is an unpleasant matter, and I cherish thy smile, which I would not diminish with my news." After tearing off a piece of bread, he dipped it into the sop and then brought it to her mouth, which she accepted. "But the time has come to take action against thy father and de Mravec."

"What hast thou planned?" she asked between bites. "Wherefore art thou hesitant to share thy burden?"

"Because I must detail thy father's involvement, and the consequences could be dire for him and thy brother." Arucard pressed his lips to her forehead and then tipped her chin to meet her gaze. "In order to establish thy innocence, I must apprise His Majesty of thy ill treatment, thy wounds, and thy correspondence from thy father, as he threatens thee in each letter. With the statements taken from the injured landowners, and thy missives, I would send Demetrius to London, with all due haste. Without thy proof of the crimes committed against the citizenry, it is my word against thy father's. Dost thou understand the urgency?"

"Of course." Then she realized the source of his discomfit, inched from his hold, and strolled into the inner chamber. Lifting the bottom right corner of the mattress, she retrieved the bundled parchments. When she returned to the solar, she recovered her place in his lap and surrendered the evidence he required. "My lord, what is mine is thine."

"Dost thou trust me with thy fate?" He swallowed hard.

"Aye." Resolved to stand with her husband against her father's treachery, she discovered renewed strength such as she had never known, which quashed any lingering fears. "As always, I am at thy command, my champion."

"Mayhap we can compose a joint entreaty, if thou wilt sign it." When she framed his face, he heaved a sigh. "Isolde, if thither were any means available to keep thee from the conflict, know that I would employ it. But thy father has left me little choice, given his letters, and I must confront thy involvement and explain thy unwilling and minimal participation in the scheme."

"Then I shall affix my name to thy cause." Riding a wave of conviction, she rebuked her father's claim on her loyalties. "As thou hast promised to defend me, I would defend thee."

"Hast thou so much faith in me?" He appeared so earnest she had not the heart to tease him. "Dost thou believe in me?"

"Yea, my lord." Only a month ago, Isolde had no reason to believe in anyone or anything, and now she clung to hope for a future she never dared imagine, and Arucard had given her that—hope. And she gloried in it. "I doubt thee not."

CHAPTER TEN

"Hast thou everything thou dost require for the journey?" Arucard tied another blanket to the back of Demetrius's saddle. "And Isolde packed a substantial amount of thy favorite fare."

"Brother, thou art more nervous than a virgin on her wedding night." As he mounted his destrier, Demetrius chuckled. "Calm thyself."

"And what would thee know of such things?" The momentary levity did much to lighten the mood, but the focus quickly returned to his brother's departure, as he sent his friend into the lion's den and could only pray he survived unscathed. "Hast thou stowed the letters in a protected place, as thou must not lose them?"

"Cease thy worry, old woman." A cold November wind caught the folds of his wool cloak, and Demetrius adjusted the ermine collar. "I have my marshalsea and my sword, and we will ride hard until we reach His Majesty, wherein I shall plead thy cause with thy right and true evidence." Then he reached with his hand, which Arucard accepted in friendship. "Take care, good sirrah. Until we meet again."

"And I would have thee do the same." The rough weather boded ill tidings, as Arucard stepped back and saluted, but he had no choice in the matter. "I know not what thee can expect to find in the palace of Westminster, but I would not lose thee, if it can be helped."

"In that we can agree." As he drew rein, Demetrius dipped his chin and then heeled the flanks of his horse. In mere minutes, he traversed the first and then the second bridge, with his man in tow.

"Close the gates." After securing the entries to the castle, he sought Pellier. "I want three watches to rotate on the wall and the gatehouses must be staffed, at all times. And assign the archers to overlapping duties. Make sure the barbican is ready to defend against an assault, and devise a secret word or phrase of thy choosing, which any party must know to gain admittance. And Lady Isolde must have a full escort if she ventures forth for any reason, unless I am with her." Then he snapped his fingers. "Wait, my wife is not to travel beyond these confines without me."

"Aye, sir." Pellier nodded and rushed to the garrison.

"What is thy worry, brother?" With a countenance of confusion, Aristide folded his arms and snorted. "What dost thou fear, as thou dost fear naught?"

"I know not, and that is what troubles me." Scanning the immediate vicinity, he assessed the castle from a new perspective. As a Templar, his tasks were marked by a clearly defined goal in conflict with an equally obvious adversary, on familiar territory. In England, he knew not of hidden dangers. A battle-hardened warrior, he dreaded not Rochester or his soldiers. Indeed, the earl could not hurt Arucard, unless the bastard struck Isolde. The mere thought of his wife in peril was enough to summon the bitterness of anger he had always managed with ease. "And I must ensure Isolde's safety. That is enough to inspire concern."

Not to mention he had yet to examine the strange sensations associated with his wife.

Something about her mere presence called to him, woke the hunger impossible to satisfy, and drove him to the brink of insanity for want of her. And just when he thought he had sated his craving, it prospered anew, and he sought her sweet body at all hours of the day and night. To her credit, she never denied him, and that knowledge, alone, lured him into her arms. Her steadfast acceptance was a humbling prospect, which fostered a powerful attachment he could not quite understand.

"Thou dost care for her." With an expression of bewilderment, Aristide cleared his throat. "And thy feelings extend beyond friendship."

"I know not what I harbor for my lady." Yet he spent countless minutes in contemplation of their union, their commitment, and their marriage bed and had formulated no clear conclusion, as the matter was out of his depth. "But I will not deny a fondness I can neither comprehend nor explain."

"So thou art content in thy marriage?" Geoffrey appeared to Arucard's left. "As we art curious."

"And Demetrius threatened to remove our tongues if we asked ye." Shameless as usual, Morgan winked. "Does thy wife gratify thee between the sheets?"

"Do not disparage Lady Isolde, else I shall fulfill Demetrius's pledge." Then he spied his bride, strolling from the servant's quarters, with Margery in tow, and the peculiar but pleasant warmth sparked in his belly and spread to his limbs, enveloping him in the glow of her beguiling visage. "But she intrigues me like no other."

"So thou would recommend the marital state?" inquired Aristide. "Because we suspect the King will require us to wed, too."

"I cannot speak for His Majesty or to his plans, as I am not privy to the inner workings of the Realm." Although the Crown had indicated the Brethren would be similarly matched, Arucard would cross that bridge, as must needs. For the time being, he would not presume to know the Sire's mind, as situations changed. "But if thou art so fortunate to gain such a mate as my Isolde, then thou art truly blessed, for she is an estimable lady."

"And what of the female form?" Now Geoffrey blushed, and Arucard could not stifle a snort of laughter, as he knew well what his friend referenced. "As never have we looked on a naked woman, excepting in paintings, and I am not convinced that will suffice, when it comes to the performance of husbandly obligations."

Oh, there was much Arucard could say, in that respect.

"Take pity on us, brother." Morgan shuffled his feet. "After all, how didst thee fare on thy wedding night?"

In an instant, he remembered Isolde's brief but stunning attack with the halberd, and he chuckled. "Verily, it was not what I expected." And that was an understatement. "But I vow to counsel thee, if thou art called upon to make the same sacrifice."

"Is that what I am—thy sacrifice?" The Brethren parted to reveal Isolde, arching a brow, standing with her arms folded, and tapping her slippered foot. "Oh, but I am crushed."

And then his fellow Nautionnier knights scattered like leaves in the wind and abandoned him to his bride.

"Er, it was but a harmless manner of speaking, my lady." Then he noticed her playful grin and relaxed. "Perchance it is an accurate description, as I surrender to thee every night."

"Thou art so romantic, my champion." When she rocked on her heels and clucked her tongue, he pulled her close for a hug. "Hither I thought I surrendered to thee."

"Mayhap we could take turns." As she embraced him about his waist and burrowed beneath his cloak, he pulled the wool folds over her and kissed her forehead. "Thou dost distract me, honey flower."

"I hope to do more than that, as the guest

accommodations art ready for inspection, and I wondered if thou might assist me? We should ensure the bed frame is sturdy, and I know of a tried and true method to test it." Splaying her fingers across his tunic, she nudged him with her hips. For the past sennight, they had initiated a game, of sorts, wherein they made love in various rooms and chambers in the castle. "Unless thou hast a prior occupation of greater importance."

Ah, he would inspect something, all right.

"My lady, I am at thy service." Then he bent and flung her over his shoulder, and she shrieked. "And I intend to submit the mattress and supporting ropes to a rigorous examination."

#

A light rain fell on a dreary morrow, as the wind whistled and howled beyond the walls of the bedchamber, and Isolde cuddled closer to Arucard, after a prolonged round of lovemaking. Ever since Demetrius's departure, some four days ago, her knight's demands had grown more desperate than usual, and she had not the strength to dismiss him, so she indulged her husband whenever he beckoned. Given his suspicions, in regard to her father, their private time became far more precious, and she considered their marital activities a chance to deepen their intimacy.

As he traced circles on a particular part of her anatomy, she giggled. "Thou art hungry, my lord."

"Thy bottom is a wonder to behold." To her surprise, he flipped her onto her belly and drew back the covers. Had he ever given her reason, she would have been ashamed of her scarred flesh, but never had he mentioned it. Then he nipped her skin, and she squealed. "It is soft, yet firm, and deliciously round." When he tickled her sides, she bucked. "Yield."

"Nay." An ensuing match proved entertaining, as they tangled amid the sheets, and just as the situation grew serious, and all levity ceased, someone knocked at the door.

"Great bleeding balls of frustration." Stomping from their bed, Arucard glanced about the floor, located his robe, and shrugged into it. "Thither who goes?"

"Pellier, sir." The muffled call came from the hall.

Raking his fingers through his hair, her husband glanced at her and winked. "Whither thou art, thou shalt remain, as I will return."

Encouraged by the promise in his heated expression, she stretched long. "Do not make me wait too long, my lord."

"Admit it, thou art a sorceress." For a scarce second, he gazed at her. Then he bent, planted his palms at either side of her head, and kissed her. "And I am thy willing devotee."

Alone in their inner sanctum, she drew the sheets to her chin, wiggled her toes, and sighed. From her earliest childhood memories, Isolde had nurtured dreams of a knight in shining armor, riding to her rescue, but none had ever taken hold as she had spent so many years in isolation and loneliness, and so Arucard manifested her salvation. Studying the intricate woodwork on the ceiling, she hugged herself and dared aspire to new possibilities, as she yearned to bear his child.

After a few minutes, she sat upright. "Arucard, whither art thou?"

When he did not respond, she flung aside the blankets, jumped from the mattress, foraged for her nightgown, which she rarely used because her husband preferred her naked, pulled the garment over her head, cracked open the door, and peered into the solar. To her surprise, she discovered him situated before the window that featured a view of the courtyard. As he did not acknowledge her, she moved to a position behind him and wound her arms about his waist. With her cheek pressed to his back, she squeezed him.

"Something has gone very wrong." In an instant, he

covered her hands with his. "His Majesty demands I report for questioning, in person."

"But that is a good thing, as thou canst plead thy case directly to the Crown." When he turned and faced her, she noted the strain at the corners of his blue eyes. "Thou dost make too much of the Sovereign's request. What does Sir Demetrius say on the matter?"

"I know not, as he remains a guest of the King." Now she understood her husband's concern, and fear blossomed in the pit of her belly. "And that is what troubles me, as thither is no reason to hold Demetrius, unless—"

"—Thou dost stand accused." Trepidation grew in epic proportions, and she shivered as she pondered the possibilities. "Whither dost thou depart for London?"

"That is another interesting bit of information." Heaving a sigh, he rubbed the back of his neck. "His Majesty and his forces art camped just south of Guildford, which does not bode well, and I cannot escape the belief, however misplaced, that the Brethren and I ride into a trap."

"How soon must thou report?" In haste, she formed an imaginary list of items to complete before they commenced their journey.

"According to the King's messenger, with all due expediency." After claiming a quick kiss, Arucard strode into their bedchamber and doffed his robe. "Thus I travel, at once."

Disappointed they would not finish what they started, Isolde followed in his wake. In quiet, they washed and garbed themselves for the day's events, and while naught was spoken, much was conveyed in the occasional glance and brief touch. And then they came together for another tender kiss, which struck her as a subtle farewell, for some odd reason, and they emerged from their shared sanctuary. Thus her heart weighed heavy when she entered the kitchens, in search of Margery.

"How long dost thou expect to be gone?" The steward sampled a dish and wrinkled her nose. "Needs more salt."

"That I know not." Isolde selected various dried foods to be packed for the journey. "But I charge thee with the upkeep of Chichester Castle, in my absence."

"Aye, my lady." Snapping her fingers, Margery summoned the scullery maid. "Anne, prepare Lady Isolde's trunk, and air the navy wool cotehardie and matching cloak."

"Aye." The young woman, boasting her usual dirty cheeks and disheveled appearance, curtseyed.

"Make sure thither is plenty of food, as the knights have large appetites, and we have an additional mouth to feed." Despite Arucard's anxiety, Isolde vowed it was all for naught, as the King would not act without cause; at least, that is what she kept telling herself. Given her husband was innocent, what had she to fear? "And stow the brewets, as they travel well, and I anticipate Sir Demetrius will be glad of them."

"Doth my lady require anything else?" As she had on so many previous occasions, Margery smoothed a lock of hair from Isolde's forehead. "Mayhap thou should rest until it is time to depart."

"Nay, as thither is too much to be done, but I shall prepare Sir Arucard's belongings." And so Isolde returned to her chambers and organized her husband's personal items with care. When he appeared, with a stranger in tow, she walked into the solar. "We art almost ready, my lord. And Margery bundles suitable sustenance for our party."

"Thank ye, my lady. Allow me to present the King's messenger and sergeant, Briarus." Her husband stepped aside, and a young and handsome soldier bowed. "And I would ask a favor, which would aid our cause, if thou wilt but cooperate."

"It is my great pleasure to meet thee, Lady Isolde." With twinkling amber eyes and flaxen hair, the soldier cast a kind smile. "I have heard many complimentary things about ye."

"Thank ye, Briarus. If ye would but make thy request, I am at thy service." Curious, she set down her swaddled clothing. "What would thou have of me?"

"Forgive me, Isolde." Something in her husband's tone and countenance gave her pause, as he approached and rested his palms to her shoulders. "I have told Briarus of thy wounds suffered at the hands of thy father, but it would strengthen our argument if—"

"Wilt thou untie my laces?" Despite her embarrassment, she understood what he asked of her, so she gave Arucard her back, as she knew well his intentions, and she would not balk. In silence, he loosened her garment, and then she tugged on the ribbon of her chemise and shrugged free.

"Wait." Arucard turned her to face him, drawing her arms about his waist, and she pressed her cheek to his chest as he inched her gown to her hips. "Canst thou see what violence the earl hath wrought upon my wife?"

The cool air teased her flesh, and she shivered. On display for a stranger, she fought tears of humiliation but relaxed, when her knight kissed her temple. "I pray thou art satisfied, sir."

"By Christ's blood, that is not how I would describe what I have just witnessed." Briarus cleared his throat. "I beg thy pardon, Lady Isolde. Prithee, know it was not my purpose to shame thee, as thou art without blame."

"Thou art brave, my lady." Once Arucard righted her gown, he framed her jaw. "I am so proud of thee."

"Praise, indeed." Just like that, he relieved a burden she had long carried as a defect.

"Sir Arucard, everything is in order, per thy charge." Pellier loomed in the hall. "Shall I collect thy trunk?"

"Aye." He nodded. "If thou wilt permit me a moment in private with my wife, I would make my farewells."

"What—*wait*." Panic crushed her in its invisible clutch,

as Briarus and Pellier made a hasty exit. "But I journey with thee. Wherefore would thou bid farewell?"

"Isolde, the battlefield is no place for a woman and most especially my wife." Arucard ushered her to the table, sat on the bench, and then pulled her into his lap, and she dreaded his next words. "Even now, thou mayest carry our babe, and I will not risk thy most precious life."

"Didst thou not promise to defend me? Thou must take me with thee." Now she wept openly, and she suppressed none of her misery at the prospect of his withdrawal without her. "How canst thou protect me if we art apart? Art thou not my champion?"

"But thou hast no need of me, if thou dost remain at Chichester Castle." As she sobbed, he hugged her tight and rocked, to and fro, in a gentle rhythm. "Thou art safe within these walls, my honey flower. And with thee secure hither, I can focus on the task, convince His Majesty of thy father's guilt, and establish thy innocence."

"And thou cannot do so if I am with thee?" she inquired in a small voice. "As I cannot bear to be separated from thee. Hast thou not proclaimed we art stronger together?"

"Somehow, I knew thee would make this difficult." Arucard tipped her chin and brought her gaze to his. "Sweet Isolde, if I am to gain thy independence from thy father and his schemes, I must ride without distractions, and thy very presence captivates me, such that I can concentrate on little but thy alluring body. Pray, wilt thou remain hither, for me, so I might do my duty? Wilt thou cooperate because I ask it of thee? And the sooner I succeed in my endeavor, to our mutual benefit, the sooner I will venture home to thy cherished embrace."

"Thou dost make it quite impossible to deny thee." She sniffed, even as he dried her face. "Yet I will obey, as I pledged to do so before the archbishop, but I am not happy, as I believe naught good can come of our estrangement, however brief, and I beg thee to reconsider." In desperation, she grasped his tunic. "Arucard, I beseech ye, do not leave me, as I dread what might happen in thy absence."

"God's bones, woman, art thou blind?" When he barked, she flinched, and he groaned. "How can I make thee understand my position?" Then he sighed, speared his fingers in the hair at her nape, and held her tight. "At dawn, I force myself from our bed, as I would not relinquish ye, and I count the hours until we retire, and I lie between thy sumptuous thighs. When thou art not at my side, I wonder whither art thou, and I search for thee until I find ye. And even after I claim thy enchanting blossom, my first thought is how I desire thee again. The simple fact is I care for thee—too much, and all I want to do is make love to thee, when thou art near."

"Oh, my lord." Stunned by his admission, however graceless, her heart rejoiced, and she collapsed against him. "I care for thee, too."

"If that is true, then do as I say, and stay hither, whither I am assured of thy wellbeing." Cradling her head, he nuzzled her neck and then suckled her earlobe. "And upon my return, I would have thy promise to welcome me in the courtyard, wearing naught but thy arresting smile, a cloak, and thy slippers, as I would have thee naked and in our bed with the least amount of impediments."

Then he kissed her—hard.

Hand in hand, with nary a word spoken between them, they walked to the courtyard; whither they shared a final hug, and something within her fractured in that instant. "I bid ye an unadventurous and boring journey, my lord." Then she perched on her toes and whispered, "Prithee, come back to me. Remember, thou art my champion."

"And thou art my honey flower," he replied in a low tone. "And I miss thee already."

As a cold wind penetrated her cotehardie, she shuddered, and he released her. Without so much as a backward glance, he mounted his destrier, grasped the reins, and charged the main gatehouse and the barbican. In that second, Isolde realized thither was naught sadder than the ever-growing distance as a loved one rode away.

It dawned on her then that she loved her husband.

Breaking into a run, she called after him, but he navigated the first bridge, and the soldiers drew the traverse. So she rushed the garrison, flew up the stone steps, and hurried along the top of the curtain wall to the northwest tower. From the crenellated rooftop, she stood as a sentry until she could no longer distinguish her husband's traveling party. Shielding her eyes from the pelting raindrops, she sent him well wishes for a safe and prosperous journey.

For some reason Isolde could not fathom, she could not escape the nagging suspicion that all was not as it appeared, but she prayed her fears were unfounded and her knight would survive. With one last survey of the landscape, she closed her eyes and sent him an oath, as a shield against danger, on the chilly fall breeze, and willed him to hear her. "Arucard, I love thee."

#

After two days on the road, and as many sleepless nights, Arucard exited his tent and admired the pale watercolors that streaked the morrow sky. Isolde favored dawn, and often they rose from their bed, naked and wrapped only in a blanket, to stand before the east facing windows of the solar and delight in the sunrise. In that moment, he wondered if she shared the view, and he ached for her.

He missed her soft and inviting body splayed beneath his, her warmth as she cuddled to his side, and her cries of bliss as he pleasured her. He yearned for the reassurance of her steady heartbeat, the rush of her breath to his flesh, and the enchantment of her tender touch.

Despite years of service, battles, and hardship, he realized he had known no true suffering until he left his wife in Chichester. Invested with quiet and unassuming strength, Isolde had become indispensable, a significant part of his existence, and he relied on her sage opinions for guidance. Her absence, marked by palpable emptiness, rendered him at a loss, as a ship adrift without an anchor, and he struggled with uncharacteristic and unappreciated doubt.

Without her, to his frustration, he questioned everything.

"So how long hast thou been in love with thy wife?"

Arucard snapped to attention, and Briarus grinned. His first instinct was to deny the soldier's assertion. Instead, he scanned the dew-covered meadow and pondered the possibility, which neither troubled nor frightened him. "How dost thou know I am thus afflicted, as our acquaintance is new?"

"I suspected as much when thou didst hold thy lady, as thou displayed her wounds, and thou were gentle." Slapping his thigh, Briarus snickered. "But it was thy apology for thy actions that convinced me of thy engaged affection, given no man expresses regret for what must be done unless his heart is fixed."

"All right." Well, that seemed simple enough.

"Hast thou naught more to say on the subject?" Mouth agape, the sergeant blinked. "As most men cower in terror at the prospect."

"What have I to fear?" He scoffed at the mere thought. "My wife is the kindest and most compassionate chatelaine, and she cares for me, which she stated prior to my departure. Indeed, I am fortunate the King chose Isolde for my bride."

"His Majesty did so in hopes of fostering better relations with the earl of Rochester." Shifting his weight, Briarus compressed his lips. "It is doubtful the Sovereign possessed any knowledge of the violence inflicted upon Lady Isolde or their less than propitious kinship, else he may have selected another."

"Still, I am grateful for Isolde, and I would explain the

circumstances surrounding the burgage plots to the Crown's satisfaction." Yawning, Arucard rubbed the back of his neck. "And I would have the earl and de Mravec arrested and tried for their crimes against England."

"Arucard, I must warn thee, as I have come to discern thou art honorable." The soldier squared his shoulders. "Thither art an untold number of schemes poisoning our lands, and His Majesty receives information from various sources, which makes it difficult to trust anyone. Thou would do well to prepare thy position with concern for details and appreciable facts."

"Thank ye, Briarus." How he wished he had brought Isolde with him, as she would have manifested irrefutable evidence of her father's evil deeds. "But His Majesty will see that my cause is right and good."

"Perchance it is, but I have seen many right and good men die by the executioner's ax, at His Majesty's command." Briarus chucked Arucard's arm. "I would hate to see that happen to thee, as I believe thee to be a loyal servant of the Crown."

"What dost thou know? Am I riding into a trap?" In that instant, a chill of unease traipsed his spine, and he mulled so many outcomes, none of which inspired confidence. At once, he pondered Isolde. What would happen to her if he failed? "Wherefore hath His Majesty held Demetrius? Is my friend a prisoner?"

"I know naught of Demetrius, except he remains in the royal encampment." Thunder rumbled from the south, and Briarus and Arucard turned to discover a storm approaching. "But only the King holds all the cards in a dangerous game, Sir Arucard. Thou would do well to guard thyself and thy friends."

CHAPTER ELEVEN

A sennight had passed since Arucard's departure, and Isolde immersed herself in the daily activities associated with running the castle. Unafraid of hard drudgery and a little dirt or, in the case of the clogged drain in the garrison, a lot of foul-smelling muck, she rolled up her sleeves and joined the household staff in their chores.

"Lady Isolde, how many times must I remind thee, thou art no scullery maid?" With hands on hips, Margery shook her head and frowned. "Wherefore art thou scrubbing the buttery floor, when it is Anne's responsibility?"

"Because she hath failed to remove the mold in the back corner, and I would get it clean." Of course, Isolde welcomed the arduous toil, as it kept her mind from wandering. "And I have naught else to do, as Arucard is gone."

And that brought her full circle, from the desolation of their massive bed, which seemed empty without her husband, to the brief respite found in onerous labors, to the recollection that at the end of her grind, she would retire alone. On the thought, she sat on her heels and rested her chin to her chest.

"Oh, my lady, do not cry." Margery knelt and placed an arm about Isolde's shoulders. "I am sure everything is fine, and Sir Arucard hath been too busy to send word of the situation."

The simple statement, intended to offer solace, only inspired more anxiety, and she grasped Margery's sleeve. "Dost thou think he is injured—or worse?"

"My lady, calm thyself." The steward stood and brought Isolde upright. "Sir Arucard performs the King's bidding, and he will write thee when he has time. Until then, thou shalt not work thy fingers to the bone, as his lordship will not be pleased upon his return."

"Whenever that may be, as I know naught of his homecoming." Wiping her hands on her apron, she mulled the condition of the pantry, as she had yet to organize the contents. Then she yawned. "Mayhap I should take a nap, as I am rather tired, but I find it difficult to sleep without Arucard at my side."

"Then I shall make thee a nice pot of tea, to help thee relax." As they entered the kitchen, Isolde noted the spilt flour and scattered herbs on the table, but Margery steered for the door to the great hall. "Leave it, as one of the girls will clean the mess."

"But I may as well do it, while hither I am and able." After locating a cloth, Isolde wiped the numerous food preparation sites, while Margery set a pot of water to boil. "And how fares thy association with Pellier?"

"Thou dost know of that?" The steward blushed, and Isolde laughed. "Ah, he is a foul little man." Then Margery smiled. "Oh, very well. I find him quite entertaining, and I might even be convinced to marry him if he did not irritate me so much."

"What art thou carping about now, woman?" Speak of the devil, and Isolde bit her tongue. "And thou hadst no complaints in thy chamber, when I stoked the flames in thy hearth." When Isolde gasped in shock, he sketched a proper bow. "Sorry for my indiscretion, my lady."

"No apologies necessary, Pellier." To Margery, Isolde said, "And I believe I will take that nap."

"Beg thy pardon, Lady Isolde, but I require thy assistance." The marshalsea scratched his cheek and shuffled his feet. "A matter of some urgency requires thy right and good judgment."

"Have I been remiss in my duties?" She searched her mind but could seize upon naught she had overlooked. "Regardless, I am at thy service, Pellier."

"It is not serious, my lady." He ushered her into the great hall, whither a young maid and a soldier from the garrison waited. "If thou wilt take thy place on the dais, thy approval or disapproval is needed, but first thy servants must plead their cause."

"I am curious." Sitting in her chair, and ignoring the empty space to her right, she reclined. "How can I help thee?"

"My name is Grimbaud Van Daalen, and I am one of thy lancers, my lady." The guard bowed. "I would humbly ask thy permission to court Miss Isotta."

Well that was an unforeseen development she never would have predicted, and she knew not how to respond. Then again, the chatelaine had final say in such affairs involving the staff, absent his lordship, and she could not surrender the decision to another. So Isolde pondered the one query that would determine her ruling.

Leveling her gaze on the dignified soldier, she cleared her throat. "Art thou in love, Grimbaud?"

For a few seconds, he appeared to examine her question. Then he glanced at Isotta and smiled. "Aye, Lady Isolde."

How Isolde wished she had declared her engaged affection to Arucard, prior to his departure. While she admitted she cared for him, and he proclaimed a similar attachment, she did not explain the depth of her regard, and now she feared she might never get the chance. "And doth Isotta welcome Grimbaud's suit?"

Without hesitation, the maid nodded and took her beau's hand. "I do, my lady. As I love Grimbaud."

"Then as chatelaine of Chichester Castle, I hereby grant consent in Sir Arucard's stead." But Isolde wagged a finger in caution. "However, thou must observe all proscribed strictures in advance of thy wedding. Treat thy future wife with kindness and respect, Grimbaud. And I insist we celebrate thy nuptials hither, with a special supper, which I am certain His Lordship would approve."

"Gramercy, Lady Isolde." With a fist pressed to his chest, Grimbaud dipped his chin, and Isotta curtseyed. "By thy leave."

"Thou art dismissed." When the couple reached the narrow passage that led to the domestic apartments, Grimbaud lifted Isotta into his arms and whirled in circles, and Isolde laughed. "They seem very happy."

"My lady, a messenger hath just delivered a letter for thee." Pellier charged the dais. "Mayhap it is news from Sir Arucard."

"Pray it is so." But as she stared at the writing, Isolde flinched, as it was what she dreaded. "*No.*"

"Do not tell me it is from the earl." Margery swallowed hard.

"Indeed." While she preferred to toss the missive into the hearth, and intuition told her to do just that, she could not disregard the threat her father posed. So Isolde broke the seal, unfolded the parchment, read the note, shuddered, and whispered, "Arucard."

"My lady, if I may." Pellier stepped forward. "What doth it say?"

Anger—not fear, burned as a steady flame, surged in her veins, and her fingers trembled as she passed Pellier the letter. Nay, she would not yield, despite her father's claims to her allegiance. But a certain aspect of his message rocked the earth beneath her feet. "According to Father, I need no longer consider myself married."

#

The royal encampment dotted an otherwise pristine pasture, and a sea of tents bespoke an army of considerable size. Countless soldiers noted the latest arrivals, which sparked Arucard's nerves and fighting instincts. As he rode into what struck him as enemy territory, for some odd reason he could not shake, he assessed the terrain in search of a hasty exit, should the situation merit escape.

"Follow me to His Majesty's lodging, and I shall announce thee." Briarus took the lead. "The King commands thy immediate audience."

The Crown's men closed about the Brethren, as the ocean overtook a sinking ship, enfolding it in a watery grave, and Arucard struggled with the weight of the unsettling scrutiny. He glanced at Aristide. "We art popular, brother."

"Aye." Frowning, Aristide nodded once. "I noticed. What would thou have us do?"

"Naught, as we are surrounded." Every instinct screamed at Arucard to flee, but he had to apprise the King of the earl's schemes and Isolde's innocence, so he stayed the course. "Keep calm, my friend."

Dismounting, he surrendered his destrier and peered at Geoffrey, who signaled Morgan, who prompted Aristide. On watch for the slightest attack, they walked the plush rug that disappeared into the large tent embroidered with the royal crest. Behind him, a maid secured the outer flaps. Then two servants tied back a partition, revealing a full compliment of armed soldiers, and Arucard unsheathed his sword.

"Lower thy weapon, Sir Arucard." Briarus positioned himself between his comrades the Nautionnier knights. "And stand down, as no lives will be taken today."

"Brave words from our sergeant, as thy charge hath

much to answer for, in light of recent revelations." The soldiers parted, and His Majesty perched on a somewhat small throne. "And what hath Sir Arucard to say for himself, after we saved him from certain death and bestowed upon him our friendship? How hast thou shown thy appreciation of our benevolence? Thou hast conspired with our enemies to steal lands and attacked our loyal citizens without our permission."

"Majesty, I have purloined naught." With his sword leveled at the nearest guard's neck, Arucard poised for battle. "I sent my man to meet with thee and deliver proof of the earl of Rochester's evil plans. And if the Crown references the assault on my caravan, which occurred as my party neared Chichester, it was a misunderstanding brought about by the counterfeit burgage plots. But I secured sworn testimony to that purpose, which Sir Demetrius was tasked to convey to thee. Whither is my friend?"

"He is safe, for now, and we shall conduct thy interrogation." The King stood and narrowed his stare. "We have been aware of questionable dealings in Chichester and Winchester for some time, and we dispatched our agents to gain evidence, yet none proved successful. The previous earl of Sussex connived with a mysterious partner we had yet to discover, but he took that secret to his grave, much to our disappointment. Then thou didst promise to investigate and bring to justice the unknown villain, and we had high hopes for thee, given thy professed honor and religious beliefs. Imagine our surprise when we were informed of thy traitorous behavior."

"I am no traitor." Leashing his fury, Arucard rolled his shoulders and chose his words with care. "Sovereign, I remain thy faithful servant, and any claims to the contrary art false. While my life is of little significance, and I will not beg for my continued existence, I would plead for the soul of my gentle wife, Lady Isolde, that thou might have mercy on her. The earl of Rochester schemes with a man named Juraj de Mravec to misappropriate lands thou hast awarded, in order to undermine thy authority in the area and incite revolution. Lord Rochester hath solicited her involvement, which is minimal, but she fears him on equitable grounds. She hath born the wrath of her father and his deeds, and I would ask Sire to spare and shield her, in my absence, if thou dost deem it necessary to send me to the hereafter."

"A noble request, and thy argument is sound." The King rubbed his jaw and studied the ground. "But I have correspondence that implicates thee in the deception."

"Then I would ask His Majesty to consider the source, as I am unjustly accused and the unworthy recipient of thy ill-founded suspicions." And it appeared the earl had struck the first blow, so how could Arucard sway the Sovereign? What more could he do? "In fact, thy sergeant can attest to the validity of my statements."

"Sir Arucard is correct, Sire." Briarus glanced at Arucard and nodded. "I witnessed, with my own eyes, the abuse inflicted upon Lady Isolde." Slowly, Briarus detailed the wounds on Isolde's back, and Arucard recalled holding her, as he bared her twisted flesh. Again, he ached for her, and he summoned her sweet and reassuring image. The next thing he knew, the soldiers stowed their weapons. "My King, I speak honestly when I say I believe Sir Arucard. If someone hath misled thee, it was with nefarious purposes in mind."

Tension hung in the air, as the Crown paced. Arucard gripped the hilt of his sword and tensed, as he remained alert. At his back, the Brethren shifted.

"Thou art in luck, as we are in a mood to show compassion." At last, His Majesty eased to his throne. "We will seek additional information before we determine thy fate. Take the Brethren into custody."

#

It was a cold and dark afternoon, as Isolde assisted

Margery and the physic in the herbarium. A host of illnesses plagued her small community, which the steward declared normal when groups of people were confined to such close quarters, but she permitted no violation of Arucard's commands. Per her husband's orders, no one ventured beyond the walls of Chichester Castle.

Of course, many questioned her continued adherence to Arucard's demands, given she had received naught of his whereabouts since he departed in November. But she remained resolute in her responsibilities as chatelaine and kept the bridges drawn.

"We have little horehound, flax, and saffron in store, my lady. Yet the line of patients only grows." The physic examined the clusters of dried plants. "If the situation remains the same, I will run out of my most critical medicines, unless I am allowed to purchase more provisions, as the early snowfall either damaged or destroyed the new garden in the courtyard before we could harvest what few herbs grew."

"While I understand thy concerns, and I admire thy dedication to treating our sick and injured, we must abide his lordship's dictates, until Sir Arucard returns and rescinds the restrictions." If only she had some idea when that happy day would occur, and she refused to consider the contrary conclusion. "In the meantime, we will make do with what we have and tend our people. Mayhap thou could employ secondary treatments, or devise new remedies."

"Aye, my lady." The physic nodded his assent. "I will do my best, but I am no miracle worker."

"My lady, come quickly." A soldier wiped his brow. "The marshalsea requests thy presence in the courtyard."

"Of course." Curious, Isolde wiped her hands on her apron, rushed through the kitchen, ran across the great hall, and pushed ajar the heavy door that led to the open-air square. To her horror, a slew of soldiers, including a standard-bearer carrying an all too familiar ensign, filled the grand expanse. "Oh, no. How can this be?"

"Lady Isolde, I could not stop them." Pellier drew her toward the well. "Young Grimbaud convinced a guard to lower the bridges, that Grimbaud might venture to town and procure a gift for Isotta. When Grimbaud navigated the first traverse, the earl's soldiers overtook our lancer. They threatened to kill Grimbaud if our watch did not open the main gate, so our men relented."

It was her worst nightmare, as she had yet to respond to her father's most recent letter. And her instincts told her that, whatever he was about, he was up to no good.

"Come hither, Pellier." She grabbed the marshalsea's arm and led him to the stables. Availing herself of the confusion and activity amid the unexpected arrivals, Isolde summoned additional assistance. To the Master of the Horse, she said, "Hurry. Thou must saddle our fastest mount, and send thy apprentice to the rear guards to lower the postern bridge, per my directive."

"My lady, I am at thy service." Pellier peered over her shoulder and frowned. "But if I try to leave the castle, thy father will see me."

"Not if thou dost exit the rear gate—now." As her plan formed and took shape, Isolde attempted to anticipate his needs and clapped twice as Margery, out of breath, stumbled into the stall. "Return to the kitchen and pack foods that travel well, and make haste."

"Whither doth Pellier journey?" Pale, Margery swallowed hard. "And wherefore hath thy father traveled hither?"

"Anon, I will explain, and I know not my father's aim." Isolde shoved her friend. "But do not delay, as I suspect my life, and that of Sir Arucard, hangs in the balance."

"Aye, my lady." Margery disappeared as fast as she had appeared.

A shiver of unease danced along her spine, but Isolde shook off the disconcerting sensation and focused her efforts, as now was no time for panic. She had but a single opportunity to send for help, and if Pellier failed, she might never reunite with her husband again. When the hand led a stallion into the yard, she wound her arm about Pellier's. "Let us stroll, under shield of calamity, to avoid attracting unnecessary attention."

"My lady, while I shall not challenge thee, I do not like this." The marshalsea scowled, as they navigated the throng. "I am charged with thy safety, and I would not abandon thee to thine enemy."

"That is thy first mistake, Pellier." When they gained the small, unremarkable gatehouse, which blended into the background, to her good fortune, with none the wiser, Isolde uttered a silent prayer of thanks. "Thou art not abandoning me. Thou art my lone chance for survival if thou canst locate my husband."

"I grabbed everything I could find that would not spoil in thy belly." Margery conveyed a bundle, which she tied to the saddle. "Try not to consume it all by dusk, as thou dost eat enough for three." Then she sniffed and stared at the ground. "Take care, Pellier."

"Woman, thou wilt not be rid of me so easily." To Isolde's surprise, Pellier cupped Margery's cheek and bestowed upon her a thorough kiss. "Perchance I might marry thee when I return."

"Thou should be so blessed." The steward smoothed the folds of his cloak and then hugged him. "If thou dost come back, I will be thy wife."

"Ah, that alone is reason to fight." The ground shook as the drawbridge extended, and he jumped into the saddle, drew rein, and turned the stallion. To Isolde, he said, "My lady, I will not fail ye."

"I have faith in ye." Isolde clasped hands with Margery. "Tell Sir Arucard I need him."

With that, Pellier dipped his chin and charged the traverse. As soon as he had safely crossed the expanse, Isolde glanced at the guard. "Raise the bridge."

"My lady, what shall we do now?" Margery asked, as

they returned to the courtyard, which manifested a beehive of activity.

"Ready the guest rooms." Her father descended his great black stallion, and Isolde inhaled a calming breath. "And have the cook prepare pykes in brasey and a mushroom pasty for supper."

"The earl's favorite." Margery frowned, as he spied them and waved. "My lady, I will do whatever thou dost require, but I ask ye not to trust his lordship."

"I know better than that, old friend. I will see thee at dinner." Marching into the breach, Isolde dreaded each consecutive step she took, which brought her closer to her adversary. With images of Arucard flashing in her mind, she invoked his strength to meet her foe. "Father, what a lovely surprise." The epitome of elegance and refinement, she curtseyed, even as her heart plummeted. "Welcome to Chichester Castle."

CHAPTER TWELVE

Two days had passed since the fateful confrontation in the Sovereign's tent, and Arucard seethed in silence and under guard, as the royal forces marched east. Despite His Majesty's promise to keep the Brethren safe from harm, naught was said regarding the length of such hospitality, and Arucard knew too well the dangers of powerful rulers and fickle favor.

"I am so glad I expended considerable worry for thy welfare, as we journeyed hither." Aristide snorted and glared at Demetrius. "As the King's food and drink poses a dire threat to the size of thy waist."

"Do not confuse my appetite with indifference, as I am just as concerned as thee." Demetrius tossed aside a chicken bone. "But I see no reason to starve myself, if I am but to die."

"Thou hast always thought with thy belly." Geoffrey kicked over a platter of fruit. "Dost thou not care for our necks, and what of Lady Isolde?"

"I understand the risks." Demetrius shot to his feet and squared off with Geoffrey. "Dost thou question my honor?"

"What honor?" Aristide inquired.

"Cease thy arguments." As their leader, Arucard situated himself in the middle of the fray, as he pondered how long it would take before someone struck a blow. "We will not do this. We will not permit anyone to put us at odds, when we art not enemies."

The misplaced anger did not surprise him, given their close quarters. Add to that the restlessness of an unknown future, and it was no small wonder his fellow knights had not already clashed.

It was, perchance, for that reason he was infinitely glad of his decision to leave Isolde in Chichester, whither she was safe from harm. If the worst happened, and he was executed, thither remained the outside chance she would survive the baseless charges. As long as she lived, all was not lost.

"I am sorry, brother." Demetrius extended a hand in camaraderie, which Aristide accepted. "But the uncertainty of our predicament gnaws at my gut."

"My apologies." With a chuckle, Aristide chucked Demetrius. "Thou hast always been a nervous eater."

Arms splayed wide, Geoffrey winked. "Give us a kiss, pretty one."

"I am anxious, not crazy." Demetrius grimaced. "And I would sooner have my head separated from my body than kiss thy ugly face."

"Easy, friend. Thou mayest yet get thy wish." And so Arucard heaved a sigh of relief—until Briarus entered the tent. "What say ye, sirrah?"

"His Majesty commands thy presence." The sergeant bowed. When Demetrius, Geoffrey, and Aristide loomed behind Arucard, Briarus stated, "My apologies, but only Sir Arucard is summoned."

"Whither my brother goes, so go I." Demetrius stretched to his full height. "Would thou attack us, one by one? Art thou a coward?"

"Stand down, men. Hither thou shalt remain, as I confront the Sire's judgment." Having surrendered his sword, Arucard possessed naught but the strength of his conviction and faith, as he walked to the exit. At the last second, he peered into the corner and rolled his eyes. "And someone wake Morgan."

Outside, he shielded his gaze from the sunlight and noticed the servants and soldiers rushing to dismantle tents, put out fires, and pack the encampment. To the left, he observed a makeshift pen and the Brethren horses. Numerous opportunities for escape flashed in his brain, now that he had located their mounts; as the prisoner knights had been transported in a wagon since falling from favor, and he formed a strategy, should a chance at liberty prevail.

In the King's huge lodging, Arucard discovered no garrison of soldiers. Instead, only the Sovereign waited. As customary, Arucard knelt, bowed his head, and pressed a fist to his chest.

"Rise, Sir Arucard." As Arucard gained his feet, His Majesty displayed two parchments, one of which he passed to Arucard. "The burden of rule presents us with a seemingly endless supply of enemies in quest for our throne, and we must depend on our judgment to determine who we can and cannot trust. We art gratified to learn we can rely upon thee."

Scanning the contents of the missive, Arucard clenched his teeth and simmered with rage, given the outright lies contained in the document. "Majesty, on my life, never have I—"

"Keep reading, Sir Arucard." The King smiled and then poured two goblets of wine.

As he neared the closing, Arucard paused, sighed in relief, and then chuckled, as the traitor, in his zeal to deflect blame and condemn an innocent, had unwittingly provided too much information and all but heralded his own culpability. "The earl of Rochester knows naught of my affiliations or my history."

"And therein lies his downfall." His Majesty rubbed his chin and narrowed his stare. "At the time thou were supposed to have committed thy heinous infractions against our authority, thou were, in fact, our guest in White Tower. Thus thou could not have perpetrated the crimes of which thou dost stand accused. And Aeduuard de Cadby supports thy account of the skirmish in Chichester as an unfortunate misunderstanding."

"Lord, be praised." For the first time since departing Chichester Castle, Arucard relaxed. "Sire, if I may, I would like to ride for Rochester."

"Sir Arucard, thither we have journeyed, since thou joined our caravan." The revelation stunned Arucard, as the King descended his traveling throne and stretched upright. "And we would ask our Nautionnier knights to drive ahead, as we art but a day's ride from thy wife's childhood home."

And Arucard could arrest the earl for offenses against the Realm, if not for Isolde's abuse. At the prospect, he rejoiced. "Majesty, it would be my pleasure."

#

It was just after dawn when Isolde emerged from her chambers, clothed in a green cotehardie and with her hair plaited. While most homes opted to forgo a morning meal, her father always demanded a sop, bread, and tea, so she prepared the fare, herself, to spare the cook and Margery any complaints. But she coveted other motives, as she preferred to keep him isolated, in the event her servants divulged precious information that might harm Arucard. So to avoid any additional protests, she delivered the food.

"Good morrow, Father." She set the tray on the bedside table and turned to exit.

"Come in and pull up a chair, chitty-face, as I would have words with thee." How she hated it when he called her that, but she would not protest and incite his anger, as she found comfort in his disdain. Garbed in a robe, he sat at the edge of the mattress and draped a blanket over his legs. "Wherefore hast thou not answered my last letter?"

"I did not realize it required a response, as thou didst not ask for one." Given he thought her dull-witted, she saw no reason to disabuse him of the notion, especially when it aided her cause. So she would play her part to perfection and, mayhap, save her husband. "Art thou comfortable in thy accommodations? Is this not a grand castle? Sir Arucard hath many plans for improvements, we shall purchase new oak benches for the great hall, and I should love to plant roses in the spring." Smoothing her skirts, she bounced. "And dost thou favor my new fashions?"

"Stupid girl, I did not travel hither to discuss the furnishings or thy attire." He scowled, as sop trickled down his chin, and she yearned to vomit, but she maintained her false veil. "What hast thou learned of thy husband's fortune? And how hath he earned the King's favor?"

"I know not, Father." She blinked and shrugged, but inside she laughed at his ignorance. "As Sir Arucard doth not discuss such things in my presence, as I am but a woman." It physically hurt to proclaim such a falsehood, given Arucard shared everything with her, but Father would never learn her husband's secrets from her. To reinforce her act, she giggled and toyed with the cuff of her sleeve, knowing such behavior would incite him. "Hast thou admired the tapestries? Art they not very fine? And hast thou noticed we have glazed windows? Is that not a wonder?"

"That thou art my issue is the wonder." The ire in his tone left her shaking, as she feared a lashing. "Get thee gone, as thy mere existence annoys me."

"Aye, Father." He did not know it, but that was just what she wanted—his condescension and dismissal. If she could fool her father until her husband returned, she would survive. For good measure, she skipped to the door and added, "Have a lovely day."

As expected, he didn't even acknowledge her. So Isolde returned to the kitchen to plan supper. But just as she gathered the ingredients for her special herb bread, a soldier approached, and his expression conveyed ill tidings.

"My lady, a visitor is just arrived." The guard shuffled his feet. "He claims an acquaintance with Lord Rochester, and the earl's men permitted entry, despite our protests."

"But thou didst make the right choice." So many decisions had fallen to her judgment, and never had she foreseen assuming such responsibility prior to her marriage. And while Arucard had not written, she maintained their home and their people. Given her father's troops outnumbered the garrison of Chichester, by a majority of two to one, Isolde had instructed her husband's soldiers to yield, as she would not risk unnecessary violence. "Whither is our guest?"

"In the great hall, my lady." The young soldier speared his fingers through his hair and sputtered. "It seems he expects thee to provide lodging."

"Oh." Fear sparked and grew, as she contemplated housing her father's ally, and she loathed another villain in their midst, but she recalled her position and the power invested therein. "Then summon Margery and have her prepare an additional chamber."

"Aye, my lady." The guard saluted, and she laughed.

When she entered the primary seat of dining, drinking, and celebrating, she was surprised to find a tall and handsome man waiting. With the garb of a noble, ebony hair, and foreign features, the stranger gazed on her and smiled.

"Welcome to Chichester Castle." She extended her hand, and he bowed and placed a chaste kiss on her knuckles. "I am Lady Isolde de Villiers, the chatelaine."

"I have heard much of thee, my lady." When she attempted to retreat, he squeezed her fingers, and she swallowed her trepidation, lest she panic. "Thy father neglected to mention thou art beauteous. Permit me to introduce myself. I am Juraj de Mravec."

#

The journey to Rochester had been arduous, given the weather had turned, but Arucard uttered a prayer of thanks when they arrived. Quaint but rugged, Isolde's childhood home presented an odd mix of quiet beauty and austere resilience. A rolling hill hugged the manor house, which was protected by a large ditch at the base of the outer wall. To his surprise, the lone gatehouse remained open, and he rode into the courtyard with no resistance, just before sunset. As he studied the natural stone structure that boasted a single crenellated tower, an elderly man and woman emerged from a large entry.

"Good eventide, sir." The grey-haired servant bowed. "I am Hervisse, Lord Rochester's majordomo. How may I be of assistance?"

"I am the earl of Sussex and thy master's son-in-law." After descending his destrier, he peered left and then right, as the yard was eerily quiet and empty, which worried him. "Is Lord Rochester in residence?"

"Nay, my lord." Hervisse whispered to the woman, and she curtseyed and then scurried into the house. "Wilt thou not come inside and take thy ease?"

"Thank ye." He was in no mood to partake of the earl's hospitality, but he cooperated. To Demetrius, Arucard said, "Search the garrison, the stables, and any other structures. Report what ye dost find."

"Aye, brother." Demetrius signaled the Brethren.

When Arucard strolled into the grand residence, which opened into a massive gallery, he noted numerous paintings of what he presumed were de Tyreswelles past and present, but he failed to locate any portrait of his wife. While he recognized the earl, the heir, and what he would have guessed was the countess, in light of her resemblance to Isolde, thither were no images of his lady.

"Hither she is not, my lord." The bespectacled woman wiped a stray tear from her cheek. "The earl of Rochester commissioned no renderings of his daughter, the Lady Isolde, God bless her kind spirit." Then she drew a handkerchief from her fitchet and daubed her nose. "If I might infringe on thy generosity, mayest I prevail upon thee to convey my lady's personal belongings to her? The earl commanded I destroy Lady Isolde's things, but I had not the heart to abide his order."

"Of course, I will transport them to her." When she indicated a very small trunk, he frowned. "Is that all of it?"

"Yea, my lord." She bent, unlatched the lock, and lifted the lid. "My lady never had much, but she never complained."

Tattered garb bespoke a pauper's life, not the daughter of a wealthy nobleman, and telltale stains to the chemises betrayed the hardship she suffered long before they married. A broken comb, a well-worn brush, a bundle of lace-edged squares, and a frayed Bartholomew baby, which inspired a smile, constituted the whole of her existence, and he counted it a precious treasure. "I will see to it my wife receives the items."

"My lord, if I may inquire after her health and happiness." The old woman clutched her throat. "And art thou pleased with thy union?"

"Infe, thou must not ask such questions." Hervisse grabbed her arm. "Remain in the kitchen, if thou cannot show proper respect and hold thy tongue. I apologize, your lordship."

"Wait, as I am not offended." Arucard understood the servant's concern. Just as Isolde had won Margery's loyalty, along with everyone else's in the castle, she had charmed her former attendants, and he sought to allay their fears. "My wife was very unhappy with me, when last I saw her, as I departed Chichester without her. But Isolde counts our steward a friend, as the woman once worked for the earl, so she is not alone. Mayhap thou art familiar with Margery."

Infe gave vent to a startling shriek, and Hervisse flinched and then hugged her. With a watery gaze, the majordomo opened and then closed his mouth. "Forgive us, Lord Sussex, but Margery is our daughter, and we have had no word of her, since the earl dismissed her from employ. We knew naught of her fate and feared the worst."

"Then permit me to reassure thee of Margery's continued well-being, and she seems a vast deal more than content." And after swiping a linen kerchief, he pressed it to his nose and inhaled Isolde's scent. "As for my nuptials, I count myself quite fortunate, as I love my bride."

"Oh, my lord." Again, Infe sobbed. "Thou hast given us a most treasured gift, and we art in thy debt."

"How can we serve thee?" Hervisse patted Infe's cheek and set her aside. "Wherefore art thou hither?"

"Whither hath Lord Rochester gone?" Naught seemed as it should, as the home was all but deserted, and he could not shake the unease nestled atop his shoulders. "Dost thou know of his plans, as it is important that I speak with him?"

"I apologize, my lord. But the earl never discusses his schedule with us." The majordomo closed and refastened Isolde's trunk. "However, his lordship's pursuivant remains in the garrison, as he is young, and Lord Rochester hath no patience for the boy."

Just then, Demetrius and Aristide charged into the residence, and the expression on Demetrius's face bespoke trouble. "Arucard, we know whither the earl hath gone."

"The news is dreadful, brother." Aristide shook his head. "The earl rides for Chichester."

Arucard's gut clenched, his ears rang, and terror struck his heart. "*Isolde.*"

CHAPTER THIRTEEN

At the end of another day, Isolde presided over supper, although she had yielded her place of honor at the dais, as her father and his friend de Mravec claimed the positions of prominence. Yet she would not object to such minor insults, as her father was capable of much worse than what she deemed a mere slight.

"Unhand me." Nearby, a maid struggled with an intoxicated and amorous soldier from the Rochester garrison, and the guards of Chichester took note.

"Let go of my servant." Before war broke out in the great hall, Isolde addressed the offender. "Prithee, in this great household, we treat our workers with respect and kindness. If thou cannot obey our directives, thou canst take thy meals in the stable, with the other animals."

A full compliment of troops jumped to their feet, but she stood her ground. To her relief, Grimbaud and the remaining lancers positioned themselves behind her. Just as it appeared the opposing sides would clash, the Rochesters retreated. To diffuse the situation, she signaled the minstrel, but before he could commence recitation of his poem, a loud pounding snared the attention of the crowd, and a lull fell on the sea of revelers.

"How dare thee reprimand my men? In thy husband's absence, I am the lord of Chichester Castle, and thou wilt obey my commands." Her father scowled and then nodded to his sergeant. "Finish thy sup, and gather thy belongings, as we depart tonight for Winchester under cover of darkness."

With a sigh of gratitude, Isolde pondered his words, as she had prayed for his departure since he arrived, and she could have shouted her joy from the top of the northwest tower. To garner the regard of her staff, she clapped once. "Quickly, we must assist Lord Rochester. Prepare provisions, pack their things, and saddle their horses"

For the next hour or so, she organized and supervised the activities, as she could not remove the enemy from her home fast enough. After stowing Father's trunk, she followed a servant into the courtyard. With the final items secured, she located Margery. "Make a thorough search of the premises, as I would leave them no reason to return." Then Isolde flagged Grimbaud. "Ensure the bridges art drawn as soon as the earl's men have cleared the castle."

"Yea, my lady." The lancer signaled a collective. "Guard the gates."

The cold December wind cut through her wool cloak, as she studied the full moon, which cast shadows framed in silvery light on the grounds. Clutching the folds about her, she whisked aside a stray tendril and tucked it behind her ear. As always, her thoughts turned to Arucard. So many nights, she enjoyed the view with her husband after they made love, but nature's beauty inspired naught more than sorrow, as she yearned for him.

Juraj de Mravec gained his saddle, as did her father, and she mustered a smile. Beneath the weight of his stare, unusual in its intensity, she shivered. When he dipped his chin, she made to bid him farewell—just as two soldiers grabbed her.

"What art thou doing? Release me." Kicking and flailing against her would-be captors, she fought hard, dragging her feet in the dirt. "I order thee to set me free, as I am Lady Isolde of Chichester Castle."

"Turn loose my lady, thou villain." Margery scratched an assaulter, but he struck her in the mouth, and she dropped, unmoving, on her face.

"Bind her," Father shouted.

"Prithee, no." As the soldier wound rope about her wrists, Isolde wrestled with her assailant. "And what hast thou done to Margery?"

Then the Chichester garrison responded with full weaponry, and the Rochester guards squared off, in a show of hostility. When Grimbaud advanced, two foes struck him down, but they did not kill him. Isotta screamed and ran to her beau, and the Chichesters responded with unveiled anger. The situation rapidly spun out of control, especially when her father issued a dire request.

"Light the torches." The earl raised his right hand. "Once we have evacuated, we shall set fire to the castle and burn its inhabitants herein."

"Wait." After her attacker shoved her atop a horse, Isolde realized resistance constituted an exercise in futility, and she would not allow her people to sacrifice themselves, in vain. "If I promise to go with thee willingly, and make no attempt at escape, wilt thou spare Chichester Castle and its occupants?"

"Thou dost bargain on behalf of thy citizenry?" Her father sneered and motioned to his soldiers. "Thou hast more fortitude than I anticipated, though thou should expend thy worry for thy fate. Mayhap thou art of my loins, after all."

"Pray, Father." Tasked with the safety of those left in her care, she would not surrender without ensuring their protection. "Let them live, as they art innocent, and I will cause thee no trouble. I will do as thou dost ask, and they will not hinder thee." She scanned the crowd to impress upon them her pact with the devil. "Thou hast my word, as chatelaine."

With a clenched fist pressed to their chest, and sober expressions, the Chichester men nodded their assent, as the women wept. Slowly, her guards retreated, and two maids rushed to help Margery.

"Very well." Father turned his mount, and the dragoons steered for the barbican. "Rochesters, let us ride."

With a final survey of her home, which she vowed to see again, Isolde heeled the flanks of her horse and charged into the indigo blanket of night and equally dark uncertainty.

#

The road manifested a lethal combination of muddy ruts and furrows, which slowed the trip to Chichester. But Arucard pushed hard, leaving behind His Majesty and the royal troops, as the caravan traveled at a snail's pace. As a wicked December storm dumped snow on the terrain, the treacherous conditions forced him to break his journey at night, or risk a lame horse, much to his frustration.

A howling gale battered his tent, as he sat upright in his makeshift bed. Light from a single brazier cast a saffron glow about the small accommodation, and he stretched. On the other side of the temporary dwelling, Demetrius propped on an elbow.

"Canst thou not sleep, either?" Arucard rubbed the back of his neck.

"Nay." Demetrius fluffed and resituated his pillow. "I am hungry, as the boiled chicken scarcely dented my empty belly."

"Wherefore am I not surprised?" He might have laughed, were he not so worried. It was an awesome responsibility to care for another, and the sacrament tasked him with Isolde's welfare. Yet he could not shake the feeling that he had failed her, and he would not yield until he held her in his arms. "Would that the sky was clear and the moon high, as I would wake our brothers and drive to Sussex, without stopping."

"Ah, how I miss Lady Isolde's brewets." Even in the dimness, Arucard noted Demetrius's flinch. "Sorry, brother. I should have said naught."

"Never should I have left her." All manner of torment haunted his conscience, as his nightmares taunted him with images of Isolde in her father's evil clutch. No matter how hard he tried, he could not shake the unease that had settled as a lead ball in belly. And a singular refrain played a disturbing melody, as she invoked his name, again and again, as a plea for salvation, which he vowed to answer. "Never should I have abandoned her, after she begged me to take her with me."

"At the peril of my own hide, might I suggest thou art weaving unsustainable conclusions based on irrational fears motivated by thy passionate attachment, as thou didst not abandon her? Thou didst act in her best interest; given the battlefield is no place for a woman, which thou didst correctly assert. We have no idea what Rochester plans, and our information regarding his land thefts is vague. Thither is no reason to believe he intends to harm his daughter." Demetrius arched a brow. "Mayhap I will try to rest."

"Nay, my friend." He needed to talk to someone, needed to share the burden he carried; else he might devolve into insanity. "Something is not right, and I cannot explain my logic, as I understand it not. But a deep sense of foreboding chills me to the bone, and I know Isolde is in trouble as sure as I know my name. Do not ask me how I can be certain, as I cannot interpret my instincts—but thou canst attest to the fact that in such instances I am never wrong."

For a long while, Demetrius said naught, and Arucard presumed his brother slept.

"Arucard, we should get an early start in the morrow." With that, Demetrius rolled onto his side.

"A rider approaches." The call came from outside, as Morgan stood watch.

In seconds, Arucard leaped from his straw-stuffed mattress, tugged on his boots, grabbed his cloak, and plunged into the tempest, followed by Demetrius.

"Thither who goes?" He shielded his eyes and just made out the profile of a horse. "Art thou sure the saddle is occupied, as I see no one."

"I am not sure." Morgan tried but failed to relight his torch in the dwindling campfire. "But I would rather be safe than sorry."

The poor beast, with an accumulation of froth about its mouth, trotted into their midst, and it was then Arucard spied the slumped body. As Geoffrey grabbed the reins, Aristide and Demetrius retrieved the unknown person. Together, they carried their uninvited guest into Arucard's tent, whither they put him in Demetrius's bed.

When they removed the traveler's hat, Arucard's gut clenched. "God's bones, it is Pellier."

"Fetch some water." Demetrius stripped off the soaked cloak and tunic. "Arucard, give me thy blanket."

"Of course." As he tucked the cover about his marshalsea, Arucard studied Pellier's face.

Gaunt in appearance, his flesh showed signs of severe weathering, and his lips were cracked and bleeding. Arucard wet a cloth and wiped Pellier's forehead and cheeks, and the marshalsea groaned.

For the next few hours, Arucard anchored at his friend's side, and Pellier's incoherent babble interspersed with a mention of Isolde stimulated intense anxiety and endless queries for which Arucard had no answer. Why had his friend abandoned his post and left Chichester? What manner of distress sent Pellier in pursuit of Arucard? As the first hint of dawn streaked the sky in pale yellow, Pellier choked and sputtered.

"Easy, sirrah." Supporting his friend's head, Arucard held a cup of water to Pellier's mouth. "Sip slowly."

"Christ's blood, art thou trying to kill me?" With a grimace, Pellier coughed and opened his eyes. "That is Adam's ale. Have ye no beer?"

"I would say he is fine." Demetrius chuckled.

After a few minutes, Pellier eased upright and scratched his chin. As he made to speak, he sneezed and blew his nose on his tunic. "Sir, I have searched for ye, high and low."

"To what purpose?" Arucard braced himself. "Is it Isolde?"

"Aye, sir. Her ladyship asks me to tell ye that she needs ye." Pellier met Arucard's stare. "Lord Rochester hath taken Chichester Castle."

#

When Father forced her to journey with him, Isolde wondered about his motives, as thither remained no love lost between them, and he had made no secret of his utter disdain for her. But the answer to her quandary became evident, when he proclaimed his plan to prosecute her for crimes against the citizenry. In short, she was to shoulder the blame for her sire's conspiracy, thereby positioning him as Winchester's savior.

The hasty trial, a mockery of justice, had lasted two days in Winchester, with her father acting as judge and jury. Pronounced guilty of conspiring with her husband to steal lands, using the counterfeit burgage plots, Isolde was sentenced to a public lashing. Given she had endured and survived countless such whippings, she accepted the decision with calm confidence. But what irritated her was Father's outright refusal to grant her the opportunity to plead her innocence before a crowd that viewed her as the enemy. And neither was she permitted to defend Arucard.

As she knelt in the corner of her small room, which featured a single bed, a table, a matched set of chairs, and a washstand, she leaned against the wall. A seemingly harmless drain functioned as a herald, of sorts, as it carried her father's voice, along with that of Juraj de Mravec, from the chamber below, revealing the details of their nefarious plans.

"Dost thou verily intend to beat thy daughter?" Juraj inquired. "As I would be willing to enter into a marriage contract to solidify our connections. Thither is no need for violence."

The very suggestion struck terror in her heart, as she had a husband she dearly loved.

"Hast thou lost thy mind?" Father scoffed. "She must be punished for our ruse to succeed. If we art to place blame on the Crown, undermine the King's authority, and win the support of the citizenry, we must sacrifice Isolde on the altar of rebellion. Trust me, the people want blood, and blood we will give them."

She expected no less from her father.

"How wilt thou defend against Sir Arucard?"

"Given our most recent communication from thy spies reports he is currently imprisoned by the King, thanks to our fortuitous letter, which inflamed His Majesty's temper, we need not fear de Villiers."

In that moment, Isolde bowed her head, bit her lip, shivered, and let the tears flow. First, she wept for Arucard, as she loved him, yet she had not told him so. Second, while Father's intense dislike was naught new, never had she imagined he would subject her husband to such brutality, in his illegitimate quest for power. In short, thither was no limit to his degeneracy.

"And what of the Lancasters?"

"They will support my son's ascendance to the throne, and William rallies the troops. Which begs the question, whither art thy men?"

So Father had involved her brother in the dastardly plot. Was there no end to his depravity? Would he not be satisfied until he destroyed their entire family?

"Given the weather hath turned, their departure was delayed. If thou wilt but wait another day or two, my soldiers should arrive to reinforce thy position."

"Thou hast thy requisite postponement but no more, as I am anxious to secure Winchester for our mighty cause and celebrate my son's ascendance to the throne."

The remainder of their conversation degenerated into a vulgar discussion of women, so Isolde moved to stand by the window, which overlooked the town square. At center, a platform held a large stake, and she shuddered, as she envisioned what her father intended. Then she studied the night sky and hugged herself.

Nay, she would not yield, and Arucard would not fall. He was a good man, and the King would see that. His Majesty had to see that.

"Oh, Arucard, whither art thou?" She sniffed and then vowed to fight. "Thou wilt come for me. I believe in thee, and I will do so until I die."

CHAPTER FOURTEEN

All was not as he had anticipated, and something was most definitely wrong as he soared over the verge. Evidence of the recent occupation surrounded Chichester Castle, as Arucard noted the remnants of numerous campfires dotting the meadow. That he expected. What surprised him was the absence of Lord Rochester's troops, as it was obvious the earl had departed.

Was it as Demetrius claimed? Had Arucard worried for naught? But when both drawbridges lowered before he could offer the secret phrase, which his lady had suggested, permitting a hasty entrance, and the head of the guard rushed forth, Arucard feared the worst.

As he drew rein in the courtyard, he searched for the one person he most wanted to welcome him home, but his wife remained conspicuously absent. When he spied Margery, and noted the black bruise to her left eye, his anxiety grew by leaps and bounds.

"Whither is Isolde?" He jumped from the saddle, grabbed Margery, and shook her. "Whither is my wife?"

"Gone, sir." With tears welling, Margery peered over

his shoulder and shrieked. *"Pellier."*

"Woman, what happened to thy face?" The marshalsea dismounted and ran to the steward. "Who injured thee, as I will slit the bastard's throat?"

"Oh, thou art my funny little man, and I have missed thy wit. I am grateful thou art well." Then, to his surprise, Margery kissed Pellier, and Arucard envied their reunion. "Come inside, and I will tell thee everything."

While his staff celebrated the Brethren's return, Arucard navigated the crowd gathered to receive him and walked to his chambers, as he was in no mood to socialize. In the solar, the sitting room had been tidied, but the psalter he gifted his bride on their wedding night sat on the table near the windows, whither she often read. As he opened the double-door portal to the inner sanctum, he found Isolde's robe draped across the foot of the bed they shared.

Perched at the edge of the mattress, he caressed the linen garment and then held it to his nose. Inhaling her scent, he closed his eyes and invoked her sweet face, framed by her shimmering smile. Then her pleas to journey with him filled his ears, as a morbid refrain, and his heart broke. Never should he have abandoned her.

"Lord Rochester took my lady almost a sennight ago, sir. He declared an intent to journey to Winchester, but that is all I know, and we have had no word of her, since." With an expression of sorrow, Margery loomed in the entry, and Pellier stood to her right. "The earl threatened to burn the castle, so Lady Isolde made a pact with the devil, himself, to spare us."

"Of course, she did." Oh, he could just imagine his valorous heroine, with her blazing green gaze, her fists clenched at her sides, and her adorable chin thrust high. With care, he spread her robe whither she left it, as she would want it when he brought her back. He would not permit himself to think otherwise. "Pellier, have fresh horses saddled for the Brethren, and pack our armor."

Pellier clenched his fists. "Sir, I would go with ye, as—
"

"Thou wilt remain hither, and guard this castle with thy life." Arucard flipped through his belongings and located a clean tunic. After washing his face, he shaved. "How is Grimbaud?"

"Better, sir. But he blames himself for what happened." Margery collected his soiled garment. "Shall I bring thy meal hither? Or wilt thou dine in the great hall?"

"I want no food." He tossed aside the towel and strode into the narrow passage. "And it is not his fault, as Rochester would have found a way to invade Chichester Castle, which might have resulted in costly damage to the curtain walls and rendered us vulnerable to additional attacks."

Various torments plagued his thoughts, as he pondered the tortures the earl might inflict on Isolde. Of course, naught would have happened to her, had he abided her pleas and taken her with him. While he had sought to protect her, he had, in fact, delivered her unto the earl and very real danger. That was a grave mistake he would never repeat.

"Brother, Pellier tells me thou dost intend to ride for Winchester, now." With hands on hips, Demetrius frowned. "We have been traveling for weeks, and thou art not thyself. Rest and eat. Can we not take the day to recover, else thou mayest not be fit to rescue Lady Isolde?"

In the vast meeting room, his fellow knights gathered around a large table. For a hairsbreadth, he considered Demetrius's suggestion, as the men looked to Arucard for guidance. But then he recalled her scarred flesh, and he shook his head. "Isolde may not have another day."

#

A multitude of angry Winchester citizens lined the street and filled the square, bombarding her with all manner of spoiled food and calling for her death, as Isolde marched to the platform, and the miserable journey seemed never-ending. With her wrists bound, she lost her balance, as a soldier shoved her up the steps, and she tripped and fell to her knees.

"Beat her."

"Make her pay."

"Burn her."

Clothed only in her linen chemise, hose, and leather calf boots, she shivered as the icy December wind chilled her to the marrow, and her teeth chattered. In truth, she also shuddered in stark fear. While she refused to cry, terror struck at her heart, as never had she suffered the unrelenting hatred, however displaced, of so many.

An irate man hit her in the forehead with a rotten egg, and she gagged, bent, and vomited. In a flash, she wrenched free and lurched to the edge of the morbid stage, of sorts. "Prithee, people of Winchester, I am innocent of the charges for which I stand accused and convicted. Thou must believe me. And Lord Sussex works to restore thy lands—"

A screaming woman launched a gourd, which smashed into Isolde's nose, knocking her backwards. The world spun on end, and she teetered but did not fall.

"I will hear no more of thy lies, as thou hast shown by thy disgraceful offenses that thou art without shame." Father lorded over her, she spat in his face, and he punched her in the cheek. For a second, she thought she might faint. With a scowl, he shoved a rag between her teeth, muting her protests. Holding a book of prayer, he stretched tall. "Friends, we art come hither today to dispense justice well deserved for crimes committed by Lady Isolde de Villiers, countess of Sussex, who hath been judged guilty for conspiring with her husband, Arucard de Villiers, earl of Sussex, to deprive the honest and forthright servants of His Majesty of their fortune and legacy."

Cheers echoed on the shop edifices.

Father nodded, the guards turned her to face the stake,

and a soldier lifted her arms to hook the binding at her wrists on a pike that jutted on high. Raw terror enveloped her, swallowing her whole, and she pledged not to scream. Father wanted a spectacle, and she would deny him that. To add to her humiliation, her father used a dagger to cut open the chemise and bare her back. "Acting as the Crown's faithful attendant, I sentence Isolde de Villiers to forty lashes."

Another deafening roar filled her ears.

Focusing on the sky, Isolde uttered a silent prayer for strength, clasped her hands, and braced for the first blow, which always seemed the worst. For a moment, time stood still, and she held her breath. Then with the leather whip he thrashed her flesh, and the searing agony, so painfully familiar, invested her. Again and again, Father scourged her, and adrift in misery she lost count of the blows. Slowly, her knees failed her, and she faltered, until a blissful chasm of darkness blanketed her in an abyss of oblivion.

#

The main gate heralding the modest town of Winchester sat open and unmanned, as the Brethren of the Coast arrived. As they navigated the narrow streets, dusted with new fallen snow, the shops, with their windows festooned in holly and evergreen, appeared closed, and their doors were shut, which struck Arucard as odd, given the time of day. It should have been the most profitable hours for exchange. And every now and then, a strange cheer erupted ahead, but they moved slow and steady, as they traversed the city.

"I do not like this, brother." Aristide assessed a farm stand, which displayed various fall crop yields. Yet no trader staffed the tiny market. "Whither hath everyone gone?"

"I know not what to make of this place." Again the eerie cheer echoed, and Demetrius drew his sword. "What inspires the commotion?"

"Mayhap thither is an early festival, of some sort, in celebration of Christmastide." Morgan peered left and then right. "Although the holiday is not for a fortnight."

The hair on the back of Arucard's neck stood, as another sinister clamor hung in the air, but he advanced. At a quaint tavern with its door ajar, he signaled his brothers, and they drew rein. After tying his horse, he pulled off his gloves and strolled into the dark establishment, from which the distinct aroma of roasted goose wafted. An attendant acknowledged their entrance, as they occupied a table and two benches near the hearth.

"Welcome to the Goat in Boots." A red-haired character with a noticeable limp tossed a cloth over his shoulder. "I am Orthaeus, the owner. What can I serve ye?"

So many responses filled Arucard's brain that he could not form a coherent response. Sharing polite pleasantries while Isolde lingered in the earl's grip struck him as offensive.

"How is thy wassail?" Geoffrey inquired, as Morgan blanched.

"Like me." The jolly server laughed, and his round belly shook. "Spicy and spirited, as I use an ancient family mixture of special ingredients, so I highly recommend it."

"Sounds delicious." Geoffrey smiled. "We will take five flagons, good sirrah."

"An excellent choice." Their host ladled the portions and hobbled back. "Wilt thou care for any food, as my wife cooks a savory pourcelet farci."

"Perchance, we may consider thy fare." Arucard glanced over his shoulder and then gazed at the tavern keep. "I journeyed to Winchester in search of a gift—a new comb, for my bride, but the merchandry is closed. Mayhap thou dost know the location of thy townspeople, as the streets art deserted?"

"Ah, it is a foul affair and quite unusual." Sitting at the next table, Orthaeus grimaced. "Methinks the citizenry attends the public flaying of a noblewoman judged a traitor for stealing lands, using counterfeit burgage plots." He scratched his cheek and snorted. "I chose to forgo the spectacle, because I have no stomach for it, and the lady hath done naught to me."

Without doubt, Orthaeus referenced Isolde, and Arucard prepared to charge, but Aristide stayed him.

"How unfortunate but fascinating, all the same." Demetrius elbowed Arucard, and he realized he had crushed the handle of his mug. "Dost thou know her name?"

"I believe she is known as the countess of Sussex." Orthaeus narrowed his stare. "Isolde—that is what she is called, and I suspect the judge plans to execute her."

CHAPTER FIFTEEN

Small merchandries dealing in various goods and trades lined the square, and a large crowd occupied the sidewalks. Christmastide garlands of evergreen, ivy, and holly draped the shop windows, in peculiar contradiction to the violence enacted at the heart of the city. As Arucard emerged from a side street, a gut-wrenching scene came into view, and for a moment he paused, in shock from the vicious sight he confronted.

At the center of the action, and surrounded by the earl's guards, loomed a platform, which bore a huge stake. Tied to the post, and hanging eerily limp, was Isolde. Clothed only in her chemise and leather shoes, her slip had been torn from the waist up, and her back presented a bloody mass of abused flesh, such as he had never seen. Not even the beating she suffered the night before their wedding could rival her current wounds. At random, the throng pelted his wife with rotting food, and he clenched his fists and gritted his teeth. When he made to attack, a hand covered his mouth, and he found himself set upon by his brothers.

"Hold him," Demetrius whispered, and his fellow knights grappled with Arucard's limbs as he fought. "Calm thyself, Arucard. I understand thy anger, but look about thee. We art outnumbered, and thy lady is badly injured. Wilt thou enact a battle we cannot win and thy lady could not possibly survive in her condition? In thy haste to act, wilt thou sign her death warrant?"

Pure unadulterated rage churned in his gut, and he languished in fury, burning white hot, as it distracted him from the desire to assault his friends. But he wanted to maim. He wanted to behead. He wanted to kill. Never before had he craved death, but in that moment he hungered for revenge on anyone who had hurt Isolde. And chief on that list of offenders was the earl of Rochester.

"Thou art a master of strategy, but thou art verily outraged." Aristide pinned Arucard's left shoulder to a wall. "Use thy righteous indignation and plot our attack, as we will rescue thy wife."

"Good people of Winchester, I have dispensed thy justice, and the criminal fainted, cheating thee of thy reward." The earl quieted the throng, and the Brethren peered at the stage. "Juraj de Mravec and I have attempted to compensate thee for thy loss. Art thou appeased?"

Arucard noted the second gentlemen previously identified by Aeduuard de Cadby as the earl's co-conspirator. And the earl's letters and His Majesty's report also named the same villain, which Arucard counted as another enemy.

"Nay." A chorus of witnesses shouted their objection.

"What more doth the bastard want from her?" Arucard glanced at Demetrius, who shrugged.

"While I understand thy displeasure, as I cannot restore thy pilfered acres, and thy injury remains, what more wilt thou ask of thy humble servant?" With an expression of sympathy, which did not fool Arucard for a second, Rochester splayed his hands. "If thou dost command it, I would sacrifice myself for thee, but who would protect thee from the King's greedy minions?"

"Burn her," bellowed an old man.

"Hang her," screamed a woman.

"God's bones." Arucard swallowed hard. "He doth intend to kill her."

Now he comprehended the full extent of Lord Rochester's plans. The earl stole their property and fixed the blame on Isolde, with the Crown as her leader. And in so doing, her father posited himself as Winchester's champion. It was a wily scheme, as naught incited revolution like the theft of land, and Arucard swore under his breath.

A monstrous refrain played in the town, as the earl fed their lust for savagery on an innocent. "Hang, hang, hang, hang…"

"Hear me." The earl waved to silence the throng. "Though Lady Isolde is my kin, I am prepared to forfeit her life, in reparation for her heinous actions that have hurt so many, as I am ashamed to call her family."

"I would argue the reverse is true." Arucard vowed vengeance on his in-law.

"But we have no gallows." As de Mravec signaled soldiers to cut down Isolde, he whispered to the earl and then nodded. "Citizens, let us build a proper support this eventide, that we might fulfill thy demands in the morrow, as we would not be cruel."

That had to be the understatement of the century.

So Arucard had the night to prevail, but he had an insufficient tally of collaborators, given de Mravec and the earl's combined forces. In that instant, Arucard seized on an idea, and a plan of action took shape. Retreating to an alley, he assessed the time needed to gather the various elements and then assembled his knights. "Brothers, the earl hath won the first battle, but he knows not with whom he fights, and we shall take the war, as we will save Isolde."

#

It took a while for Isolde to recognize that she had been returned to her tiny temporary prison. As she sat upright in bed, she gritted her teeth and sobbed. The pitcher on the table seemed so far away, as she thirsted for a measure of relief from her dry throat. Rolling onto her side, she winced and slid to the floor. On her hands and knees, she crawled across the rug and used a chair to gain her feet.

Memories and bits of time assaulted her, the angry crowd, the platform with the stake, the sting of the lash, and she swayed. With a tight grip on the ewer, she poured a glass of water, which she gulped. How long she had slept she knew not, but the shadows on the floor suggested sunset grew nigh. When the door to her room opened to reveal a stranger, she retreated to the large window. "Who art thou, and wherefore art thou hither?"

"Relax, Lady Isolde, as I am not thy enemy. I am Paganus, the physic." After setting his bag of medics and potions on the table, he removed his spectacles, wiped them clean, and then resituated them on his nose. "I have come to treat thy wounds, at the behest of Juraj de Mravec, that thou wilt stand for thy punishment in the morrow."

"How kind of him." Then she snapped to attention. "Wait—what? I endured my father's dispensation and thought I might be returned to my home. What hath changed? Of what dost thou speak?"

"Hath no one told thee?" With a countenance of sadness, he flicked his fingers. "Come hither, my lady, as I will not hurt thee."

As she needed his kindness just then, she obeyed. Perched at one end of a bench, she hissed, as he cleaned her torn flesh. But he was gentle, much like Margery, and Isolde tried but failed to stifle tears. "Though innocent of the charges, I have come to discover truth matters not to evil men. Good Paganus, what am I to face? What hath my father decreed?"

"Allow me to smooth some salve on thy rent skin." When she whimpered, he paused. "Sorry, my lady. The earl condemns thee to hang at dawn."

Grim acceptance enveloped her, when she should have pilloried her father. Whither previously she would have panicked, now she remained calm. While the situation looked hopeless, she hoped. While she could have lost faith, she believed. And although her fate seemed sealed against her, she clung to the unexplainable prescience of a future with Arucard. "All right."

"Lady Isolde, thither is not much I can do for thee in so little time, as it will take a fortnight, at least, for the worst of thy damage to heal." Then he sighed and tapped her shoulder. "But I have something I can offer thee. It is quick and painless, and thou wilt feel naught."

"Thou would have me take my own life?" Of course, she realized he only wanted to help her. "I thank ye, for thy charity, Paganus. But I would save my soul, despite my father's judgment, as I have committed no crimes, and my maker knows that."

"Well then, I will leave thee to thy reflection." After collecting his remedies, he studied her and then cupped her cheek. "May God have mercy on thee."

Alone, so very alone, Isolde simply stared at the pattern on the thick rug. Smiling, she recalled her wedding night and Arucard's attempt to sleep on the floor. Their first real kiss elicited a snicker, as it was quite clumsy on both parts. The eventide when he claimed her maidenhead had her giggling, especially when she remembered her husband's hearty bellow of passion after he achieved completion on the second thrust of his hips. Then she savored the sweet visions of that glorious afternoon on the hillside, when he suckled the flesh between her legs and took her to new heights of pleasure she never knew existed. Anon, he took her atop a barrel in the undercroft. And thither was the fierce warrior who fought the bandits and de Cadby, yet he showed compassion and heard their complaints.

Yea, Arucard could be kind and gentle, but he could also be ruthless, and it was the latter incarnation she prayed would come for her.

CHAPTER SIXTEEN

As the workmen labored to build the platform from which she would hang, the steady beat of the hammer kept Isolde awake all night, not that she could have rested, given the agony of her injuries and constant visions of Arucard. By first light, she gazed at the clear sky, uttered a silent prayer, and made her peace. Yet she hoped for the rescue that still eluded her.

Clinging to the promise her husband made, she remained entrenched in the belief that Arucard would save her. He would not let her die at Father's hands. All she had to do was survive, and her champion would free her. So despite the fact that she was not hungry, she ate the sop, grapes, and bread a servant delivered, to maintain her strength.

When the rasp of the lock signaled an arrival, she stood and folded her arms. To her amazement, a bishop entered her makeshift prison and smiled.

"Good morrow, Lady Isolde." Garbed in the traditional robe, he bowed. "I have come to hear thy confession, that ye might find absolution and salvation."

"I beg thy pardon?" The world seemed to spin beyond control, her ears rang, and she clutched the edge of the table for support, as she feared she might faint. "What have I to confess, as I am innocent of the allegations leveled against me?"

"My child, I am told thy father shall be lenient, show compassion, and offer thee a quick death, if thou wilt but admit thy guilt before the citizens of Winchester." The book in his grasp only highlighted the hypocrisy of his statement, given no one associated with her father's foul deeds evaded accountability. "Declare thy sins, and I shall grant thee dispensation for thy transgressions."

"I am not thy child, and if thou dost conspire with my father, thou art not without crimes against Our Lord." Drawing herself up with noble refinement, she stared down her nose. "Hear me well. I have met pious men, and thou art not one. If my father intends to deflect blame for his actions, he will not do so with my assistance. And while he may take my life, the truth of his involvement remains very much alive, and he will atone for his misdeeds in this world or the next."

With a scowl, the bishop gestured with his hand. "May the Almighty have mercy on thee."

"No." She clenched her fists and stood proud. "May God have mercy on thee, as thou wilt, no doubt, need it."

It was not until the so-called religious man exited that she faltered, as the pain of her wounds weakened her. And then voices echoed from the drain. Hugging the corner, she bent and laughed, as her father cursed her.

"Then let her swing, if she is so intent," he yelled. "I will be glad to be rid of her."

The revelation that her father desired her death should have hurt her, but she suspected he would kill her, with or without a confession. Instead, his hatred did naught but kindle her longing for Arucard. Returning to the window, she conjured her husband's image, fierce in battle against young de Cadby. If possible, her knight would come for her—she would believe that until she drew her last breath.

And so she braided her hair and tugged on her leather calf boots. Just as she tied the lace, Juraj de Mravec appeared, along with a compliment of soldiers. "Lady Isolde, it is time."

#

With her wrists bound in front of her, and a gag tied about her head, Isolde stood proud and strong on the gallows. And while on the outside she portrayed an image of calm, inside she screamed her husband's name. Disgusted, she glared at the crowd that had gathered to see her executed for crimes she did not commit.

"Good citizens of Winchester, thou hast been wronged by my own kin." Father should have been a thespian, as he belonged on a stage, and his ability to fool the masses impressed her. With a hand pressed to his chest, he sighed. "Would that I had known the evil she would mete upon thee, with her husband, the earl of Sussex, as I might have prevented it."

The throng hissed.

"But I will no longer be silent on the evil all but sanctioned by the Crown." Her father strolled to one end of the platform. "Thou hast been abandoned by he who hath been tasked with thy protection. Thou hast been betrayed. No one defends thee."

The crowd jeered and pelted Isolde with rotting refuse. Yet she persisted, refusing to embarrass herself with a public display of terror, as they craved that.

"I have failed ye." Father sobbed. "I should offer myself on the block for thy judgment."

The people composed a malevolent chorale.

"Nay."

"Thou art benevolent."

"Thou art honorable."

"We will follow thee."

How smoothly he lured them, feeding their desires and fears, and she pitied them when she should have hated them.

"Alas, I am old and feeble, though my mind is sharp." He had the poor, unsuspecting dupes in his grasp, and she admired his persuasive skills. "Yet my son is young and robust. If thou wilt but swear allegiance to the same, William would lead thee into prosperity and return thy stolen lands and legacy."

A piercing roar demonstrated the flock's assent, and a tear coursed Isolde's cheek, as the horror played out before her.

"Then let us punish the traitor." In that instant, Father cast her a vicious scowl. "As she hath earned her just reward."

The escort shoved her forward, and the noose slapped her face. The rush of her breath filled her ears, and her heart pounded, as a soldier slipped the rope about her neck.

Then a driverless wagon charged into the square, crashing into various merchant carts, and a wave of panic struck the multitude of subjects assembled to witness her death. Screams reverberated, and de Mravec scrambled to the fore.

"Protect the earl." The eloquent villain wrenched a guard. "Surround Lord Rochester."

Unattended, Isolde flinched, when an unknown attacker swept her from the platform and threw her to a hooded figure. Quick as a flash, the mysterious assailant yanked the gag from her mouth and lifted his head.

"*Aeduuard.*" She rejoiced, and then he grabbed her bound wrists, and they fled. "Whither is Arucard?"

"Hurry, my lady." Signaling his friends, he veered toward an alley but pulled her left to avoid a mountain of casks. "We must reach the main gate before thy father's men capture us."

Together, they bolted down a side street and charged an unfortunate peddler, who shouted a warning. Soon the guard sounded the alarm, and thunderous hoofbeats declared their pursuit. They dashed into the front of a store and exited the rear, but they confronted her father's men at every turn. At one point, de Cadby ducked into a small tavern, until the soldiers passed, and then he retraced their steps and navigated another passage. When two guards challenged them, Aeduuard kicked an enemy into an applecart and then struck the other with a fist.

A slew of townspeople swamped the thoroughfares, and some recognized her. But the sheer confusion provided shelter, as she disappeared into the throng as quickly as she was identified. And all the while she sought Arucard, yet he remained absent.

As they negotiated a maze of lanes, she lost her direction, but her liberator pushed her faster and faster. Nauseated, as her lungs burned for air, she huffed and puffed but refused to yield. Her pulse raced, and at times she thought she might faint, but she launched herself forward and swallowed the bitterness rising in her throat.

In what seemed as several hours, but was in reality only a few minutes, Isolde clung to her rescuer, as they winded and wended their way through the town, with Father's guards in their wake. At last, the decorated egress loomed, and Aeduuard waved a piece of red cloth. With the troops nipping at her heels, she tasted freedom and permitted herself a glimmer of hope.

The weighty wooden panels, a very real obstacle to her liberation, opened and spread wide before her, and Isolde ran straight into a royal patrol. "*No*."

CHAPTER SEVENTEEN

Dressed in the signature black garb of his trade, including the menacing hood, the largest executioner Isolde had ever seen heeled his horse, advanced on her even as she retreated, bent, and scooped her up in one fail swoop. Sitting astride in the lap of a creature every bit as imposing as her husband, she struck his chest with her bound fists. "Brute." Then she glanced at the King's guard and helmeted knights in impressive armor. "Prithee, good sirrah. Sir Arucard is innocent of the baseless charges levied against him, and thou cannot condemn him without a trial. If thou wilt permit me to plead my true and righteous cause before the Crown, I would—"

"His Majesty is aware of the extent of his servant's involvement in the crimes against the Realm and has taken swift and appropriate action." To her father and de Mravec, who had pushed to the front of the crowd, he said, "We will take the culpable parties into custody, and deliver unto them their just punishment." Without hesitation, the guard directed the soldiers, who surrounded her would-be rescuers, and then addressed the executioner with a nod. "Deal with her."

"Wait. Pray, do not harm my people, as they only wanted to help me." Desperate, she peered from side to side, searching for the escape that evaded her. It was in that moment she feared the end of her life, not because she dreaded death but because never again would she look on Arucard's face. That exceptional understanding was enough to send terror into her heart, which she had ruthlessly fortified, so she inhaled a calming gulp of air and resolved to meet her fate on her terms. Locating de Cadby, she mustered a smile. "Thank ye, for trying to save me. And if thou dost not think me ungrateful, I would ask a favor. If thou dost see him, tell my lord Arucard that I love him, and with my last breath his name shall pass my lips."

"My lady." Young Aeduuard opened his mouth, gritted his teeth, and then huffed in apparent frustration. "Believe me, Sir Arucard hears thy plea."

The man who would dispatch her to her maker stretched an arm about her belly, gripped her hip, which mercifully avoided her injuries, and held her tight, as his mount broke into a gallop, taking her from her friends and the possibility of the prayed-for reprieve. With the troops in their wake, they coursed the lane to the outlying and sparsely populated areas of Winchester, whither she surmised he would do the deed.

When her captor discovered her attempting to free her wrists, which had rendered her flesh raw and bloody, he drew rein. As he produced a small dagger, she suspected she had hastened her demise, and so she prepared herself. After a final survey of the surrounding countryside, Isolde focused on the clear cerulean sky and commenced her farewell. "Arucard, I love thee. Arucard. Arucard—"

"Honey flower, I love thee, too."

The cherished declaration had come to her once, in a dream. It had blanketed her in soothing heat. But in that instant she imagined naught, as he cut the ties that bound her. In shock, she shrieked and gazed at the executioner. Grasping his shoulders, she met his stare, and she would know his blue eyes anywhere. "*Arucard.*"

"Easy, Isolde." Wrenching the heavy mask that shrouded his head, she yanked and pulled. "Woman, wilt thou send us tumbling to the ground, whither we might break our necks?"

"Take off thy disguise." While he untied the laces, she twisted, situated her legs at either side of his hips, and scooted ever closer. When he revealed the familiar visage she so treasured, she sobbed in relief, framed his cheeks, and kissed him.

Even though the guard had joined them, she refused to relinquish her knight. It had been too long since she tasted her husband, and she savored the warmth of his flesh, the reassuring strength of his embrace, and the spicy scent that was uniquely his, as it all but surrounded her.

"Isolde, let go, as we must ride, and I have a fresh horse for thee." As Arucard attempted to loosen her grip, she fought him. "Pray, we must return to Chichester, as the King's men march on Winchester to confront thy father, and I would protect thee, yet I expect no confidence, given I have failed ye so miserably."

"How hast thou failed me, and wherefore didst thou not reveal thyself?" Every time he tried to break free, she shifted and gained a better position. "I am alive and in thy arms, whither I belong, and whither I shall stay. Tell me how thou hast foundered?"

"Pray, I could not betray my identity so close to town, as thy father's spies are everywhere. And never should I have parted from thee, as thou didst beg me not to leave thee, and thy father took thee whilst I was away, thus I am to blame for thy suffering." At last, he must have realized the futility of his endeavor, signaled by a sigh of exasperation she knew well, as he tucked his cloak about her, draped a blanket over her legs, cupped her bottom, and cradled her head. "Canst thou ever forgive me?"

"But thou didst come for me, as thou didst promise." Burying her face in his leather tunic, she yawned as the bone-wearying exhaustion took its toll, yet she rejoiced. "And if thou wilt but swear thou wilt keep me at thy side for the remains of thy days, thou art pardoned of thy unfounded transgression."

As blissful sleep beckoned, he proclaimed, "By my troth, thou wilt never be separated from me again."

\#

The journey to Chichester Castle seemed never-ending, as Arucard, with Isolde tucked safe in his lap, drove his stallion harder and faster than ever before. Only once would he stop to relieve himself and doff the leather tunic, that he might warm his wife with his body. To his relief, she never stirred, not even when he handed her to Demetrius. It was then he glimpsed the bloodstained chemise, torn and tattered, as he wrapped her in a borrowed blanket, regained his saddle, and claimed her from his friend.

In a familiar formation, the Brethren of the Coast rode, constructing a protective barrier about Isolde, which each Nautionnier knight would defend to his death. Whereas on previous occasions they often engaged in spirited discourse, that day they remained hushed, and Arucard embraced the silence.

The sun sat low on the horizon when he broke from the King's guard, along with the Brethren, and cut through the meadow of rolling hills. As the Nautionnier knights charged the last embankment, a familiar and welcoming silhouette, precious because it was whither he had first made love to his bride, came into view, and he uttered a silent prayer of thanks.

At the west bank of the moat, Arucard cupped his mouth. "Thither, ho."

"Whither thou dost go?" The call came from the outer gatehouse.

"So go I," Arucard replied. The simple phrase, stark in

its clarity as it symbolized the depth of their union, had been Isolde's idea.

In what seemed an eternity, the drawbridge lowered, and he navigated to the tiny island. As per his commands, the secondary traverse descended only after the first was raised. When he rode into the courtyard, Margery and Pellier emerged.

"Bring thy medicines, as well as the physic, to my chambers." With Isolde in his clutch, he slid from the saddle and carried her into the castle. In seconds, he ran up the stairs and swept her into the solar, just as she woke.

"My lord, we art home." A feminine smile graced her lips, as she gazed at him. But soon he wished she had remained blissfully unaware of her surroundings, as Margery attempted to remove the chemise, which had dried and stuck to the wounds on his wife's back.

Initially, the steward tried to peel off the fabric, as Arucard sat on the bench in the solar, with Isolde facing him and astride in his lap. Resting her chin on his shoulder, his valiant bride flinched and tried but failed to stifle her cries of agony, but he felt every one as a mortal blow, and he suffered each successive whimper as a stain on his heart and mind. At last, mercifully, she fainted and fell limp in his hold.

"Mayhap we should wet the material." Wiping her tears, Margery summoned the servants, who prepared the ancere for Isolde's bath. "Ease her into the water, my lord. But thou must be careful to support her."

"Do what must needs." Kneeling at one end of the tub, he braced Isolde beneath her arms and kissed her, when her head rolled to the side. "Perchance the physic should assist thee."

"Nay, my lord." The steward frowned. "I have nursed my lady since she was but a child. Trust my skills, as she will heal."

Little by little, Margery inched the garment from Isolde's injuries, and then the steward washed away the grime and blood, revealing a foul sight he would never forget, as he almost vomited to contemplate what his wife endured. Words could not describe the evidence of the earl's barbarity, and neither could they adequately encompass the depth of Arucard's rage.

"Oh, my lady." At that moment, Margery pressed a clenched fist to her mouth and sniffed. "Look what her father hath wrought upon her."

"Prithee, finish thy work." It began then—the lust for revenge. The festering hatred. In opposition to the gentle purity of his wife, a malevolent sickness infested his senses. Unfurling slow and steady, as the velvety petals of a delicate spring rose, a foreign but insatiable hunger grew in his belly and spread, investing every fiber of his being until he could taste the repulsive malignance. Given his faith and his oath, he should have repressed such dark inclinations, but he resisted not. Instead, he reveled in the bitterness. As an old friend, he welcomed the plague on his soul. He embraced the malice. Despite his long held beliefs, he would violate his convictions and avenge Isolde.

"My lord, I am done." With a strange expression, Margery shook him. "If thou wilt set Lady Isolde on the bed, on her belly, I can treat her."

Lost in a haze of confusion, Arucard blinked and assessed the situation, as he would not risk rousing his wife. "Summon Demetrius."

"Aye, sir." Margery strolled into the hall but returned minutes later.

"How can I help thee?" Demetrius glanced at Isolde's condition, compressed his lips, and swallowed hard. "By God's bones, Arucard. How could any man visit such violence on a woman, much less his daughter?"

That was a question Arucard no longer asked, as thither was no adequate answer.

"Take her feet, brother." Arucard stood upright, lifting her with him, and she moaned, as Margery dried his wife with a towel. "Have care," he whispered, "as I would not wake her."

"Of course," Demetrius replied in a low voice.

Together, they conveyed Isolde to the bed, and with caution they turned her facedown and lowered her to the mattress. Margery pulled a sheet to Isolde's hips. After situating a chair, the steward began the difficult task of smoothing salve to his wife's back.

"This will require some time, my lord." Margery began her work at the left shoulder. "Mayhap thou might use the boar's hair brush to remove the tangles from thy wife's locks, as they will dry faster, and I will braid them."

"Arucard, if thou dost need me, I will be in the great hall." Shuffling his feet, Demetrius gazed at Isolde and rubbed his neck. "I am more sorry than I can say, as she is a very fine, kind-hearted lady."

"Thank ye, brother." On the outside, all appeared calm as Arucard retrieved Isolde's simple appurtenance, which he had seen her use on countless nights, before they retired. But inside a tempest of unutterable contempt waged war for his soul, and Lord Rochester would rue Arucard's wrath. Yet he perched on the opposite side and drew the brush through Isolde's hair, in slow and repetitive movements. The simple occupation should have soothed his ire, but it only fueled it.

Molten fury poured through his veins and festered in his senses, in stark contrast to his wife's motionless form. As the minutes ticked past, the rage smoldered and gathered strength. And while he toiled in silence, a primitive howl echoed in his brain.

"Thither, it is done." With her job complete, Margery draped strips of boiled linen over Isolde's back and then drew the sheet and blankets to his wife's neck. "When she wakes, I will give her some hops and thyme in her tea, to make her sleep, as she needs to heal and recover."

"Canst thou keep her unaware of my temporary absence?" A plot formed, a means of securing retribution took shape, as he pondered the King's plans, but he would abandon his scheme if it caused Isolde added trauma. "I must join His Majesty's guard, but I will return in a matter of days, a sennight at most."

"Aye, sir." For a while, Margery studied him. Then she sobered and nodded once. "Thou mayest rely on me, as Pellier and I will guard the Lady Isolde with our lives."

"Thank ye." With steely determination as a shield, he bent and kissed his brave heroine. In her ear, he whispered, "Rest easy, honey flower. I am with thee always."

Then he stood, strode from his chambers, and marched into the great hall. The center of activity in the grand castle usually reverberated with mirth and cheer, but not on that eventide. Palpable sadness as thick as London fog hung over the cavernous room. Evidence of Isolde's benevolence surrounded him, visible in the faces of those for whom she cared and nurtured.

"Arucard, thither is food and drink." Aristide offered a tankard of ale, but Arucard refused it.

"Fill thy belly, as duty calls." To Pellier, Arucard said, "Saddle fresh horses and pack our armor, as we would travel light with all due haste." Then he pounded a table, and a hush fell on the crowd. "Hear me well. Thy Lady Isolde hath returned, and thou art to defend these walls at any expense. Whosoever permits anyone to breach our home shall pay with his life, as thy last mistake almost cost my wife hers. Now make ready, as tonight the Brethren ride into battle." Thrusting his fist into the air, Arucard proclaimed, "For King, for Chichester, and for Isolde."

#

The battle for control of Winchester commenced the following morrow. Side by side, in an impressive display of military might, the Nautionnier Knights of the Brethren of the Coast rode into the storm, wearing the unique ailette with the wind-star design. Yet Arucard fought not for His Majesty, his faith, or his honor.

As he charged into the fray, unconcerned for his own

being, he suspected he had left the noblest part of himself in Chichester, with Isolde, to shield her whilst she recovered, as he owed her that much. That bit of himself, unspoiled and unsullied, belonged to her. What remained was the beast inside him, and the animal was hungry on that fateful day.

Killing indiscriminately, he maimed, beheaded, impaled, and slaughtered untold numbers, ignoring their cries for mercy, as no one had spared his wife. Whereas before he always struggled with guilt when taking a life, in those miserable hours he suffered no such compunction and, therefore, tempered not his rage.

Given no one had pardoned her, he would extend no reprieve. Every enemy combatant he struck down he counted as right and good retribution for Isolde, as none of them had defended her, and no matter how many souls he claimed it was not enough. It would never be enough. Not until he came face to face with the person responsible for her suffering—the earl of Rochester.

"*Tyreswelle.*" Arucard urged his destrier into a gallop. "Thou art mine."

Metal clashed with metal, as they waged war amid the stench of damp earth mixed with blood, and sunlight flickered on the flat of the blades, but it was no contest, given the villain posed no real threat to a man unafraid of death. With a single swing of his sword, Arucard knocked Isolde's father from his horse. As Arucard could have predicted, the pathetic bastard surrendered without so much as a single challenge.

"I yield." The earl tossed down his weapon and splayed his palms. "And I demand thee deliver me unto His Majesty."

"Thou art in no position to make demands." Arucard leaped from his saddle and assumed a provocative stance. "Now pick up thy sword."

"Nay." The bastard spat at Arucard's feet. "I am the earl of Rochester, Reinfrid de Tyreswelle, and head of one of England's oldest noble families. Whither art thou from, and who art thy connections, de Villiers?"

"The Sovereign is my connection." Arucard lowered his chin and bared his teeth. "And I ride straight from hell to claim recompense for thy daughter." Then he lunged.

"Sir Arucard, wait." Briarus drove his horse between Arucard and his prey. "Prithee, good sirrah. Remember, His Majesty commands we take the earl alive."

"Am I not allowed to touch him? Am I granted no measure of retribution?" Gripping the hilt of his sword, he threw off his helmet. "What of his treachery? And what of de Mravec? Will the Crown pardon their evil deeds? Thither is no justice in this land?"

"While I understand thy anger, and I share thy views, I must obey the King's orders." The sergeant drew a section of rope from his sack and tossed it to Arucard. "If thou wilt bind his wrists, that I may transport Rochester to His Majesty's encampment."

"I told thee." With a sneer, the earl presented his arms. "We art a civilized people, Sir Arucard. And I am far too valuable to kill like some commoner."

It would have been so easy to slide the blade of his sword into the small indention at the base of his father-in-law's neck. With a simple twist and tug, he could separate Rochester's head from his body, and never again could the villain harm Isolde. That was Arucard's goal, to protect his wife from the one person who should have been her most fervent champion.

"Mayhap that is true." With purpose, Arucard wound one end of the twine and tied it tight, until the earl flinched. "But if thou dost come near thy daughter again, I will slit thy noble throat." Then he tossed the rope to Briarus.

"Thank ye." The guard dipped his chin. "As the battle is won, His Majesty requests thy presence in his tent." Clucking his tongue, Briarus snickered. "And I shall join thee anon, as the earl shall walk to camp."

With Rochester's complaints echoing above the din of conflict, Arucard retrieved his helmet, jumped to the saddle of his stallion, and steered for the northern territory. Along the way, he counted his friends and sighed with relief, as the Brethren remained bloody but unscathed. As his mount soared up the embankment, he thought of Isolde, his lady, his love.

Given her father had been arrested but had cheated the Dark Angel, Arucard wondered what to tell her. As long as the earl lived, he would present a very real danger to her. Somehow, Arucard needed to scare the man. That was his primary goal when he entered the King's tent.

But rage surged anew when he discovered Juraj de Mravec kneeling before the Crown. Without hesitation, Arucard lunged, grabbed de Mravec by the neck, and struck him. As the co-conspirator slumped on the ground, Arucard drew his sword and leveled the pointed end just beneath the man's chin. "Say thy prayers."

"Sir Arucard, we demand thee halt thy attack." Waving, His Majesty summoned his guards, and Arucard found himself grossly outnumbered, but it mattered not. When the Sovereign rested a hand to Arucard's shoulder, he lowered his weapon. "We understand thy anger, but we cannot permit thee to kill our appointed servant when he hath performed to our expectations."

In that moment, naught made sense.

Confused, Arucard stumbled back and landed in a fortuitously placed chair. Leaning forward, with his elbows propped on his thighs, he stared at the intricate pattern on the rug and struggled to breathe. "Forgive me, Majesty, but de Mravec schemed with the earl to undermine thy authority and seize control of Winchester."

"And so he was directed." The King perched on his temporary throne. "The previous earl of Sussex initiated the original plan with an unknown collaborator who eluded our attempts at discovery. We dispatched our agent to investigate, befriend, and collude with the mysterious conniver."

"So he is to go free, along with de Tyreswelle?" Huffing in frustration, Arucard stood and paced. "Is no one to pay for their crimes against the Crown, if not my wife? Does the rule of law mean naught in this country?"

Rubbing his jaw, de Mravec scrambled to his feet. "Arucard—"

"*Sir* Arucard to thee, as we art not now nor shall we ever be friends." If not for the soldiers present, he would have dispatched the earl's partner in heinous deeds, despite the King's directives. "Thou art without honor, given what thou didst allow to happen to Isolde."

"Upon my word, I tried to spare her, as I am not thy enemy." As he emerged from behind the guards, de Mravec extended his hand but retreated as Arucard shook his head. "Her father is an animal, and he would have killed her when he beat her in the square, had I not interceded."

"By recommending he hang her on the following morrow." Quick as a flash, he swooped and grasped fistfuls of de Mravec's tunic. "And thou dost consider that sparing my wife?" He wrenched hard on his adversary. "Hear me well, His Majesty may call thee an associate, but if thou dost ever show thy face in Chichester, I will kill thee on sight, consequences be damned."

"Thy anger is legitimate, thus I take no offense. But thy rescue triumphed because I assisted in thy plan, and thou should think on that." Casting a mock salute, de Mravec glanced at the King. "By thy leave, Majesty." As de Mravec exited, Briarus entered.

"Didst thou know of his involvement?" Of course, he asked the question with grave trepidation, as he could abide no betrayal. "Art thou in collusion with de Mravec?"

"Nay." With a mighty scowl, Briarus narrowed his stare. "I knew naught of his affiliation until last eventide, when his messenger arrived with detailed reports regarding the number and location of Rochester's forces."

"Is our guest comfortable?" The King poured three goblets of wine. "Shall we toast to a victorious enterprise?"

"In light of Isolde's condition, I do not consider our maneuvers successful." Despite inclinations otherwise, Arucard accepted the drink. "And if His Majesty hath no further duties, I would journey to Chichester and remain at my wife's side, as she recovers."

"How long until her health improves?" Briarus inquired. "And Lord Rochester objects to the size of his accommodation, which he claims, quite vociferously, he will take up with His Majesty."

"The bastard almost beat his daughter to death and would have executed her had we not rescued her, and he grouses about his quarters?" In no mood for drink, Arucard set down the still full goblet. "He is lucky to draw breath. And Margery estimates it will take a fortnight, at minimum, for the worst injuries to heal."

"Perchance it will ease her worries to know her father will not survive to see her restored." His Majesty met Arucard's gaze and smiled. "We have always intended to execute those responsible for the illegal burgage plots, but we required proof of culpability to mete justice, as we art not cruel." The Sovereign arched a brow. "As thou dost lead thy men, thou dost know the difficulties of rule, and a king confronts all manner of insurrection, which only increases with time, from the moment he takes the throne. We must not act in haste or without reason. On that note, we would have thy promise to protect and defend our heir, should we meet our fate. Swear thy allegiance to our newborn son, and thou canst discuss with Briarus a way to secure a measure of reprisal for Lady Isolde's injuries. But have care, and do not mark Lord Rochester's face, as we would have him pretty when we display his head on a pike outside White Tower."

CHAPTER EIGHTEEN

It was late when the earl of Rochester finished his bath and stepped from the ancere. After drying himself with a towel, he searched for his robe, muttered something about the dismal conditions of his tent, and speared his fingers through his wet hair. Naked, he scowled as he continued to comb through his belongings, presumably in quest for the garment Arucard held in his grasp.

From the shadows, Arucard emerged. "Looking for something?"

"What art thou doing hither?" Sneering, the villain narrowed his stare. "Get thee gone, before I summon the King's guard and have thee arrested."

So many rebukes filled his ears, as thither Arucard stood, facing down his sworn enemy. Never in his life had he thirsted for blood—craved it, but in that moment he desired the earl's death. Yet His Majesty forbade Arucard from killing his father-in-law. But thither were other ways to make the bastard pay for his crimes against Isolde.

Quick as a wink, Arucard charged his adversary. Using the robe as a gag, he shoved the material into the man's mouth, muffling his protests. While the earl flailed and scratched, he was no match for a Nautionnier knight almost twice his size. With a discarded tunic and a towel, Arucard tied the earl's wrists to either end of the bed frame. Then he kicked the man's feet from beneath him, so he knelt on the ground.

"Thy back is pristine, so unlike thy daughter's." Trailing his fingers down the unmarred flesh, Arucard fought the urge to slit Rochester's throat. "But I wonder how thee would suffer the punishment thou hast meted without mercy upon her."

As it dawned on the earl what Arucard intended, the coward struggled against his bindings to no avail, pissed himself, and emitted a series of pathetic mewling and whimpering that only inflamed Arucard's fury. Recalling that night after he found the letter from her father, when she displayed incomparable bravery in advance of the discipline she anticipated, he resolved to complete his task. Slow and steady, he unhooked and removed his belt.

For a scarce second, he hesitated. According to his long held beliefs, vengeance was not his to dispatch, yet visions of his wife flashed before him. In his mind he conjured images of her raven hair, her shy smile, her rosy cheeks as he bathed her, and her green eyes so vivid in the early morrow sunlight. Then the memory of her limp and abused body, tied to a stake and pelted with rotting food, intruded on his thoughts and girded his resolve.

Standing at attention, he inhaled a deep breath and swung wide. Brandishing the thick leather strap, moving back and forth, again and again, he whipped the earl, dispensing the justice so righteously deserved. At last, he let go the rage, unleashed the hellfire, and purged the molten ire simmering within him. And as the sad excuse for a nobleman wept and lost his bowels, Arucard counted the tears as an insult to his wife, who bore the brutality as a valiant heroine.

Without compunction, Arucard beat his heartless foe

until he could wield no more retribution. Satisfied, he stumbled back, exhausted from overexertion, and threw his belt to the ground as he studied the bloody welts that streaked the earl's skin.

Moaning and whining, the earl flinched when Arucard grasped a fistful of the milksop's hair. Whispering into Tyreswelle's ear, Arucard said, "My sweet Isolde, for all her feminine attributes, is more a man than thou wilt ever be." With that, he stormed from the tent. Outside, he located Briarus. "Gramercy, good sirrah."

"Shall I presume his lordship prefers not to be disturbed?" The King's guard cast a lop-sided grin and snickered. "Or should I send for the physic?"

"Let him stew in his own mire, as it will do him well, given His Majesty's plans." Rubbing the back of his neck, he glanced at the full moon peeking through the thinning clouds and exhaled. "Now, I shall decamp for Chichester, as thither I would be when my wife wakes."

And never again would he part from her.

"I understand." As if sensing the urgency, Briarus led Arucard to his destrier. "Sir Demetrius packed thy armor with his, that ye might enjoy a faster ride. The roads art passable but dangerous in the dark." He grabbed a torch. "Take this to light the way."

"Thank ye." After securing his cloak against the wind and new fallen snow, Arucard leaped into his saddle. "Fare thee well, Briarus."

"And the same to thee, my lord." The guard saluted. "And I wish improved health and a quick recovery for the Lady Isolde. Prithee, convey my deepest felicitations."

"I will give her thy regard." Heeling the flanks of his stallion, Arucard rode from the encampment and veered to the south, keeping to the verge to avoid ruts, and he struggled with an emotional tempest waging battle within him as he spurred his mount. How far he had traveled he knew not, when he reached the top of a hill, reined in, and stretched. Wrestling with sorrow he could ill contain, he dismounted and strolled to the precipice of a seemingly bottomless drop. Finally, he knelt and gazed at the sky.

Countless stars flickered amid a blanket of indigo, as the earlier storm dissipated, and he bowed his head and wept. In silent reflection, he closed his eyes and made his confession, but never would he regret his actions. Unburdening his sins, he yielded to the anguish investing his frame, as thither were no winners in the day's events. "Forgive me, My Lord, if thy servant hath disappointed thee. Alas, I am but a man in love with his wife."

Braced for swift judgment and ensuing punishment, he relaxed, as a gentle breeze buffeted him, and yet time ticked past with nary a lightning strike. In that moment, he smiled and nodded once. And so Arucard regained his horse and steered for home and Isolde.

#

Her world had been consumed by a series of dreams and nightmares, some vivid in detail and others less so, which haunted Isolde's seemingly endless sleep. How many days had she languished, she knew not whether it was morrow or night? "Arucard." Beneath the covers, she shifted on her belly and reached for him. "Arucard. Whither art thou, Arucard?"

"Shh." His voice came to her through a haze of confusion brought about by Margery's special tea. "Rest easy, honey flower. As I guard thy slumber with my life."

In an instant, she awakened, as only her husband called her by the telltale pet name she cherished. To her surprise, she met his stare, as he sat on the floor beside their bed. "Hither art thou, when I have called thee, time and again, and thou hast not answered. Wherefore hast thou not responded, when I need thee?"

"His Majesty summoned me into action, but Pellier and Margery never left thee alone." Brushing a lock of hair from her face, he smiled and kissed her. "But I am returned to defend thee, sweet Isolde. And as our Heavenly Father is my witness, never again shall I part from thee."

"Thou art unusually dramatic, my champion." It was then she realized he kept a blanket, and an awful reality, which had tormented her dreams, dawned. "Wherefore art thou on the stone?"

"I would not disturb thee." He pressed his lips to her forehead, but the display of affection did nothing to dispel her worries. "And I would not risk injuring thee, so hither I shall remain."

"Verily, is it so?" Burying her face in her pillow, Isolde sobbed. "Or dost thou no longer desire me, as I am beaten, and my cheek is bruised?"

"Nay, honey flower." Arucard tried to address her, but desolation and despair encased her heart, and she wept, as she feared she had lost him. "Prithee, Isolde. Do not cry, as my concern is thy comfort."

"How can I find comfort if thou wilt not share our bed or thy body?" The mattress dipped as he joined her, and she peered at him and sniffed. "Tell me the truth. I am ugly, and thou dost find me unappealing. I knew it would happen, and Father was right. I am chitty-faced."

"Never, and I forbid thee to make such outrageous statements in my presence, as the mere suggestion is a vile abomination." With care, he reclined, lifted her atop him, and drew the covers to her chin. "Isolde, thou hast never been more beauteous than thou art now, as thou art alive, and that is my sole requirement of thee."

"Then lie with me." Naked but for the strips of boiled linen shielding her wounds, she sat upright. "Pray, take pity, as I need thee."

"Nay, Isolde." Grasping her wrists, he just stopped her from untying his garb. "Thou art weak and vulnerable, and I would not take thee in that condition, as I might cause thee pain."

"Prithee, thy rejection hurts far worse, my lord, as I love thee, and I require thy strength." At her declaration, he eased his hold, and she discovered him hard and ready for her, which somewhat belied her fears but did naught to quell the hunger for his touch. For Isolde, it was too much. To her shame, she broke. Slumping, she shed tears of relief, as her husband cupped her bottom with one hand and hugged her tenderly with the other. "It is true. Thou dost want me, when I thought otherwise."

"Aye, I ache for thee, as it hath been too long since I stirred thy sweet waters." Then he shuffled her in his embrace, doffing his tunic, breeches, and braies in an awkward and clumsy dance. "And never doubt my devotion to thee, as thou hast my heart, for two lifetimes. Yet, when today is but a memory, the whispering wind no longer kisses thy cheeks, and time ceases to exist for us, I will love thee still. Never forget that. Now scoot forward, honey flower, and let me show thee the depth of my regard."

Abiding his request, she tilted her hips, joining their bodies, and it was as if she had, at long last, come home. As Arucard stretched her flesh and filled her, he rose to support her, and she hugged him about his shoulders. Familiar heat beckoned as an old friend, spreading from the pit of her belly, fanning the flames of desire that supplanted her pain and the horrors of the past. Gaining speed, she rocked, even as he grunted and groaned in completion, but she rode him faster still. And then reality fractured and time suspended, as she clung to her husband and screamed.

After the rapturous moment passed, she sighed, as he cradled her to his chest. For a while, they simply sat thither, enjoying comfort bestowed by their tender reunion. "Margery and Pellier art to wed."

"Aye, he told me." He rubbed her scalp in a soothing rhythm. "I had thought, mayhap, Margery might write her kin and have them live hither, with us, given their current employment is ended."

"She would adore that." Then Isolde seized upon his meaning. "What news of my father?"

"He is for the ax." Shuffling her in his embrace, Arucard caressed her cheek. "I am sorry, my love, but thither is naught I can do to redeem him, thus he is condemned."

"Do not be, as his outcome is of his making." Despite what her father did to her, she did not welcome his death. "And my brother?"

"I suspect the same, as he conspired with the Lancasters to take the throne, and His Majesty is unforgiving, in that respect." He tipped her chin, brushed his lips to hers, and frowned. "But thou must have no fear, as the King knows of thy innocence."

"But I am not worried, my champion, when I am in thy arms, and hither I shall stay." Without thought, she tensed her thighs, and he hissed. Smiling, she kissed his chest and thrust her hips, and he groaned. "Thou art hungry again, and I am in a mood to feed thee thy most favored fare."

"Aye, I always want thee, but I would sooner cut my throat than risk injuring thee." As she began the delicate dance, he closed his eyes, set his forehead to hers, and gritted his teeth. "Isolde, how I love thee. And I would give thee everything thy heart desires, if thou would but share thy hopes and aspirations, that I might fulfill them."

"But thou hast already given me so much. In truth, I indulged in few fantasies, as a young girl, given my father treated me with cruelty, I knew naught of love, and I was always alone. I never conjured images of a handsome knight, riding to my rescue, but it seems fate had other plans and gifted ye." She increased her pace, and together they soared. "And with thee as my teacher, I am learning to dream."

#

Sound asleep, Isolde draped across Arucard, with their bodies still joined. It had taken two additional rounds of lovemaking, after the first brief but fiery coupling, to satisfy her, yet she refused to disengage him, as she would prolong their affinity, and he had not the strength to deny her. With a grimace, he stretched to reach the edge of the blanket but halted when his wife murmured incoherently. When a charming smiled graced her lush lips, which tempted him even now, she sighed and then quieted, he pulled the covers over them, mindful of her injured back, and tucked the bedclothes beneath her chin.

Just as he shielded them, Margery entered the chamber. With a start, she averted her stare. "I beg thy pardon, my lord. But thou didst ask me to check my lady, in the event thou didst sleep."

"It is all right," he responded in a low voice, as he set a palm to his wife's ear, that she might doze, undisturbed. "Have a light meal delivered to the solar in the morrow, and I will feed my lady when she wakes. Prepare a bath at noon, and I shall wash her. Afterward, I shall summon thee to tend her wounds. And continue to brew thy special tea, until the worst of Isolde's pain has passed, as I would spare her additional needless suffering."

"Yea, my lord." The steward curtseyed and gave him her back. "Wilt thou require anything else?"

"Aye." He snorted as the servant fidgeted, but then he checked to ensure he bared naught unintended. "I commission thee to write thy parents and bid them to live hither, at Chichester Castle, as an early wedding gift from Lord and Lady Sussex."

"God be praised." With a hand over her mouth, Margery smothered a sob, but her surprise was evident as she shook. "Thank ye, my lord. Thou art most kind."

"Thou art most welcome, and thou art excused." Drawing an extra pillow beneath his head, he adjusted his hold on his wife. "And close the inner doors, as I would ensure Isolde's uninterrupted rest."

Peaceful quiet fell on the private quarter he shared with his lady. Staring at the flames in the hearth, a sweet refrain echoed in his brain, as he revisited her boisterous exultations of pleasure, and with his finger he drew tiny circles on her bare bottom, which never failed to fascinate him. In response, she wiggled her hips and clenched her muscles, hugging him in an intimate embrace, and he wanted her again, but he would not rouse her.

Instead, he savored the obsessive desire, the constant beat of her heart, and the subtle rush of her breath to his flesh, proof that she remained very much a part of his world. It was a peculiar feeling—love. Crafty and furtive, the singular emotion seeped into his veins, simmered in his blood, and pervaded every aspect of his being, and he was powerless to stop it, not that he would. When they stood before the archbishop and made their vows, he did not anticipate the powerful commitment that now overwhelmed him. Rather, he had hoped for abiding friendship, an allegiance he deemed reasonable, in light of their arranged marriage and utter unfamiliarity. But thither was naught reasonable about the all-consuming devotion he coveted for her.

"Arucard." Gasping, Isolde shivered violently, flailed her legs, and whimpered, and her distress tore at his heart. "Whither art thou, Arucard?"

"Shh, honey flower." With his thumb, he caressed her cheek until she relaxed. "Hither am I, and hither shall I remain."

The truth of his proclamation, invested with steely resolution he would defend to his death, supplanted the most important oath he had ever sworn, excepting his nuptials. While his brothers might frown on Arucard's priorities, he owed Isolde his very existence, as she manifested his center, and he would have it no other way. So the next time he undertook the Brethren oath, in his mind he would alter the last sentence: *For love and Isolde he lived.*

EPILOGUE

"Admit it, thou art trying to kill me with pleasure." Arucard pinched Isolde's bottom, and she shrieked. "But what a way to meet my fate."

"Thou art free to reject my advances, my lusty lord." Sprawled atop her husband, she placed a kiss on his chest and then sighed. "But keep thy voice down, as thy daughter sleeps. If thou dost wake her, thou must deal with her."

"When dost thou expect Margery to collect our child?" When he hugged her tight, she cuddled close. "As I would have thee to myself, once the deed is done. And I intend to suckle thy sumptuous petals and make thee scream, this eventide."

Ah, yea. The deed.

An official proclamation arrived only yesterday, and her husband dreaded apprising Demetrius of impending events, which would forever change his life. How odd it was that Arucard would deliver the news on the first anniversary of their wedding.

"I suppose we should rise and garb ourselves for the

singular occasion." Yet Isolde shifted beneath the warm blankets. "My lord, I do love our lazy days spent in private, especially when the weather turns unseasonably cold."

"As do I." To her surprise, he sat upright and carried her with him. "Let us have done with it, that we might commence the celebration of our nuptials, to which I look forward."

"Very well." Naked, she crossed her arms and strolled to the washbasin, while he tended the fire in the hearth. As she soaped her face, he hugged her from behind and kissed the back of her neck. Rinsing the suds from her eyes, she giggled. "My insatiable lord, thou dost tempt me, and I will not be held responsible for my actions."

"Isolde, dost thou remember when I said thou dost hold my heart?" In play, he nipped the crest of her ear.

"Aye." When he cupped her breasts, she moaned, reached and grasped his thighs. "It is one of my most cherished memories."

"I was wrong." At his declaration, she turned in his grasp, preparing to protest, and he rubbed his nose to hers. "Thou art my heart."

With a cry of delight, she jumped on him, and they fell into bed.

Anon, as she again collapsed atop him, spent and sated, she started when someone knocked at the door. "My lord, I do not think I can move."

"Prithee, a moment." In one fail swoop, Arucard rolled her over, kissed her with a loud smack, and then leaped from the mattress. After retrieving his robe, he belted it tight. "Honey flower, I love thee. Now don thy attire, as thou hast promised to help me with Demetrius, and I believe he will take it better with thee in his presence."

As he stepped into the outer room, he closed the door to their inner chamber, and she reluctantly repeated her earlier grooming.

Seconds later, he reappeared and whispered, "It is Margery, come to take little Roswitha."

It warmed her that he took such tender care, as he bent and scooped their daughter into his arms, along with Isolde's cherished Bartholomew baby. When their child cooed, he smiled and kissed her forehead. Then he rocked gently, as he carried her into the solar.

With her hose in place, Isolde pulled on a chemise, just as Arucard re-entered their sanctuary. "So, it is done?"

"Aye." As she anticipated, he made straight for her. "We art alone until the morrow, when Margery will return Roswitha to us, my lady."

"And now we must tend Sir Demetrius." She expelled a breath, as he suckled her bottom lip and then chuckled. "And, between the two, I believe Margery hath the easier task." Then something occurred to her. "My lord, how didst thee react to the revelation, when it was thy turn?"

"I should clothe myself." In a flash, he whirled about and all but dove into his trunk. "I need fresh braies and hose. And I would wear my burgundy tunic, which thou didst sew with thy own sweet fingers."

"Arucard?" With hands on hips, she tapped her foot on the stone floor. "Answer me."

"In truth, I vomited before the King." Rotating until he faced her, he cast a charming pout. "It was humiliating. But, in fairness, I knew not the bounty that awaited, and never have I regretted fulfilling my duty and taking thee to wife."

"Given our union was arranged, I shared thy trepidation, though not in such spectacular fashion." After pulling a gown over her head, she gave him her back. Without prompting, he tied her laces. "Am I still thy duty?"

All activity ceased.

Biting her tongue, she turned and peered at her husband, and the pain in his visage was evident.

"Isolde, I love thee." He trailed a finger along the

curve of her cheek. "And while I admit I harbored more than a little apprehension as we took our vows, that changed when I lifted thy veil and glimpsed thee, as thou art no duty such as I have ever known. But the love and devotion came anon, when thou didst kneel on the ground and bare thy marked flesh, in preparation to receive thy punishment after I found the letter from thy father. Thou didst win me with thy bravery."

"Thou were so angry." When he flicked his fingers, she wrapped her arms about his waist, and he cradled her close. "I thought thou would never desire me, if thou didst know of my scars."

"On the contrary." Shifting her in his grasp, Arucard bent and kissed her. "Thou art glorious, and thy wounds bear testament to thy strength and courage. If I could have spared thee the torment, I would have done so. But as I cannot change what hath already happened, I would have thee no other way. And thou art not my duty. Thou art my life."

Noises in the solar signaled their meal had been delivered.

"My champion, let us impart the joyous report, that Sir Demetrius may enjoy similar good fortune." Then Isolde rubbed his crotch. "As I would savor thy company, unreservedly, for the remains of the day and night, and I want thee naked for every minute of it."

"Honey flower, I will make thee pay in coin of thy supple flesh for thy enticement." He squeezed her bottom and thrust his hips. "But now we must host my friend, and thou must play thy part."

"It will not be difficult, given I love thee." With a wink, she eased into her slippers and then set wide the doors.

At the table, an alluring feast had been served to her exacting specification, which included the burly knight's favorite dishes. Just as she poured the tankards of ale, the guest of honor arrived.

"Am I late?" Although Sir Demetrius was not as large in stature as Arucard, he was nonetheless imposing, especially in light of his unique coloring. Whereas Arucard boasted dark brown hair and deep baby blues, Demetrius was known for his raven locks and pale, almost silver eyes, which often unnerved her in their clarity, as he appeared possessed by some foul demon.

"Nay, brother." Arucard slapped Demetrius on the shoulder. "Come in and sup with my bride and I, on our special day."

"I wish ye merry and must confess I was surprised to receive thy invitation." Chuckling, Demetrius straddled the bench, and Arucard followed suit. "Rest assured, I will not linger."

While the men talked of various interests, Isolde dished ample portions. As she made to sit beside her husband, he grabbed her by the hips and lifted her to his lap.

"No worries, old friend." As a show of affection, Arucard broke off a large piece of cameline meat brewet, shoved it into her mouth, and she choked. "Ah, it is good to be a husband."

"My lord, if I may, perchance thou might offer a smaller bite?" With her napkin, she wiped her chin and coughed. "And I am more than capable of feeding myself."

"My lady, is that a sambocade cheesecake?" Demetrius licked his lips.

"Indeed." She glanced at Arucard and winked. "I dried the elderflowers, myself."

"Only a wife would think of such simple pleasures," Arucard added.

"Thou art too kind, gentlewoman." Wolfing down an impressive amount of buttered wortes, Demetrius narrowed his stare. "But what need have I of such a creature, when Lady Isolde doth indulge my preferences so well?"

Arucard gazed at Isolde, and together they blinked.

"Well, have I shown thee my new tunic?" With unmasked pride, Arucard stretched upright. "My wife created this for me."

"Ah, yea." Demetrius tugged at his collar. "She made mine, and it is a perfect fit."

When Arucard frowned at her, she shrugged.

"God's bones, brother." At last, Arucard propped his elbow on the table and groaned. Then he drew the King's letter from beneath his napkin and tossed it to Demetrius. "Soon, thou wilt have no need of my wife's skills as a cook and a tailor."

"I do not understand." Demetrius scratched his temple and peered at the missive.

"Read it." Arucard nodded once.

As Demetrius unfolded the note, Arucard caressed her bottom and pulled her closer. For some strange reason, Isolde held her breath as the tension grew.

Then Demetrius jerked, toppled his tankard, and blanched. "Great abyss of misery, I am to marry."

EXCERPT OF *LOVE WITH AN IMPROPER STRANGER*

The Descendants
Brussels, Belgium
September 30, 1814

"Hurry, Lucilla." Hefting the small trunk of her belongings, Lenore Teversham huffed and puffed, as she glanced at her younger sister and all but ran along the sidewalk. The lanes, a muddy mess after recent rains, bustled with activity, as she dodged elegantly dressed ladies and gentlemen. "We must not be late, or we may have to search out another ride home. Given our financial situation, I am not sure I can procure appropriate boarding to sustain us any longer."

After the Allies drove the French from Belgium, and their father died from wounds suffered in battle, she and her awkward sibling had begged, borrowed, and pleaded their way to the city, wherein they secured return passage to London from one of Papa's friends. While the British Army transported the war dead home, it made no provisions for survivors, and she had been left to her own enterprises.

Alone and in dire straits, Lenore had put aside pride and sold precious trinkets to purchase coach fare from Ghent to Brussels. Now all she needed was the assistance of General Stapleton Cotton and his associate, a naval captain of some estimation with space on his ship for two hapless vagabonds.

"Nag, nag, nag." Lucy clucked her tongue. "Stop crowing, Lenny. You sound like an old woman."

"I have told you numerous times not to call me that in public." When they arrived at a large intersection, she studied the road and frowned. "Oh, dear. I will never navigate that muck without soiling the hem of my dress, and I did so wish to make a good impression on our benefactor." Just then, a gust of wind caught her favorite hat, which landed amid the soggy mire in the middle of traffic.

"Well, you may kiss that goodbye." With a mischievous grin, Lucy snickered. "As you will never recover it in one piece."

"Watch me." With her steely gaze fixed on the much cherished, lavender felt fashion item, decorated with a jaunty white feather, she set down her trunk. "Stay here."

A passing team gave her pause, and then a curricle raced past, but Lenore remained determined, as she refused to cede anything by accident. On tiptoes, she evaded a large pool of water and skipped beyond the path of a brougham, but the driver shook his fist at her, which she ignored. She hopped left and then right and finally neared her goal, with nary a spot on her frock.

So focused on her prize, she scarcely heeded the hoofbeats until it was too late. The ground shook beneath her feet, a thunderous roar filled her ears, and then the largest most menacing stallion she had ever seen trounced her beloved adornment and spattered her with clumps of mud, as it sped by in a rush.

"Sorry." The rogue rider slowed.

"*Blackguard.*" To her unmitigated embarrassment, she spat dirt from her mouth and wiped her face. Then she glanced up and beheld Satan—if the Lord of Darkness sported thick brown hair and vivid blue eyes that danced with pure evil. "Look what you have done to my gown, and that beast destroyed my hat."

"Big words for a little lady, and lucky for you I do not offend easily." He reined in and circled her. Garbed with precision, her hellish antagonist sported polished Hessians, buckskin breeches, a chocolate brown waistcoat, a dark blue coat, and a pristine cravat with a diamond twinkling at center. Then his gaze traveled her from head to toe, and she shifted. "You have spirit, and I like that in my women, but I have a prior appointment, so we cannot explore the possibilities, which I suspect would be delicious."

"How dare you." Despite her somewhat disheveled appearance, she stomped her slippered foot, which became stuck in the slimy filth, and the last of her pride drowned in a pile of nasty ooze. "I will have you know my father was a hero in His Majesty's service."

"Calm yourself." He chuckled, in a rich baritone that seemed to kiss her everywhere. "I paid you a compliment, my dear. But I cannot delay, as much as I would love to become better acquainted with you. Alas, I am already late." To her shock, he saluted, reached into his pocket, retrieved a bag of coins, and flung it at her. "For your trouble."

Then he turned and heeled the flanks of his horse, which showered her in a fresh coat of silt, and Lenore gave vent to an uncharacteristic and unladylike shriek of fury. Unable to pull her shoe from the sludge, she yielded the fight and hobbled back to the sidewalk, where Lucy waited.

"If you say one word—"

"My lips are sealed, sister." But Lucy snorted, and Lenore wanted to cry, as she picked up her trunk.

It was a lengthy, miserable journey to the business district and an exercise in humiliation for Lenore, as passersby gawked at her unsavory attire. By the time they arrived at the inn where the Cotton's lodged, her hose was in tatters along with her tenacity. The servant girl who answered the door stared down her nose, and Lenore snuffled.

"The Tevershams to see General Cotton." She tried to hand the maid a card, but the rude girl retreated, as she ushered them into the stylish residence. "He is expecting us."

"Miss Lenore? Lucilla?" General Cotton strolled into the sitting room, took one look at her, and winced. "Upon my word, what happened?"

"I met with an unfortunate incident on the way here." At that point, she swayed, but an iron grip provided unfailing support, and she daubed her brow with her handkerchief. "Thank you," she said to her unknown champion. "A most dastardly villain almost trampled me beneath an equally vile creature."

"Perhaps I should order a bath, and you may change into clean clothes." Then the general glanced to her right. "That is, if there is ample time."

"By all means." A familiar voice pricked her ears, and a shiver of recognition traipsed her spine. "I will await the lady's pleasure."

"Wonderful." General Cotton snapped his fingers. "But first, permit me to make the introductions. Miss Lenore Teversham. Miss Lucilla Teversham. Allow me to present Captain Blake Elliott, of His Majesty's Navy, and your gallant escort."

When Lucilla cackled, stepped forward, and extended an arm, as would a man, she rocked on her heels. "Cap'n, you should quit right now and set sail without us."

And that confirmed Lenore's worst suspicions. Given fate had saddled them with so many hardships, she just knew luck would not have thrown her into the auspicious charity of her assailant. Swallowing hard, she inclined her head, and her unholy tormentor winked. That was it. At the end of her tether, everything inside her railed at once. "*You.*"

"Now do not frown, as it spoils your lovely face." The devilish rogue had the unqualified audacity to smirk. "Captain Elliott, most definitely at your service, Miss Teversham." Then he sketched a salute. "And may I address you as Lenore?"

"No, you most certainly may not." As she wrenched from his hold, she peered at General Cotton. "Sir, while I do not wish to seem ungrateful for your efforts, perhaps you can secure alternative passage to England for my sister and I? There must be another ship that would suit our needs, sans such onerous company."

"I am sorry, Miss Lenore." The general shook his head. "But that is out of the question, as most transports have no capacity to accommodate two single ladies of character, and it took some convincing to sway His—"

"Er, just Captain Elliott will suffice, Stapleton." The scoundrel checked his timepiece. "Given we are to be shipmates, there is no need to observe the usual proprieties." Lenore did not like the sound of that. "And on that note, do what must needs, as I intend to cast off before sunset, with or without my fair travelers."

Furrowing his brow, the general cleared his throat and shuffled his feet. "Permit me to order a bath." In haste, he strode from the room.

"Do not be silly, Lenny. As you said, we have no money, so we must avail ourselves of Captain Elliott's goodwill." To Lenore's chagrin, Lucilla snorted, even though she had just revealed the miserable state of their affairs to a total stranger. "And you can call me Lucy, as Lucilla is a vast deal too formal. Do you not agree?"

"I do, indeed." The blackguard, every bit as imposing as he was on the street, chuckled. "But to you, little Lucy, I am simply Blake." When he returned his gaze to Lenore and smiled, her knees buckled, and again he steadied her. "Easy, Miss Teversham. We would not want you to fall and bruise what I suspect is a superior posterior."

"Release me, Captain." She slapped his hand and retreated. "As it stands, you owe me a new hat, dress, and pair of slippers, as I lost one shoe in the mud, in my failed attempt to retrieve my cherished accouterment."

"Does your memory fail, Miss Teversham, as I compensated you generously for that, or would you have something else of me?" And as he did in the lane, her tormentor studied her from top to toe, and she cursed the burn of a blush in her cheeks. "Of course, I rather fancy the opportunity to clothe your shapely body, even as my thoughts tend toward the opposite objective. Shall I procure a chemise, garters, and stockings, as well?"

"I beg your pardon?" Shocked by the intimate nature of his suggestion, she almost swooned.

"She favors lavender, Captain." With a snicker, Lucilla sported a mischievous grin. "But when it comes to her delicate undergarments—"

"That is quite enough, sister." Mortified, Lenore did not notice her antagonist had moved, until he cupped her chin and wiped her face with his lace-edged kerchief, and she stiffened her spine. "What are you doing?"

"You missed a spot, Miss Teversham." With his thumb, he caressed the edge of her jaw, and she gulped, as he all but pierced her with his clear blue eyes. In another time and place, they might have been friends, or something more, as she found him devastatingly handsome. "But even beneath a coating of road muck, I find you rather appealing." Then he grimaced and sniffed the air. "Good heavens, is that you?"

"*Oh.*" In that instant, she would have stomped her foot, but she recalled her earlier disastrous display of temper and reconsidered. Just as a particularly scathing response formed in her brain, the general returned.

"Miss Lenore, the servants are ready for you." As the

resplendent military man dipped his chin, the maid at his right curtseyed. "If you would follow Daisy, she will show you the way."

"Thank you." Lenore attempted a graceful exit, but she caught her toe on the carpet and tripped, and her less than chivalrous patron shot to her aid.

"Careful, Miss Teversham." Given the captain's throaty drawl, she braced for another insult, as she glanced over her shoulder, only to discover him blatantly scrutinizing her bottom, and she screeched in protest even as he chortled. "Well, well, I am correct in my assertion."

ABOUT BARBARA DEVLIN

Bestselling author Barbara Devlin was born a storyteller, but it was a weeklong vacation to Bethany Beach, DE that forever changed her life. The little house her parents rented had a collection of books by Kathleen Woodiwiss, which exposed Barbara to the world of romance, and Shanna remains a personal favorite. Barbara writes heartfelt historical romances that feature flawed heroes who may know how to seduce a woman but know nothing of marriage. And she prefers feisty but smart heroines who sometimes save the hero, before they find their happily ever after. Barbara earned an MA in English and continued a course of study for a Doctorate in Literature and Rhetoric. She happily considered herself an exceedingly eccentric English professor, until success in Indie publishing lured her into writing, full-time, featuring her fictional knighthood, the Brethren of the Coast.

Connect with Barbara Devlin at BarbaraDevlin.com, where you can sign up for her newsletter, The Knightly News.